TREATISES ON DUST

Treatises
on Dust

by

Timothy J. Jarvis

Swan River Press
Dublin, Ireland
MMXXIV

Treatises on Dust
by Timothy J. Jarvis

Published by
Swan River Press
at Æon House
Dublin, Ireland
in November MMXXIV

www.swanriverpress.ie
brian@swanriverpress.ie

Cover design by Meggan Kehrli
from "Another Coiled Soul" by øjeRum

Set in Garamond by Steve J. Shaw

Paperback Edition
ISBN 978-1-78380-781-9

Swan River Press published
a limited hardback edition of
Treatises on Dust in July 2023.

Contents

Under a Certain Old Street Lamp

For a while now I've been collecting texts that hint at strange tales. None of them are ghost stories in the traditional sense—and actually I don't really believe in spirits or an afterlife—but they're all haunting in some way. "Treatises on Dust" I call them, because dust is the stuff of all things. The very first, which got its hooks in me, set me seeking out others of its ilk, was something I came across when I was working as a temp at a Community Mental Health Centre in Kentish Town back in 2001. One day, while helping out with an office move, I pulled out a filing cabinet and found something scrawled in red ink on the wall behind. It was scarcely legible, took me some time to make out. But I'm pretty sure this is what was written there, or something very close:

An elderly man, committed several years ago for delusions and raving, told me yesterday that during the hours of darkness, under a certain old street lamp, on a quiet street in [*here the name of the place had been blotted out with thick hatching*], pebble-dash and mock Tudor and net curtains and a patina of boredom and frustration and prurience over everything, it was sometimes possible to hear faint yowling and scent the salt tang of blood or brine and the cloying perfume of bindweed flowers. Then, if you stood in the sallow cone of light and looked up at the bulb, it would sputter out and you'd see a sky, perhaps clear on an overcast night or lowering on a cloudless, and if clear, a bloated green smear of a moon and an awry spatter of stars, clustered not into the wonted ragtag menagerie, but a writhen horde. Last night, feeling constrained to go there myself, I found he'd spoken only the truth.

What the Bones Told Hecate Shrike

A few years ago now, during that season when the nights really begin to draw in, on a dismal cold Monday morning—mist roiling in the streets, rime whorls on car windscreens, a sky the flat grey of spoilt fish—a colleague and friend, Emese Tóth, failed to turn up for a lecture she was supposed to be giving. It was unlike her. She was conscientious, always let someone know when she was unable to make it in, was ill or had some emergency. Her mobile just rang and rang when we tried the number. We were all a bit concerned. But we had busy teaching schedules and, having put up notices to let students know the rest of her classes were cancelled, went about our days. It was not till evening then, that a couple of us went round to her flat, me and the academic she shared an office with, a pleasant bumbling man in his late fifties called Peter Grummitt, who had a pasty gaunt face, was balding and kept his skull shaved. Emese lived above a grocer's on a quiet residential street about ten minutes' walk from the university.

When we got there, we rang the doorbell. There was no answer, so we craned our necks to look up at the windows. They were dark. Peter said he thought he caught movement within, but I didn't see anything. Then the shopkeeper, an older woman, Pakistani, wearing a bright headscarf, a vivid fuchsia—I remember that because it clashed with the dull green of the shapeless dress she wore—came out of her shop and stood with her arms crossed, scowling at us. Peter coughed and ran his hand over his stubbly scalp.

"We're looking for Emese."

The grocer cocked her head, raised an eyebrow. "She's gone."

"What?" I asked. "When?"

"Friends of hers?"

"We work with her at the university."

"Day before yesterday. She settled her rent, said goodbye, said she wouldn't be coming back." The shopkeeper tutted. "Thing is, she's left all her stuff, hasn't she?"

The Friday before, Emese and I had gone drinking after work in Luton's High Town, a place called the Bricklayers Arms, the Brickies, a homely pub with good beer, sporting memorabilia on the walls, a TV for the football, two or three fruit and quiz machines. The front room was busy, but Emese spotted a table in back. I went up to the bar, bought a couple of ales, some crisps and nuts, and took them over. We sat drinking our pints, eating the crisps and nuts, and talking about work. Emese had a funny way with beer—she'd take big gulps and every time wipe the froth from her lips with the back of her hand and sigh. She'd a broad flat, but pretty face, and always wore her hair up in an old-fashioned braided chignon.

We were both having tough terms, our teaching loads heavy, and we'd both gone through breakups not long before, which though not hard had been sad, and I guess we were kind of throwing back the beer. Once we'd finished griping about work, we discussed again Béla Tarr's staggering *The Turin Horse*, its strange oneiric imagery—

bleak, so bleak, relentless; we'd both been harrowed but compelled by the film when we'd seen it at a small festival in an arts venue in town a few weeks before.

Then, a couple of hours into the evening, by which time we'd had three or four pints and were quite pissed, Emese rummaged in her bag and pulled out a small chapbook, waved it in my face. I leant back, peered at it. It was bound in black cloth. There was no lettering, just two sigils, sheeny black against the matt, glinting in the fitful flickering of a fruit machine by our table. One was an inverted ankh, the other, the outline of a small bird.

"What's that?" I asked.

"Have you heard of Hecate Shrike?"

"No. Minor eighties Goth band?"

"Hah. No, she's a poet. Was a poet. Maybe was a poet."

"Maybe was?"

Emese gave me a meaningful look, took another long swill of her beer, wiped her lips, sighed.

"So," she went on, "I think you'll like this. It's strange, uncanny."

Shrike, Emese told me, was a writer whose work she'd first come across on a blog devoted to radical literature. "I found," she said, "a strange violence in those four syllables, technically a quartus paeon. They set my pineal gland thrumming."

"Steady on," I said and grinned.

Emese waved her hand, shushed me. Shrike's practice, she explained, combined elements of contemporary innovative poetry with motifs drawn from the occult. "Imagine," she said, "a Shirley Jackson, working not in unsettling stories and novels, but bizarre prose poetry and verse. Or a Burroughs, but a Burroughs without the obsessions with pulp fiction and boys and masturbating. Or an Acker, but with a fixation on crones, rather than pirates." She paused, munched on a handful of dry roasted peanuts from the packet open on the table between us. On the screen of the fruit machine anthropomorphic lemons, oranges, and clusters of grapes danced about, somewhat suggestively. "I guess the closest comparison would be a modern-day Yeats, but one more interested in linguistic deformation than tradition. And without the flirtation with Fascism."

In fact, she went on, Shrike was collective, anti-corporate, anti-capitalist. A reader of Deleuze and Guattari who once wrote a poem in which a monstrous fleshy huddle slopped around the streets of the City of London engulfing howling bankers and share traders. A poem written as a curse. Her work, like Kathy Acker's, incorporated violent radical feminist elements and these manifested in a celebration of witchcraft, a little like that found in Shirley Jackson's writing, a celebration both ironical and intensely profound.

"Hence Hecate?" I asked. Emese nodded.

Obviously Hecate Shrike wasn't a given name. The poet had started using it when at university in her late teens. The shrike had been her totem, images of the bird recurring again and again in her work. She'd identified with it, had called her first published collection *The Larder* and in interviews given at the time described the verses in that book as, "living things impaled on the thorn bush of my mind".

Emese held the chapbook up again. "This is the last thing Shrike published. The poems are just a little different from stuff she'd written previously. A bit more direct. There's also a loose narrative running through, which was something new for her."

The volume had been an attempt to work through a troubling influence, Emese explained, a book of poetry,

Day's Horse Descend, by a minor French Decadent, Hendrick Van der Decken, a rare volume Shrike had found by chance in an obscure translation in a secondhand bookshop in Bedford.

"Something about *Day's Horse Descend* really got under Shrike's skin. Almost drove her mad. She talked in interviews about its 'baleful inspiration'. Apparently she wrote this"—Emese brandished the chapbook again—"using something she'd learned of Van der Decken's method, as an attempt at a kind of exorcism."

Emese explained that Shrike hadn't given the collection a title, bar the esoteric glyphs, but that it was known as *The Bone Antenna* after its central conceit.

"You see," she said, "the opening poem tells of Shrike constructing some weird artefact in her back garden." She pinched her lower lip between thumb and forefinger. "Hang on, why don't I just read it to you." She opened the chapbook, cleared her throat:

> I've been building an antenna in my back garden,
> from the bones of small creatures that
>   come to me at night,
> yield to my butcher's knife or my gloved hands
> as to a great comfort.
>
> Mewling, whining, whimpering,
> they come to me at night.
>
> I stab hearts or wring necks,
> then take the carcasses into my shed,
> where I flay hides
> and throw
> pink-and-white mottles of flesh
> into my simmering pots,

then hose down the blood.
Magpies, starlings, and parakeets,
foxes, badgers, cats, and dogs,
woodpeckers, geese,
squirrels and hamsters,
field mice,
caimans and terrapins,
rats, bats, and owls,
cuckoos, swans, slow-worms, and adders,
all the small lives that scurry, crawl, slither,
    prowl, soar, or swoop
hereabouts.

All come to me,
mewling, whining, whimpering,
in the hours of darkness,
tap with beaks and talons
    on the panes of my French windows,
or scratch with teeth and claws
    on the panels of my kitchen door.
Drawn by my tender heart,
and the mercy of my boning knife
    and gardening gloves.

When flesh has been stewed from bones,
I fish out from the pots
a clumped mass,
break it up,
spread it out on the floor to dry, to harden.

A woodpecker's skull like bone callipers,
a pug's, a snarling brute,
a rat's ribcage like an elfin coracle,
snakes' vertebrae like dice,

a cat's pelvis like a ritual mask.
I cement each new bone into place
    with a glue dredged from the bottom of the vats.
I writhe . . .

Emese trailed off, looked up at me. "Well, you get the idea. I can lend it to you if you'd like? The poem goes on to tell how Shrike at first can't get her artefact to work. But then a shrike, a butcher bird, comes to her, lets her throttle it. When she places its skull on top of her tower of bone"—here Emese glanced down at the open chapbook—"as she tells it, the antenna sets her 'pineal gland thrumming' and begins directing her to sites where 'the membrane is thin'. The rest of the poems in the collection describe her visiting those places."

"Sounds bizarre," I said.

"It is. Shrike sets down in verse and prose poetry her experiences at the sites the antenna directs her to. These accounts get increasingly odd. Here's one."

Emese flipped to a page in the middle of the chapbook, began to read:

The bones told me, in a low croak that rattled the sigils of my middle ear, of a certain old street lamp, on a quiet suburban street, a place of listless stone cladding and yellowing uPVC conservatories, a place gritty with tedium and outrage and misery, a place of wretched folk—twitchers of net, venerators of the sacred gogglebox, drivers of cars with heated seats and dread-rune logos on their grilles, bathers in beaten egg and blood.

From time to time, at night,
said the bones,

those folk spew from their houses,
like silverfish from under the skirting boards
of dank and dingy bathrooms, to walk the streets.
The elderly pushing bulging tartan shopping trolleys,
    grunting with the effort,
muffled whatever the season in thick coats,
    scarves, and woollen hats.
Families dragging one or two children
in gnarled masks,
mum baring bright fangs, raking the air
    with talons of garish lacquer,
dad holding his car keys out in front of him,
    fob dangling as if it were a talisman.
Teenagers huffing nitrous oxide from balloons,
leaving a trail of shiny seeds behind them.

The bones cackled or groaned, one of the two.
It might appear,
they went on,
those folk wander aimless,
but they are guided by arcane ritual,
beat bounds long forgotten by all but them,
the fillings in their teeth
whining and buzzing.

Emese stopped, put the book down. "Well, you get the idea."

"No," I said. "Go on."

She smiled, nodded, picked it up again:

The bones told me to go to the house of an old woman calling herself Ethel, on a night when the moon waned gibbous, they were very specific about that, to go bearing a soft toy thieved from a child's grave, and to present it still damp with night dew or tears.

And so I did. Ethel answered the door to my nervous rap. She had a kindly look and a mauve wen on her cheek. She seized my offering in a liver-spotted claw, tore it from my grasp before I'd even had the chance to speak, scampered off upstairs. Moments later I heard a gurgle of glee, deep and hoarse. Then Ethel returned.

She invited me in, took me by the elbow and led me through to her sitting room, chintz and lace and drab. On the mantelpiece, photographs of young children fleering and holding out toads crammed in jars, and a little model Spanish guitar from Seville that played a tune when a key jutting from its side was wound—"Clair de Lune", but stuttering and somehow wrong.

Ethel sat me down on an armchair with a crochet antimacassar draped over the back, greasy imprints of many heads upon it. I held myself awkwardly, hunched forward, elbows on knees.

Ethel stood leering down at me.

I leave poisoned bait
out for the local foxes,
she said,
her false teeth too even, too big for her mouth.
Once they've died
convulsing on my patio,
I take their mangy carcasses,
bury them in my compost heap to rot and sweeten.
In return for your tribute,
I'll give you a lump
of the squirming meat.

She pointed at a hazy glow
thrown on the net hanging in the window.
There's a street light outside.
Go, stand beneath it, hold the rank fox
flesh over your head, and wait.

She fetched the carrion for me, a grey maggoty
hunk, yellowed bone jutting, and I took it and
went outside.

Standing beneath the street light, I heard faint
yowling and scented the salt tang of blood or brine
and the cloying perfume of bindweed flowers, even
over the high stink of the meat dripping into my
hair.

Then, as I stood there in the sallow cone of
light, looking up, the bulb sputtered out, the moon
bloated and took on a greenish hue like mouldy
cheese, and the constellations whirled and spattered
into new forms, awry and bleak.

And something came screeching out of the dark
and took the rotten gobbet in its talons. Grasping
the slimy bone, I was lifted bodily aloft, dragged
through the rushing air.

After a brief lurching flight, I lost my grip, fell,
and landed in a heap.

I wasn't in London anymore,
but on a plain of mud,
where large rocks
skited over the earth
in looping reels.

In the figures they danced,
there was something of madness,

something of the Void,
and something of the Beyond.
I began digging with my hands,
delved into the clag,
burrowed through the dank and dark,
broke in upon a hollow place,
a great cave.

In that cavern was a vast lake,
a sunless sea.
I crossed to its shore.

Creatures snaggletoothed and bristling with spines,
scuttled, squirmed, and swam in the shallows.
Further out, great beasts,
with humps and tentacles,
and sad rolling eyes,
fought with beak and maw, roiling the waters.

I walked along the black strand,
and came upon a fane consecrated to dire rites,
where, on a stone altar,
between two black candles set in bone holders,
was a triptych,
depicting a garden of ecstatic transmutation,
with, above the scene in gilt blackletter, a legend:

"From the small bones of the middle ear—
    the hammer, anvil, and stirrup—
    can be fashioned a key."

Emese closed the chapbook, put it down, looked to me
for a response.
    "I liked that," I said. "Odd."

Emese nodded. "The whole is really strange. I find it compelling. It's a shame it was her last work."

"You said. Why? What happened?"

Emese leant back in her chair. The fruit machine's lights glimmered on her face.

"In 2002, Shrike failed to show up for a shift at the bookshop where she worked. She could be unreliable though, and the owner, who was a friend, tended to turn a blind eye. It wasn't then, till a few days later, she tried Hecate's mobile. Apparently it was answered, but there was only static and a faint yammering at the other end. Afterwards it was found Hecate wasn't at home, that no one, none of her other friends or her family, knew where she was. She's never turned up. No trace of her has yet been found."

"That tired trope."

"Tired, but in this case true. And there's more. Hang on a moment."

She drained the dregs of the pint she was drinking, then stood.

"Like another?"

I nodded.

Once Emese returned from the bar with our drinks and sat back down, she went on.

"So, there's been lots of speculation about what happened to Shrike. Many read *The Bone Antenna* not as allegory, but factual account. You see, though nothing like the artefact was discovered, when the police dug up Shrike's garden they found the bones of a large number of small animals buried in the overrun vegetable plots."

I paused mid swig, looked askance at Emese. She ignored me, carried on.

"The most widespread theory about Shrike's disappearance has to do with the last poem in *The Bone Antenna*. Let me read it to you. This one is only short."

Emese opened the chapbook again, found the page she was seeking. I drank my beer, sat back in my chair. She began to read:

The bones are telling me
to travel to Luton,
for, though named for light,
it is a place of darkness,
where I can cross over to
a blasted place,
a waste grim and bone strewn,
where brute creatures scrap and die,
creatures brute and dread and olden,
creatures writhen and hulking,
a blasted place
where I might collect giant bones
for an antenna
like a spiring claw
to rend the belly of the sky
and spill its guts,
and flood this world, this miserable world,
    with revelation and ecstasy.

"What people think," Emese said, staring at me, elbows on the table, chin resting in her hands, "is that Shrike came here, to Luton, crossed over to that other place, and could not get back."

"What do you think?" I asked.

"I've done some digging and found that Shrike did actually come to Luton, not long before she disappeared." She looked up at me. "You'll never guess why."

I shrugged. "To go to the airport?"

Emese grinned. "No! She came to read to a group of

students at the university. It was the University of Luton back then."

Emese had discovered that a colleague of ours from the English Department, Fiona Simon, had actually been at the reading. Fiona couldn't recollect who'd organised it, or much about it, but she did remember that something strange had happened towards the end. Apparently Shrike had glanced out the window and, seemingly transfixed, had stopped partway through a poem, midway through a word in fact, and gone into a trance, picked up a pen and begun drawing strange symbols on the white board, staring outside the while and saying, under her breath, words that no one could quite catch. Fiona had assumed it all part of the performance. The pen had been a permanent marker, she recalled, and there'd been some fuss about that, for the signs Shrike had drawn couldn't be completely cleaned from the board, left faint traces, and though just squiggles, had somehow been very upsetting, and students had complained till the board was taken down. Also, a photocopier in a nearby office had apparently begun acting up after Shrike's reading, at odd times spewing sheets on which were blotches of toner, smears and mottles that, though they seemed abstract, were fraught somehow with menace.

"Fiona told me where the reading had been held," Emese said, leaning forwards, grabbing my hand. We were both very drunk by then. Slurring our words. "It was in one of the rooms on the top floor of the A block, on the south side. I've been up there a few times to take a look, but I've not seen anything yet. But I now think I know *how* to see."

"Take a look for what?" I asked.

Emese ignored me, reached down, delved in her bag, and took out a pack of cigarettes, stark design in red and white. "Want one?" she said. "Hungarian brand."

I don't really smoke now, but it used to be a habit and I still feel the pull when I've been drinking. I nodded.

We went outside, into the small paved area at the back of the pub, sat down at a table. Emese took a cigarette from the pack, passed it to me, then held out her lighter, thumbed the flint wheel. I leaned in, touched the end of my cigarette to the flame, and drew till I had an ember burning.

Emese then lit her cigarette, and we puffed away in silence. The first few drags made me light headed, they were strong cigarettes, but the taste was good, and it was pleasant to feel woozy, to feel the world lazily wheel. Emese pulled on her cigarette, blew smoke rings. When she'd smoked it to the filter, she crushed it out in the ashtray, cocked her head, and peered at me.

"What do you think?"

I took a last drag, put out the cigarette, held up the stubbed butt.

"Good. Stronger than I'm used to, but a good flavour."

"Yes, it's Helikon brand. A very popular brand in Hungary. I remember when I was a child there was an old faded advert on the side of a building near my parents' place. A poet sitting at his desk smoking, being struck in the head by the hoof of a miniature winged horse. The slogan read, 'Smoke Helikon brand for inspiration!' Pretty obscure, huh?"

"Yes. I don't get it."

"Look it up on the internet later. But I wasn't asking about the cigarette. I meant what do you think about Shrike's disappearance? *The Bone Antenna*? Luton?"

"Well," I said, "this is a strange town. Pasteboard. I often feel that if you were to prod things here too hard, your finger might go through. Like the brickmaker in *Heart of Darkness*, that papier-mâché Mephistopheles."

"What are you running on about?"

I squinted at her. "I just mean I wouldn't be surprised if this *was* one of those places where"—and I scratched the quotes in the air with my fingers—" 'the membrane is thin'."

"So. I think I know how to find the place Shrike went. Do you think I should try?"

I thought we were talking nonsense by that point.

"Of course! Think about it. To travel beyond ordinary ken! To see the occulted world!"

"Yes, yes," Emese said, "I think you're right." Then she shook her head as if to clear it. "It's cold. Let's go back in. And get us another pint will you?"

We did, and I did, and we drank till closing time, talking about our failed relationships, other things. We didn't discuss Shrike again. I forgot to ask Emese if I could borrow the chapbook. The next day I felt rough and lay in bed till lunchtime, headsore, queasy. I regretted not having eaten dinner the previous evening. At some point that day, Emese walked out of her flat with only the clothes and coat she was wearing, and presumably *The Bone Antenna*, which was not apparently found among her things. All the rest of her stuff, she left. She said goodbye to her landlady. The police investigation is still ongoing, but I can tell they think Emese either walked out of her life or killed herself and are not really prioritising the case.

I've sought a copy of the chapbook, but haven't been able to track one down. And people get very cagey whenever I mention Hecate Shrike.

I've told the police everything. Or almost everything. I've not told them about the dream I had one night, a couple of weeks after Emese went missing. Or about what I saw the following day. The police aren't interested in such things.

In the dream, I was stood looking out over a patch of land down by the River Lea, now earmarked for the site of some new student halls and surrounded by hoardings painted a lurid green, but then open wasteground, quag sown with rubble. It's on my route to the university, I go by it most days. I dreamt that somehow the skin of that place had been flayed and beneath, like a grinning skull, was a plain, wreathed in fog, blasted, bone strewn. Among the bones I saw the skulls of animals I could identify or thought I could: the skulls of cattle, sheep, and swine; many birds' skulls, some of which I recognised by their beaks—a raven's, a cockatiel's, a hoopoe's; a skull I think was a large dog's or possibly a badger's; a stag's skull, with branching antlers. And there were human skulls too. A great many human skulls. But there were also giant bones, strange massy skulls, with one orbit or three, bristling with involute horns, vicious incurving tusks.

And there were figures skittering through the haze. I could hear faint yowling and scent the salt tang of blood or brine and the cloying perfume of bindweed flowers. In the distance, very faint, a tower of yellowing bone. Things swarming upon it. My pineal gland throbbed.

I woke then and, thirsty, downed the glass of water I have always on my nightstand.

The next day, on my walk to work, when I passed that patch of wasteland on the other side of the road, I recalled my dream, glanced over. I saw, just off the path, an old piece of machinery sinking into the mud, a rusty block of iron with prongs jutting from it. Then noticed, with a queasy lurch, that there were animals impaled on some of those barbs. A little way away, but I could see them clearly—a frog, slick green skin, a hind leg still kicking out, a pigeon, wings torn off, and a squirrel, ripped open, steaming yet. Looking up, I caught movement a bit beyond. A figure, moving swift with an odd hopping gait, on legs that bent backwards at the knees, I think, though I couldn't really see. It was as if I looked through heavy mist. The figure then turned its face to me. I still couldn't make out much, but I knew. I almost called out to her, but my words were choked in my throat.

A white van drove by, blocked my view a moment. Once it had passed, I darted across the road. As I ran, I saw that the figure and the staked frog, pigeon, and squirrel were gone. There was just that block of machinery, its iron spikes jutting.

What I saw must simply have been a figment, born of tiredness, of worry, of a loss I couldn't really articulate, still can't. Part of me wishes it hadn't been. The world just now could do with a dose of darkling bliss. But nearing the block, I saw those prongs were stark, no trace of gore.

I suppose, though, they could have been licked clean.

We Recognise Our Own

It was still early in the day, but the sun blazed down. Stepping forth, at the crest of a rise, from wooded shade into blinding light and building heat, into dust and the buzzing of flies, Angélique stood breathing hard. The way she'd come up, through the trees, under bowering branches, had been a hard slog, clambering over rocks furred with dank moss, up a path she'd guess would be a stream in spate in the wet season. Shading her eyes with her right hand, she looked out over the sweep before her. Rolling volcanic hills, grasses and scrub still green from the spring rains, but yellowing with the summer parch; a few small communes, stone buildings clustered about squat churches; some herds of grazing cattle; goats stepping fleet and light higher up the slopes. Down in the valley, beech and walnut trees, a canopy of green rolling off to the south, where rose up far and faint the snow-capped Pyrenees. A little way away she could see the village where she and her friends were staying, a daub of pale masonry on the side of a hill crowned by the jagged ruins of an ancient keep, which, in the hazy warmth, wavered like a guttering flame. She couldn't quite make out the cottage that had once belonged to her grandmother, but she knew it was there, amid that little knot of buildings.

Close by, on Angélique's left, was a small mountain chapel, blocks of weathered, lichen-stippled stone, a square spire. It was largely plain, but a Romanesque relief, zigzags and dots, arched over the iron-battened wooden door. There was a small cemetery by the side of the church, ancient monuments, weeping angels and urns. Angélique felt a hitch in her chest looking on it. To her right was a farmstead—a house with square windows hewn into the walls, a tiled roof, a corrugated iron cowshed, and a wooden barn, rotting and slumped. There were donkeys in a small paddock, tearing at the grass, chewing. Each had a bell round its neck and as they lowered their big sad skulls to the sward these would clatter.

Somewhere a bit further off could be heard the bellowing of bulls, a sound filled with rage and pain. Nearer at hand, flies buzzed, mosquitos whined past, and cicadas chirred in the trees.

In front of the house, an old woman was hanging washing, from a heap in an old wicker basket, out to dry over a line stretched between a dead tree and a metal pole—shirts, trousers, a couple of shapeless smocks, greying underwear, all worn, all going to rags. She wore a dress with ruched skirts, material patterned with crosses against a darker background, perhaps once bright yellow on blue, but now faded and threadbare. On her head was a cloth bonnet, grey and filthy. White wisps of hair curled from under it. A tightly rolled cheroot was clamped in the corner of her mouth and a ribbon of smoke rose into the clear sky. The woman's feet, in the dirt, were bare.

And she was singing something low, around the cheroot. Angélique stood listening a moment. A cracked, but tuneful voice; a melody sweet and sad. A droning chant in Occitan, with a refrain that ran through the vowels. "*Lo Boièr*", Angélique thought, and smiled. It was a song her *mémé* had sung to her as a child. She knew it was steeped in symbolism, but had forgotten just what.

Then the old woman looked up, saw Angélique. She stopped singing, hung the shirt she was holding, and crossed over to the low stone wall surrounding the farmstead. There was something wrong with her legs, twisted in childhood by rickets maybe, and she walked with an odd hopping gait, right up on her toes. Reaching the wall, she stood, hands on hips, glaring. Angélique smiled and nodded at her, but the old woman's face did not soften. Turning, Angélique started off down the track. She did not look back, but felt the old woman's stare boring into her nape till she reached the stile where she left the path.

Pamphlets written by pretentious curators had termed Angélique Bouvier an *artiste des rêves*, an oneirist, even once or twice a sibyl (though she'd never claimed there was anything mantic about her dreams). She herself always refused to name the thing she did.

But her practice consisted of this. She would sleep on a bed in the middle of an otherwise empty gallery. The lighting had to be low and the room, warm. She always used the same bed, took it with her from performance to performance. It was the bed she'd slept in at her grandmother's house as a child, a house of shabbily plastered sandy stone in a commune not far from Albi, a bed which, to her mother's annoyance, she'd insisted on them keeping during the house clearance following her *mémé*'s death shortly after Angélique had turned seventeen. Angélique hadn't seen her *mémé* for some years before that, for the family had drifted apart following an argument, and she and her mother had found out about the laryngeal tumour the size of an apple too late to make it over before her *mémé* slipped away. Sometimes Angélique still felt guilty about that. The bed was narrow with a wrought-iron bedstead and a hard mattress with creaking springs and ticking sweat-yellowed and worn threadbare in places. The bedclothes of her childhood had been lost, doubtless gone to tatters many years before, but Angélique found their likeness in a department store closing-down sale in a drab town in the English Midlands—two rough linen sheets and a heavy woollen blanket embroidered with little birds. Lying in that bed, wherever she was, she'd recall the room in her *mémé*'s cottage in the Languedoc, its high sloping ceiling and dark oak beams.

At every performance Angélique also wore the same nightgown, one that had belonged to her *mémé*, brocaded ivory cotton, with long sleeves, a high neck, lace ruffles. It was stained and tatty, but Angélique would not replace it.

She would sleep watched over by a pair of attendants who, every fifteen minutes, allowed one of the punters to wake her. Then she'd rub her eyes and sit up, and tell the throng of the dream she'd been roused from. When done, she'd slump down again, fall back to sleep and lie still, only now and again stretching out a limb, or whimpering, till woken again. To relate another dream.

Angélique's dreams always spoke particularly to the person who woke her, as if something of their psyche seeped into hers when they prodded her arm or took hold of her shoulder to shake her.

But her last show, at a gallery in an old textile mill in Mile End, hadn't gone like that. It had been set up by friends hoping to help her over the loss of her girlfriend, Alice, while Angélique was grief-stricken and strung out and in a haze. Those friends had largely meant well, but they'd been too wrapped up in what they believed was their good deed to notice how Angélique was wasting away, how wasted she was all the time. By the time she'd realised what was going on, the whole thing had been organised, money outlaid and tickets sold. She'd not then had the heart then to tell anyone that dreams hadn't come easy since Alice's death, that they'd only really come in the deep sleep following the needle's bliss, and that even then they'd been muted and dull. So she resolved to shoot up before the show and hope for the best.

At first things did go fairly well—she managed to spin striking visions out of the tawdry stuff of her reveries. But about an hour into the performance, she was woken by a man in a grey pinstriped suit and found her mind blank— she felt only the heaviness of the drug, none of its light. She sat up, against the pillows, against the headboard. He waited, holding onto her left sleeve and grinning foolishly. In a panic she started recounting the plot of a Maya Deren short.

But the man recognised it. "I know that," he said. "It's not yours." He frowned. He thought maybe she mocked him.

Angélique looked up at him, sighed. The crowd stood shuffling their feet.

"It's our money keeps you in meat and bread, isn't it?" the man said. "Collectors, I mean." He seemed hurt.

She threw back the covers, shuffled round to sit on the edge of the mattress, pushed the man with the flat of her right hand. He was somewhat the worse for wear on wine from the free bar and stumbled, then fell, still clutching the sleeve of Angélique's antique nightgown. It ripped at the shoulder seam, tore off, baring her left arm. A mess of track marks, abscesses. Snarling, she swung at the man. He backed away, cursing.

Angélique sneered round at those gathered in the gallery. "*Quoi?*" Then stripped off the nightgown, sat naked on the bed. A gasp went up. She was cankered hide stretched over an armature of bone. She'd never really been *seen* at any performance before, but she was seen then.

Her friends, the ones who'd put the show on, ran to her, bundled her up in her bedding and out of the space.

Two of those friends, Petra Sadler and Jon MacLeod, had then taken Angélique back to their Kensington townhouse. Petra was an Anglo-German art promoter, a vocal champion of Angélique's work, and Jon, a barrister, originally from Aberdeen, but in London so long his accent retained only the faintest trace of burr. A couple, they'd been together many years, for a long time before Angélique had met them. They often bickered. Angélique wasn't sure she liked them exactly, but they'd been very kind to her.

The day after the disastrous show, Petra went with Angélique to pick up her stuff from the dank room in the shared house in Stratford she'd been renting since Alice's death.

"Darling," Petra said, when she saw how Angélique had been living, saw the filthy mattress on the floor, the cardboard box beside it, needle, blackened spoon, lighter, and length of rubber hose laid out. "I hadn't realised things had got so bad."

Petra and Jon paid for a nurse to look after Angélique while she went cold turkey, and a week later she was clean, if sapped utterly. But now her veins ran with grief. And sleep was a pit—more than any high she craved dreams, even the pallid dreams of the drug had been better than this nothing.

She missed Alice dreadfully, though she knew that by the end their relationship had been mostly habit and comfort and certainly faltering. Perhaps it was the way

Alice had gone, a drop from a footbridge to the North Circular, no warning, no why and wherefore.

A Saturday in late autumn, cold but bright. Neither of them had had anything particular to do that day, but Alice set an early alarm anyway and leapt from bed when it woke her. Angélique, grumbling, tried to burrow down under the covers, but Alice pulled them off her, mock chiding her for sloth. She insisted on a quick wash and breakfast, then a walk while there was still a dawn gentleness to the light. Her mood was playful, high spirited—she gave no sign anything weighed on her, no sadness, no weariness.

On the ramp leading up to the bridge, Angélique stopped to pet a Puli with a corded coat, the dog of a man with a nose like a carving knife or beak. Alice scampered on ahead.

Angélique was hunkered down, scratching the dog behind its ears, when the man, who looked towards the bridge, gasped. Turning, Angélique saw Alice had clambered up and was stood teetering on the railings, arms spread wide and face turned to the sky.

Of the jump, the tumble through the air, the smack of the body on the tarmac, Angélique had no memory. But she knew she'd never forget looking down from the bridge after, at Alice's body lying on the road. She'd been lying on her back, perfect as always, as if she might just get up and walk away, except for the spreading pool of blood about her, and that her legs had been mangled under the wheels of a lorry.

After a month of living at Petra and Jon's place, Angélique had put back on most of the weight she'd lost and was looking healthy, even sleek. But still she wouldn't leave the house, wouldn't do anything. Petra tried to chivvy her along, but got nowhere. Then one evening, determined to cheer her up, Petra insisted on taking Angélique out, first to show at a disused warehouse, huge fibreglass toys that dwarfed the viewer, then on to eat at a new Sri Lankan place. Over dinner they talked mostly superficially, a bit about the exhibition, which Angélique had liked but Petra had thought derivative, and then about Petra's plans to open a gallery in the West End, a space for showcasing the work of the bravest contemporary artists, among whom, Petra said, Angélique was a High Priestess.

But after dinner, over cocktails at a bar down the street, Petra finally coaxed Angélique into talking about Alice. Angélique told Petra about the guilt and anguish. She also told her about her empty nights, how she no longer dreamed.

"But darling," Petra said. "You've such a gift!"

It was torment, the not-dreaming, but Angélique couldn't really have cared less if she never did another show. So she shrugged. Petra frowned, but said nothing.

A couple of days later though, Petra came into the guest drawing room, where Angélique was sitting idly thumbing through a collection of writings by Ithell Colquhoun.

"Angélique," Petra said. "I've had a thought."

Angélique put the book down on a side table.

"Why don't we stay at your grandmother's old place this summer?"

Angélique peered up at her. "Why?"

"You said last you heard it was being let out, yes?"

Angélique nodded. "But *why?*"

"You'd dream there. In your childhood room."

"I don't know. And it might be fully booked for the season. Or no longer rented out. That was a while ago."

"We could at least try?"

Picking up the Colquhoun collection again, Angélique opened it at random and read: "When we turned to regain the surface of the earth the father told me with burning eyes that I should never be the same again."

"What?"

"It's called bibliomancy, darling." Angélique sarcastically rolled the "r".

"Don't you like the idea?" Petra seemed hurt.

Looking up at her, Angélique relented. "No, I do. I'm sorry."

That evening they found the house on a website listing *gîtes* in the region. In the picture, clematis still climbed all over the front. But it was already booked through the summer as Angélique had suspected it might be. That night she lay awake listening for the ticking of deathwatch beetles in old beams far, far off. But the next day Jon sent an email to make a deal with the owner, offering a generous sum for the use of the place in July and August. The owner, delighted, agreed, other stays were cancelled, and Jon, Petra, and Angélique were booked in.

For about a week, Angélique lay awake at night fretting. She knew the plan was well intentioned, but she had her doubts about whether she could really put up with Petra and Jon for a couple of months isolated in the south of France. It was one thing in London, but . . . Petra wearied her and Jon could be a bit of a creep. And moreover, she wasn't sure she really wanted to stay in her *mémé*'s old place, felt odd about it. But after a bit she stopped worrying and resigned herself.

By the time Angélique got back from her early walk, still thinking about the old woman's fierce stare and the meaning of that ancient song, "*Lo Boièr*", it was already so close it felt hard to breathe and sweat beaded on her forehead. By lunchtime the air was hot and thick as soup, and neither she, nor Petra and Jon, who'd spent most of the morning lounging in bed, could muster up the energy to leave the house. The cottage was one of those old places with thick stone walls that generally stay cool, but it had been oppressive for so many days the heat had seeped in. The three of them were in the large open living space downstairs, a rustic room with rush matting and stone flags on the floor, dark beams overhead, a dusty chandelier with chipped and missing crystal, and a wood-burning stove in the big fireplace. It was charming, though not as lovely, Angélique thought, as it had been in the days when the house had been her grandmother's.

She was sprawled on a rattan sofa reading, or trying to read, though her head was woozy from the two glasses of wine she'd drunk with lunch. The book in her hands was a collection of surrealist verse by an enigmatic London poet and witch, who'd gone by the name Hecate Shrike, a writer who'd walked away from literature and out of her own life some years before. Angélique wished she were brave enough to quit her own art, start fresh, but she felt dreaming might be all she was good for. Petra and Jon were sitting on either side of the battered oak dining table, Petra sketching the skull of a small bird Angélique had found that morning on her walk, and Jon flipping through a French guidebook to the region he'd taken down from the cottage's bookshelves. All was quiet save the rustle of Angélique turning pages, the skritching of Petra's pencil, and the whispering of Jon's fingers running under the lines of text as he tried to make sense of them.

Then Jon turned a page and started. "Hmm. That's weird."

"Whatever are you muttering about?" Petra asked.

"Look at this." Jon held the guidebook up, splayed open at a page about the history of the Cathars. He pointed out a medieval painting depicting the butchery at Béziers during the Albigensian Crusade. Crusaders were dragging out those who'd sought refuge in a church and slaughtering them. Angélique came up behind Petra to look too. In the foreground of the picture, a young woman in a blue robe was being run through with a sword. The face of the girl, shocking in its calm, bore an uncanny resemblance to Alice. Petra stood, grabbed the book from Jon's hands, slammed it shut, put it down.

"You moron! What were you thinking?"

Jon sat looking up at her. Angélique took up the guidebook, found the page again, and studied the image. Arching over the top of the burning church, picked out in gold script, were the words: "*Caedite eos. Novit enim Dominus qui sunt eius.*" She thought about this a moment, then put the book down and went off out of the house for a walk.

She wandered up through the village to the top of the hill, past the ruined keep, which was like the rotten tooth of a giant, and down the other side, where she struck off from the road down a footpath. The heat of the day was finally waning, but the sun still beat down on her like a cudgel (*comme un gourdin*, she thought). The path dwindled, but she pushed on, through a landscape of scrubby pine, regal heather, myrtle, and sprawling bramble snares.

Then, standing on its own in a clearing, just bare earth about as if nothing could grow near, she came across a big old thorn bush. It was sere, barely alive, its wood gnarled and galled. She stood a while, contemplating its stark writhen branches, before heading back to the house.

That night Angélique's sleep was fitful, though still dreamless. She'd been set up in the bedroom she'd slept in as a child and with her childhood bed—they'd come over with the mattress and frame in a hired van especially—but no dreams had yet come. Angélique wondered if they ever would again.

After waking, she went downstairs and found Jon and Petra siting at the table, having already eaten breakfast, though it was early. They said they'd been woken by the heat. It was already well on the way to sweltering.

Angélique, as usual in the morning, ate a hunk of baguette with butter and apricot jam and drank a bowl of hot chocolate. Jon was sipping a coffee and Petra a green tea. Conversation was desultory. Jon was especially quiet. He kept glancing at Angélique. She had the impression Petra was nudging him every so often under the table. In the end he looked over and said, "Sorry. That was callous of me."

"Huh?"

"Yesterday. I just wasn't thinking."

"It's okay. It really did look like her."

Jon nodded.

"It's really not okay," Petra said.

Angélique sighed. "Don't worry. I'm fine."

No one said anything for a little while, then Angélique asked, "Did either of you see the Latin phrase written above the picture?"

"I did," Jon replied. "No clue what it meant, though."

" 'Kill them all. The Lord will recognise His own.' Something Amalric, the commander of the crusaders, is supposed to have said before the massacre."

Petra looked bemused. "The Lord will recognise His own?"

"Béziers was mostly Catholic, but rather than risk any heretics escaping slaughter, Amalric thought it best to put the whole town to the sword, let God sort the dead."

Jon frowned. "Really?"

"Yes. Grotesque, isn't it?"

"Yes, darling," Petra drawled. "But that was the Middle Ages for you."

After breakfast, the three of them sat as they had the previous afternoon, Petra sketching, a sheaf of asparagus this time, and Jon and Angélique reading—Jon back, for some reason, at the guidebook, and Angélique onto a collection of short stories she'd brought with her, Michael Ashman's *The Salvage Song of the Larks, and Other Stories*, a bleak set of tales of crime and occult revelation set in the rubble of post-war London, an obscure title she'd come across in a secondhand bookshop and been compelled to buy on the strength of the savage opening paragraph of its first story.

At the back of the house, by the dining table, was a big window. Though the room was on the ground floor as you entered the house from the road, at the rear the land fell sharply away, and this window looked out on the upper branches of some mature fig trees.

At some point Jon got up to fling the casement wide and let in some air. There was a slight breeze, which helped.

A little while later, birds started flocking to a limb laden with figs, just outside. They began to squabble over the fruit. As the noise grew louder, Petra got up and shut the casement.

Jon looked up from the guidebook. "Leave the window open, sweetheart. It's so hot."

Petra paused, turned back to Jon. "Not with those birds out there. What if one flies in?"

"That won't happen."

"It might."

"Well say it did. We'd just shoo it out again."

Angélique flipped a page, though she wasn't really reading anymore. But she glanced down and saw she'd turned to a story entitled, "Egg Tooth".

Hissing, Petra flapped her arms, gestured about. Her voice had a frantic edge to it. "And you'd have feathers and bird shit all over the place, and the day would be ruined."

"I'm sure we'd cope."

"I hate how scared they get when they're trapped. Beating against the walls." She seemed on the brink of tears.

Rubbing his eyes, Jon sighed. "What's going on? What's really the matter?"

"Shut up," Petra said, through clenched teeth. Her hands were balled into fists.

Jon grimaced. "Open the window again. Seriously."

Cringing, Angélique sank down into the couch.

Petra stood, hands on hips. "I'm not that hot."

Taking up Petra's sketch pad, Jon began to fan his face. "I'm sweltering. I'm pouring sweat."

"You must be ill."

"Christ Petra! It's like an oven in here."

Jon still sounded calm, but his face was flushed, and not just with the heat.

"Don't exaggerate." Petra rolled her eyes. Then she sat down, snatched the pad back, and returned to her sketching.

A minute or two passed, then Jon got up, pushing back his chair so the legs shrieked on the stone flags of the floor, and crossed to the window.

"Don't open it!" Petra cried out.

"Look," Jon said, pausing before the casement. "The birds out there are happily feasting on figs. They're not going to fly in here. Besides, they're just sparrows, thrushes, and I don't know, pipits and larks. They're not going to harm anyone. Don't be irrational."

"So you're being completely reasonable?"

"I am! I'm on the verge of heatstroke."

"Heatstroke? Don't be ridiculous."

"Ridiculous? You're the one who's terrified of some sparrows. What's wrong with you?" And he opened the window.

Petra stared, lip quivering, then her eyes welled, and she broke down in sobs. Jon glanced over at Angélique, clenched his teeth, went over to Petra, put his arm round her shoulder. "Look, I'm sorry love. Come on."

Petra sniffed, wiped the tears from her eyes. "Okay. But shut the window."

"What if I were to promise to protect you from any sparrows that tried to attack us. I'll fend them off with my trusty pen." He picked up a ballpoint from the table. "After all, they do say it's mightier than the sword."

Petra gritted her teeth, took a deep breath. "Oh fuck off. I'm serious, shut the fucking window. If you're so hot, why don't you go have a cold shower or something."

Jon backed away from her. "It's stifling in here. I'll get a headache."

Getting to her feet, Petra walked towards him, bristling. "I don't care. Just shut the window."

Angélique put her book down, sat up, called out. "Hey, come on. *Arrêtez!*" But Petra held up a hand to shush her.

"Sparrows." Jon sighed.

"Not just sparrows. You see those two perched on that branch there?" Petra pointed. "White, dun, and grey, with a black stripe across the eyes?"

"I see them."

"Do you know what they are?"

"No."

"They're shrikes. Also known as butcher birds. Know why?"

Jon nodded. "They keep a larder, impale their catches on thorns, on barbed wire."

Petra glared at him. "Yes, well done." Then she turned to Angélique. "They lack talons, you see." Back to Jon. "I don't like them."

"Darling, don't be silly," he said, shaking his head. "Now you're just upsetting yourself."

"I'm in deadly earnest," Petra said. Angélique saw she was trembling. "Shut the window, now, or I'm going to leave."

The last word hung in the air. It wasn't clear whether she meant the room, the cottage, or perhaps Jon himself.

Jon looked sheepishly over at Angélique, though he wouldn't meet her eye. Then stared back at Petra, resentful. But he pulled the casement to.

Some time passed. They read and sketched in tense silence. Then Petra turned to Angélique. "Sorry for the squabble, darling. Jon can be so awfully pig-headed."

He kept leafing through the guidebook, didn't look up. But Angélique thought she could hear him muttering low.

Petra came over and sat down on the couch, took one of Angélique's hands, peered at her with concern. "I meant to ask, sweetie, how have you been sleeping?"

"Well, it's been a bit hot, but yes, fine I suppose."

"Any dreams?"

Angélique had of course known what Petra meant, but the question had irritated her, especially coming on the heels of the argument. But then, yielding, she shook her head. "Not yet."

"Don't worry, I'm sure it will happen. Just give it time."

"I'm not sure I really care anymore." She really was starting to get used to her empty nights.

"Angélique," Petra said. "Now don't be so selfish."

"Selfish? How is that selfish?"

Petra pursed her lips. "Come on now. You know we've put a lot of effort into getting you out here, setting everything up just right. We only want to help."

Jon looked up from the guidebook, over at Angélique. "What she means is that some of the backers of her new gallery are only on board because she told them she had an exclusive contract or something worked out with you." He smiled at Petra. "Isn't that right, love?"

Angélique snatched her hand away from Petra. "Is that true?"

Petra turned to Jon. "You stupid arsehole." Then she looked back to Angélique. "Of course it isn't true! I'm doing all this because I care about you, because I can't stand to see you so miserable."

"Really. Is that right."

"Angélique, I swear." She made to reach out for Angélique's hand again, but Angélique folded her arms.

"Look," Petra said. "I think your practice is compelling, okay, but there are other artists who would jump at the chance to work with me, and who are much bigger draws than you."

Angélique rolled her eyes, got to her feet, and left the house.

She meandered back over the hill, passing by the ruined keep, her steps leading her again, though she didn't realise it, to the big old thorn bush. As she neared, she could see that something was different. It squirmed. On almost every spine was impaled a small thing. Circling, peering close, Angélique saw hornets, moths, crickets and cicadas, small lizards with iridescent markings, a tiny green frog, a baby mouse, blind and hairless, a hatchling, perhaps even dragged from its smashed egg, some dead, but many more still writhing. It seemed the thorn had become a shrike larder.

She sat down on a log. As she watched, transfixed, the throes, she thought she heard someone, or rather several people, singing, in harmony, that old Occitan song, "*Lo Boièr*".

She had no idea how long she sat there, but by the time she got up to head back to the cottage the sun was setting and the day was over.

Angélique's sleep that night was again dreamless. But it was deep, and she slept through her alarm. When she woke the next day, a bit later than usual, she found the weather had turned, and there was a scumble of thin cloud in the sky. It was still close, but it did feel a touch cooler with the sun hazed behind this scrim. Going down for breakfast, she found Jon sitting in the kitchen alone, looking sullen.

"Where's Petra?"

"Morning. She's resting. A migraine."

Angélique nodded.

She had her habitual breakfast. Jon sat with her, drinking his strong black coffee. They sat in silence. After Angélique had finished eating, she also poured herself a cup of coffee, then got up, threw open the big window, and threw herself down in one of the rattan chairs in front of it. She sat, with her feet up on the sill, sipping the bitter brew and looking out the window. All the figs had been stripped from the branches outside.

After a short while, Jon came over to her with the guidebook in his hand. "Yesterday evening, I found something in here. Something about the Crusade, and this village, I think. But I didn't fully understand it. Perhaps you could translate it for me?"

Angélique looked up. "Sure. Show me."

Jon passed her the guidebook, held open. A photo of the ruined keep on a sunny day took up half the left-hand page. Angélique took the book and ran her eyes over the text, grimacing as she read. Jon pulled up another of the rattan chairs and sat peering at her closely.

"What?" he asked.

"It's an old folk tale, about the Albigensian Crusade, as you thought. Apparently this place was a community of Cathars back then."

"What happened?"

So Angélique told him. About how it was said that sometime in the summer of 1210 crusaders had ridden down upon the commune. That the villagers, warned of the knights' coming, had gone to ground, and the crusaders, finding the place deserted, would have galloped on, had not a young woman from a neighbouring place, who happened to be walking by, betrayed the Cathars. This woman led the crusaders to two tunnels set into the hill, inconspicuous holes in the ground that looked like nothing more than badger setts. The woman's reward was to be stripped and beaten, and almost to be hanged as a witch when an extra teat was found on her right flank. But the crusaders knew she was truthful, for the tunnels smelled of fear, rank and acrid. So they settled for flogging her some more and sending her on her way.

The knights decided they would smoke the heretics out, so lit two big fires before the tunnel mouths and waited. When smoke began to drift down to the cavern in the heart of the hill where the Cathars were hiding, they knew something was wrong, and straining their ears heard the crackle of the flames and the cruel chatter of the crusaders. There was no other way out, so they got down on their knees to pray. They were then all, by some miracle, or so the story goes, transmuted into small birds—pipits, buntings, thrushes, sparrows, and shrikes—and flew out through the flames and over the heads of the knights. To this day it is said the area has more of these species than any neighbouring region.

Just as Angélique finished translating the tale for Jon, they were startled by a loud screech, and turning, saw a shrike perched on the ledge of the open window, peering at them, head cocked on one side. Angélique shuddered, and Jon got up to scare it off and close the window.

Petra was still moaning and clutching her head after Angélique and Jon had read in the living room for an hour or so more, so Jon suggested they leave her in peace and, since it was still overcast and a fitful mizzle now fell, not nice enough to sit out in the garden of the house under the fig trees, that they head into Albi to explore the town. Angélique agreed—she really wanted to see the Toulouse-Lautrec Museum, which she recalled visiting as a child.

"I feel an affinity for those cabaret singers and dancers, you know?"

What she really meant was she felt an affinity for Toulouse-Lautrec himself, the melancholy freak.

So, leaving Petra laid up in the darkened bedroom, they took the van and drove to the city. When they crested a rise and saw the place before them, Angélique gasped. With its austere, hulking cathedral on a hill, Gothic turrets, and arched bridges over the glassy waters of the Tarn, Albi looked like a place out of a fairy tale. She hadn't remembered it being so beautiful.

They parked in a narrow cobbled backstreet and walked down to the museum on the banks of the river. Only to find it closed for the day.

Jon gestured up at the sky. "At least it's clearing up a bit. Why don't we get a coffee?"

Jon had a *café noir*, Angélique a mint tea. They sat outside a street-corner café sipping their drinks and watching passers-by.

Jon looked up at the cathedral looming above them. "Why was it the Church felt so threatened by the Cathar faith anyway?"

"There's some debate actually among historians," Angélique replied, "about whether there really was a recognisable group of heretics or if it was just a way the clergy at the time could lump together disparate groups of dissidents." She paused to stir more sugar into her tea. "But it was said that the Cathars believed in two principles in the universe, one good and the other evil. For them, the god of the New Testament represented the good in the cosmos and was creator of spiritual things. They believed the god of the Old Testament evil, and the maker of the material realm. They called him Satan."

The sun had come out, and Jon squinted at her against the light.

"In their creed, this Satan had trapped angels in the base world, who, sexless and pure, yearned to be free. These yearning spirits were the souls of men. Men and women. These souls were born to die over and over, till they gained salvation through a rite of baptism performed when they were near death." She looked up. There was a faint rainbow in the sky, arcing over the roof of the cathedral. "The Cathars were supposed to have called that ritual *consolamentum*. Isn't that beautiful? *Consolamentum*."

"We're fed up to the back teeth with each other," Jon said.

Angélique, pulled out of her reverie, peered at him. "Huh?"

"You know, couples who've been together a long time . . . " He trailed off, sat blinking in the sun.

"Why are you telling me this? I couldn't care less."

It was getting humid again, so Angélique went into the café, into the toilet, and put on the pair of shorts she'd brought with her.

When she went back outside, Jon had his sunglasses on. The lenses were dark, and she couldn't see his eyes, but felt he was leering at her legs, and regretted changing.

But even in shorts, Angélique felt like she was going to melt, so it was with relief she followed Jon into the cavernous, dark, and cool interior of the cathedral. As she entered, an attendant looked at her shorts and bare skin, and made as if to approach her, but then seeing something in her face, backed away. She wandered behind Jon as he made his way up the nave towards the ornate rood screen. It was intricately sculpted in a dark hardwood, details picked out in gold leaf and inlaid ivory, finely wrought in black iron. With sculptures in niches, and a crucifix overhead.

Angélique looked about her. Above, the vaults were deep blue with curling fronds among which little birds perched, looking down at them. On the western wall was a fresco of the Last Judgement. She crossed over, stood gazing at it. There, among the condemned sinners, she saw Alice again. Her mien peaceful, beatific, though she was naked and bound to a wheel and had snakes coiling about her and biting her flesh. Then Alice smiled, the painted mouth smiled, and Angélique staggered back, bumping into Jon, knocking from his hands the mobile phone he was holding out to take a picture—the newest model, it was always the newest model with Jon, of course. It fell to the flags. Hunkering down, he picked it up. The screen was shattered. Hushed, hissing, he began to berate Angélique.

She ignored him. A brew of smells—the sharp acridity of a serpent of smoke wafting from an extinguished taper, the heady reek of incense, the salt tang of cold marble, the rich scent of decay given off by old wood, the must of old books—evoked something for Angélique, something from a dream maybe, she wasn't sure. She shook her head, turned to Jon, and said, "I want to go back." Then grinned a grin that took the fight out of him.

He put his smashed phone in his pocket and nodded.

On their way back, Jon pulled off the road into a little parking spot where there was a Black Madonna in a grotto in a chalk scarp, offerings strewn at her feet—sheafs of lavender, dried lemons, and the papery husks of cicadas, crickets, and hornets. He switched off the ignition.

"It's not just about the new gallery, you know? I *was* being an arsehole. Petra's sick. She's been pining away since you stopped dreaming, since you've not had any dreams to tell her. The headaches, everything."

"I don't get it."

"Why should you? Why should you get it? After all, you're only a dreamer."

"I'm not."

"What else then? What else are you?"

The infant cradled in the Madonna's arms had red eyes, Angélique now saw, pieces of red cut glass. They looked like an insect's eyes.

She turned to look at Jon. "I meant, I'm not even a dreamer. If I'm anything at all, it's a poor oxherd's wife."

Jon shrugged. "Okay. If you say so." He leant over and put his hand high up on her bare thigh. She let him, though inwardly she seethed.

When they got back to the house, Jon went straight upstairs to see how Petra was, and Angélique wandered into the living area. She was uncomfortable, sticky, so she opened the big window, and sat there before it, looking out at the birds chattering in the branches of the fig trees and feeling the breeze dry the sweat from her skin. After a bit, Jon came back downstairs.

"She's still not feeling well," he said. "I'm going to take her up something to eat and sit with her a bit."

After he'd gone again, Angélique took a *saucisson* from the larder, and sat in the window gnawing on it and reading more of Hecate Shrike's verse. The sweat on her skin dried to whorls of salt. Then, when it started to cool down a little, the sun a daub of ochre low in the western sky, she got up and went out for a walk.

She maundered without aim, but her feet took her back to the old thorn bush once more. By the time she reached it, the sun had set, but even in the twilight she could see at a glance it had been picked clean of the carrion fruit. She stood there a moment, breathing in the dusk, then heard someone nearby singing that old song, "*Lo Boièr*". She followed the sound of the voice.

The singer was a woman in late-middle age, with the deeply scored face of a heavy smoker, but a bright life in her eyes. She was sitting on a log in a clearing. The shapeless linen dress she wore was rumpled and stained. She smiled up at Angélique and patted the log beside her. Angélique sat.

"I knew your *mémé*," the woman said. She was speaking French.

Angélique started. "How do you know me?"
"We recognise our own."
Angélique nodded.

"My name is Madeleine." She smiled. "It was I who washed her clean when the time came, when her throat was all swollen with the cancer. Like a turkey's craw. She was *parfaite* at the end and went to her reward."

Angélique nodded. She didn't really feel anything, but a few tears welled and ran down her cheeks.

"*Ma pauvre petite*," Madeleine said. And she stroked Angélique's hair and sang "*Lo Boièr*" to her in a low coo.

When Angélique woke the next morning, the sun was just cresting the horizon, and it was still fresh and cool. She was a little stiff from sleeping out in the open on packed dirt, sheltered only by the log at her back. In the night, she'd dreamed. But it hadn't brought the relief she'd thought it would.

She walked back up the hill, past the keep, and then down the other side, through the commune. When she entered her grandmother's house, all was quiet and still. She called out.

"Angélique?" Petra shouted down from upstairs. "Is that you?"

"Yes."

"Come up."

"Let me just make myself a hot chocolate and I will."

Chocolate made, Angélique climbed the stairs, cupping the steaming bowl in her hands. Petra called out again, and Angélique saw that the door to her and Jon's bedroom stood ajar. After crossing over, Angélique put her head round. The windows were open and the shutters closed, and it was shady and cool in there. Petra languished in bed, sheets pulled up to her chin. She was dishevelled, looked tired, irritated, but somehow relieved. When she saw Angélique, she limply waved an arm.

"Have you seen him?" she asked. "He got up in the night, said he was going downstairs to read, but I heard him leave the house. He's not come back."

Angélique took a sip of her hot chocolate, then nodded.

"He's always doing this." Petra hissed. "I could murder him." She sat up a little in bed, against the pillows, and ran her hands through her tangled hair. "Where have you been anyway?"

Angélique smiled. "I slept outside."

Petra peered at her. "Why?"

"I had a dream."

"You did? That's wonderful!"

"Actually, Jon was in it."

Petra beckoned. "Come in," she said. "Tell me."

Angélique stepped into the room. But she kept to the shadows by the door, away from the gentle early morning light that flowed in around the closed shutters, washed over Petra in the bed. And she told Petra of her dream . . .

In the dream it was spring, but cold, and Angélique was walking through ancient forest. Tall firs, their upper branches lost to distance and the haze in the chill air, a soft carpet of dead needles and rotting pinecones on the floor. She was dressed warmly, thick overcoat, scarf, woolly hat, and hands in an old-fashioned white muff that had belonged to her grandmother. She'd just crossed a glade where the spears of grass were white with hoarfrost and crunched underfoot, and gone back in under the spiring trees, when she heard a faint cry, barely audible. She stopped, looked around, and, not seeing anyone, was about to continue on her way, when the voice came again, again feeble. This time she realised it was coming from overhead, and looked up.

Jon dangled there, upside down, impaled through the meat of one calf on a sharpened pine branch, his face some distance above her head. A sheet of paper had been pinned to his shirt, on which were scrawled the words, "*Rex Mundi*". In the dream, Angélique couldn't guess the meaning of those words, but waking she knew. Jon weakly waved one arm at her. The other hung useless, a spur of bright bone jutting from a rent near the shoulder. Blood dripped, slow and thick, from the back of his head. It looked bad, but she couldn't really see—the wound was hidden by his hair, which, dark brown in life, was a shock of white in the dream and tinged red about the gash. The blood drops mottled the wild hyacinths, starred the dock leaves at her feet.

She tilted her head, raised her ear to him, craned. He spoke again. In a strained whisper, but all else was still, other than the rustle of small creatures in the underbrush, and she could make out what he said.

"There's a certain illustrated manuscript . . . "

He wheezed, struggling for breath, lisped and drooled blood. Some of this bloody slobber fell onto her upraised cheek, and she wiped it off absentmindedly with her *mémé*'s muff.

Then, with effort, Jon went on.

"It's a fourteenth-century traveller's tale, an account of a tribe who dwelt in the foothills of the Pyrenees."

Angélique shrugged.

"The scribes drew these terrifying pictures in the margins."

She nodded.

"Do you know what those pictures are of?"

She shook her head.

"Ordinary enough folk. But they've feathers in their hair, and . . . " He choked, spluttered. Some of the blood spraying from his lips spattered Angélique's chin. She darted out a tongue to lick it off.

Jon peered at her. "Oh," he said.

"Oh," she mimicked, smiling sweetly.

He then closed his eyes, sighed soft. Above and about him, the dead and dying hung, skewered on branches.

When the dream was told, Petra, who'd listened rapt, clapped her hands. There was a brightness in her eyes.

"I knew it!"

Angélique squinted at her, then drank a swallow of her chocolate, which had cooled down enough to gulp.

"When my headache lifted in the night. It seemed a sign."

"Well, I'm happy for you."

"That's not important. The important thing's that you're dreaming again."

"Why do you care?"

"Darling, of course I care."

"What if I don't?"

Petra sat up then, against the headboard of the bed, pushed the sheets from her. She was dressed only in underwear and a silk gown, which hung open. Angélique saw there was a mole or birthmark low down on her right flank.

"But it's your gift. Your art."

"It makes me a whore."

"It keeps you fed and watered. *We* keep you fed and watered."

Angélique sneered. "Fed and watered." She hawked and spat on the dusty boards at her feet.

Shivering a little, Petra slumped back down in the bed, pulled the sheets up over her again.

Angélique shook her head. "Look, I'm sorry. Didn't mean to be a bitch."

"Didn't you?"

"No. I appreciate everything you've done for me, really I do." She took another mouthful of her chocolate. Some dribbled down her chin, and she absently licked it off.

Scrabbling with her feet, Petra cringed back, drew the sheets up to her chin. "Where's Jon?" There was a break in her voice.

"I don't know."

"What have you done with him?"

"Nothing. I've not done anything with him." She started out of the shadows to hop over to where Petra lay in bed.

"What?" Petra stammered. "Your legs!"

And the shrikes in the branches of the fig trees behind the cottage began to shriek, to goad. Angélique stopped, stood, head cocked on one side, peering at Petra, who'd fainted away, and thought about when, as a small child, she'd jump up and down on that old bed in the room down the landing, about the racket it would make, and how she'd feel then like she could fly.

Three Relics

I. Cast a Cold Eye

Though grave-diggers' toil is long,
Sharp their spades, their muscle strong,
They but thrust their buried men
Back in the human mind again.

– "Under Ben Bulben"

In summer, one of the city's most pleasant spots is a park on the shores of the Bosphorus. Cedars grow thickly there, and it is cool beneath their shade and in the breeze blowing off the sea. In this park, atop a squat knoll, is an artificial tree of gleaming silver. Flurries soughing through its filigree leaves make a soft music. Wedged in a fork of this tree is a lumpish skull. Hammered gold wraps it and it has been given horns of whetted obsidian. With the garnets set in its sockets, it looks out over the water, where dolphins sport and sunlight on the chop makes a tracery of fire.

A clockwork contraption hidden inside the skull's brainpan wags its jawbone and makes it speak in a fluting brogue, low and solemn. During the hot season, the mechanism is wound each morning before dawn by the city watch, and folk gather every day to hear the skull declaim verse and tell tales of times long past. They hunker rapt in the glade about the tree, from sunrise out over the hills on the other side of the strait, till red dusk throws the cupolas, onion domes, and minarets of the city into stark silhouette. Only then, when a booming gong sounds out from that great bell, Cracked Mary, high up in the crooked tower of the Cathedral, calling the faithful to prayers, does the skull fall silent and the crowd disperse.

But in winter, when snow bows the boughs of the cedars and keen-honed gusts off the water yowl in the branches of the silver tree, the sentries, knowing no one will come to hear it speak, do not wind the skull. During those mute, cold months, it broods, broods on the tale it would relate to the summer throngs were it not constrained by the mechanism to rote recital.

Under bare Ben Bulben's head, the skull would tell, if only it could, in Drumcliff churchyard, beneath a graved slab, was laid, in a coffin of bright wood, on foreign soil soldered shut and aspergillum spattered, a haphazard freak. Though the bulky skull was like enough to the crotchety poet's, its brow hadn't ever been adorned with the laurels—it was a peasant farmer's, a man of Alpine stock, known for his gentle way with cattle, the pungency of the tobacco he smoked in his clay pipe, and the sharpness of his chess game. From an Englishman writhen by Pott's disease had come a rib cage and gnarled spine encased in a steel-and-leather surgical truss, rusting, rotting, similar to but more elaborate than the one worn by the poet for his herniated gut. The bones of one foot, the left, frail and twisted, were from a club-footed butcher, and the long yellowed right humerus, from a tuna fisherman. The pelvis had belonged to a banker, a cruel man. The whole had been cobbled together by a forensic doctor from bones taken from an ossuary in a hilltop cemetery in the south of France. The poet had been interred there in his own plot, but then war had come, and in the chaos his remains had been dug up and thrown into the mass tomb. It was only by pure chance that one of the bones returned to Mother Ireland had actually belonged to him—this was a phalanx from the index finger of the right hand, a bone crooked from years of holding a pen. All the bones that were buried in Drumcliff, save that phalanx, are long since dust. The phalanx lies still underground, awaiting once more its pen.

When the doors of the ossuary had first been thrown open to him, the mayor of the local village, seeing the relics within mixed pell-mell, had groaned and wrung his hands. Frustrated and chagrined before the police inspector come from the capital to oversee the exhumation, he'd seized up the first long bone that came to hand, a femur, and set about the sexton with it, clubbing him bloody, before casting it into a thicket of myrtle. It just so happened that thigh bone was the poet's.

An undertaker, who was also there, ignored the mayor's tantrum and wandered into the ossuary. He nonchalantly kicked a few bones about, then took a vertebra at random from a pile in a niche and tossed it hand to hand a bit before putting it into the pocket of his waistcoat. Later, when he got home, he put it in pride of place on his mantelpiece. He told visitors ever after that it was a vertebra from the famous foreign poet, finally in old age coming to believe this lie himself. But, though he'd no way of knowing it, it wasn't in fact a lie—the bone *had* come from the poet.

On the undertaker's death, he left the vertebra to his favourite son. This sullen and ungrateful lad cared little for poetry so, on a whim, had the bone carved into a dice, which he used for playing at craps. It brought him good fortune, though he little deserved it, and that dice has been passed down through the generations, and is famed for the luck it brings. It is reputed to be used in games of hazard in this city to this day.

Many years after the hotchpotch of bones had been sealed into a coffin and shipped back to the Land of Saints and Scholars, a miserable vagrant gyrfalcon, flying south, strayed far from its hunting grounds of the arctic tundra, driven off by peregrines who, with the warming of the climate, had expanded their territory to the north, struck a corkscrew updraft over the hilltop cemetery. It spread its white-flecked brown wings and wheeled there a time. The place was by then a melancholy wreck, overgrown with bramble, ferns, and myrtle, the mausolea all ruins, the stones all canted and shattered, like a mouthful of smashed teeth. Thinking it saw the scurrying of some small creature amid a tangle of scrub, the gyrfalcon stooped, but found nothing, save the thigh bone the mayor had tossed into the bushes. The gyrfalcon snatched up the bone, then whooped into the air seeking rocks or a patch of old concrete on which to let it fall, hoping to crack it, get at the marrow. But the sad bird was mobbed by crows and dropped the femur so it could better fend them off.

The bone fell and struck the roof of an old tin shack where lived a madwoman who haunted the cemetery and the village below, telling fortunes in exchange for coin. She carried about with her always a marble putto that had broken off a monument in the graveyard and which she kept swaddled in a dirty cloth and dandled as if it were a real baby. Hearing the clunk overhead, she put down her "child" and went outside. She found the poet's thigh bone lying in the dirt before her door. She chuckled and rubbed her hands, then picked it up and took it back into her hovel. She rummaged through a pile of old rags she had in a corner, found a tattered old jacket, pulled it from the heap. Then draped it over the bone, went outside, and began to dance a surprisingly graceful waltz with that shabby coat hooked over the old bone.

She was unaware she was being watched by a moony young man, who often hid in the bushes outside her shack to gaze on her. Seeing her dancing so elegantly with the bone, his heart yearned for her still the more. He knew that to get her notice he would need to pay her tribute and cudgelled his brains over what might be a suitable gift. Then it came to him and he scampered off.

One of the village elders was a cruel haughty man who bullied and belittled all about him. For the madwoman, he had an especial scorn. Many times had he mocked her and many times pelted her with rotten fruit and even stones. That very night the young man crept into the elder's cottage while he was sleeping and, with a pair of rusty garden shears, clipped his ears from his head. Then he ran off before the elder's squeals could wake the others of the tribe. He clambered up the hill to the graveyard and left his tribute before the madwoman's door.

But she was never to see it, because, before she woke the next day, some of the villagers, stalking the night, the beams of their electric torches carving up the dark, came to her hut and found the severed ears. They dragged her off and chained her up in the village square, where she howled for several days and nights before, sore irked, they hurled her off a cliff into the sea. The cemetery they razed. Appalled by the heaped bones of the ossuary, they took armfuls and cast them also into the water. The young man, when they found him hiding in a cave down by the shore, they hung upside down from a dead tree by one ankle and left to the carrion birds.

The bones, the remainder of the poet's among them, were dispersed by the tides.

One day an elderly woman, a witch who lived in an old stone cottage on Sicily on a hill overlooking the sea, wandered down to the beach for an early morning walk. A bevy of swans strutted and hissed mournfully on the pale strand. The old woman stopped to watch them a time. In amongst their black legs and webbed feet, she sighted a yellow flash of bone and crossed over, shooing the birds, to get a closer look. It was a human collarbone, worn thin by the roiling of the water. Feeling it had some kind of talismanic power, she picked it up and put it in the pocket of her apron. It was the left clavicle of the poet.

When she got back to her cottage after the walk, the old woman took a gimlet and drilled a hole in the bone, through which she threaded a cord. She hung the bone round her neck, wore it there for the rest of her days. It brought luck and helped with her magical workings.

When she felt death was nearly upon her, she decided, knowing the power of the bone, to bury it in a lonely place, somewhere no one who might use it for ill would ever happen across it. So she trudged one wearisome summer's eve, after the heat of the day had broken, up into the hills behind the village, and interred the collarbone there in a hole as deep as she could dig. The very next day, she died. The villagers celebrated her life with a week of feasting and revelry.

But unbeknownst to the witch, there lived in the Sicilian hills, in the shell of a tumbledown villa, a ghoul, a gaunt and shambling old man, who spent his days in brooding and attempting dark rites, all of which failed. He knew of and envied the witch's magic. He saw her bury the bone and then, like a carrion dog, dug it up. He spent many months trying to tap its uncanny power. He prayed to it. He wore it round his neck and he brandished it like a wand. He even smashed open one end with a hammer and sucked on the desiccated marrow. Nothing worked. Finally, on a whim, he held the hole the old witch had bored to his right eye and peering through it saw a world transfigured, colours garish and eldritch. It bleared his vision at first, but once he was used to it he realised he could see things that were hidden from mundane sight. He climbed to the highest point of the island and surveyed the prospect in all directions, his eye to the hole in the bone. To the north, out in a bay, he saw a black rocky islet girded by a flaring nimbus. He knew there was something potent and strange there.

The very next day the old warlock rented a boat from a local fisherman and rowed out. It was warm, sunny, and he was soon red and sweaty with the effort. As he drew nearer he kept stopping to look at the islet through the hole in the collar bone. Had anyone been watching him from the shore, they would have thought him mad—he seemed awestruck by the rock, which was drab, streaked with seagull shit, encrusted with whelks and barnacles, and swagged with bladderwrack. But seen through the hole in the bone it was a lush isle of fig trees and wild rosemary and thyme, where magical unicorns gambolled with gracile nymphs clinging to their backs, and centaurs galloped whooping and hunting viridian swans with ironwood bows. And at its heart, on a hill, spiring to rend the white wisps of cloud scudding overhead, was a tower of ivory, which seemed, though it must be impossible, to be of one piece, as if the tusk of some ancient behemoth. It was ornately carved, like gargantuan scrimshaw, graved with dolphins, nudes, peacocks, and snakes, all twined together.

The warlock beached his boat, dragged it up above the waterline. The nymphs and centaurs ceased their frolics and watched him, wary but silent, from a distance, as he went up the hill to the base of the tower. When he reached it, he circled around and came across ebony doors, huge and iron studded, with carved over their arch a motto, *Daemon est Deus Inversus*. He pushed at these doors, found they opened easily, then went inside, into the cool. It was stark, save a stone staircase that wound into the heights above.

After climbing for what seemed, and maybe was, an age, the warlock came up into a room at the top of the tower, the point of the tusk. Its walls were graved, like the outside, but the designs here were darker. The Sphinx, vultures reeling about its head, turned its broken face to look out, gaze blank and pitiless as the sun. In a simple wooden crib, an infant, mouth gaping to wail. Crawling across sand and waste, a bleak chimera. Crawling towards a desert city, streets swamped with blood.

Other than the wall carvings, the room was bare save a stone altar draped in a black cloth emblazoned with that motto, *Daemon est Deus Inversus*, in gold. On this altar was set, like a venerated relic, the pelvis of the poet, and beside it lay a book of ritual.

The warlock spent many years in the room at the top of the tower poring over the book, pondering its conundrums. Silver platters of rich and gamey swan and goblets of ambrosial mead were brought to him by the nymphs—the denizens of the isle had recognised in him their destroyer, but worshipping the turning wheel of history, aided him in all ways they could. When he finally descended the tower, came out into a peaceful gloaming, and waited for night to fall, the nymphs and unicorns and centaurs gathered to watch his rite.

Once it was dark and the constellations were wheeling in the void above, the warlock held the poet's pelvis like a mask to his face and intoned, in a high cracked voice, "May this laborious stair and this stark tower become a roofless ruin that the owl may build in the cracked masonry and cry her desolation to the desolate sky."

And the holy centaurs and nymphs and unicorns were banished and fled, and the warlock fell to his knees and his parched tongue turned to dust in his throat and choked him, and the tower was revealed to be but a squat thing of loosening masonry, where bees built in the crevices, a squat thing clad in a vibrant mantle of butterflies and moths.

And again the world gyred and span. But this time, because of what the warlock had done, its still point was a skull, the poet's skull, somewhere beneath the ocean, in the belly of a leviathan. The skull talked to that whale from its guts, told it to swim into the Mediterranean and beach itself on the shore by the ruins of an ancient city on the Bosphorus and die there. And when the carcass rotted, the skull, able once more to gaze upon the welkin, fell into a reverie. That skull is the skull which now sings to you of what is passed or passing, and could sing to you of what is to come, if it so chose. That skull is the skull which, as you must deep down know, conjures you, for you are naught but figments of its dream.

The skull knows that, were it ever able to tell this truth, the word would blaze through the city. And that evening, when Cracked Mary began tolling under a dusking sky, no one would hearken. And, as overhead the stars glimmered into being one by one, the flames that flitted on the pavements, fed by resinous hearts, would sputter out. The streets would be mobbed, all the folk of the city parading doleful down to the Bosphorus, keening eerie, filthy wrappings unwinding to bare grey and withered flesh. And down in the harbour, dolphins, porpoises, and narwhals would wait, offering their backs to the wailing dead that they might carry them off to paradise.

The skull, gazing on all of this, would, unheard by any, say, "Cast a cold eye on life, on death. Horseman, pass by!"

II. Sad Presentiments of a Proud Monster

The voice of the Garonne as it carves, brute, if a little sluggish, through Bordeaux on its way to meet the Dordogne before flowing turbid through the Gironde estuary and out into the wild Atlantic, is deep and sonorous, if dog-tired. But listen closely and you'll still hear some of the high fleet fettle of the cascades of the river's youth on the slopes of the Pyrenees. The voice that issued from the massy skull when it spoke, lying canted on the warped and stained wooden floorboards of the apartment in the old quarter of the ancient city, unmistakably the great artist's voice, had the same quality of being profound, if weary, but with an undercurrent of something sprightly and mischievous.

The last of the drinkers at the cafés had long since staggered home when the young woman wearing a black lace mantilla, whose features were pretty if pinched and wan, scurried across la place Saint-Pierre. She lifted her ruffled skirts with one hand, while clutching a calfskin portfolio in the other. Passing by the Gothic edifice of the ancient church, she cast a glance at the carven saints arcing over its doorway and superstitiously crossed herself. Then she ducked into the narrow cobbled streets of the quarter and, keeping to the shadows, made her way to her witching-hour appointment.

When the warlock, who'd modelled once for the great artist and had admired and hated him for the unsparing light the portrait had shone on his flaws, had taken the skull from the crypt in le cimetière de la Chartreuse, a dank stone pit where the artist's bones and those of a friend of his, a cloth trader, had been laid out on grey slabs, there had still been a few strands of brittle wispy hair clinging to the temples. The warlock had brushed these off, and slunk out with the skull in a waxed-hide bag.

The portfolio of mottled calfskin the girl held tight contained her most prized possession, a set of prints from a series of etchings about the horrors of war and of despotism. The prints had been made privately from the copperplates and left to her by the great artist. Fearing his satire would bring reprisals down on his head, he'd not had the series published in his lifetime. The girl had got nothing else from the artist, who was her godfather and, she felt sure, her father, so she guarded the prints jealously. But the warlock had told her they were needful for the rite she'd asked him to perform. So she'd brought them with her when she'd come back to this filthy place from Spain.

A dream disturbed the young woman's nights. The same dream every night. A dream smeared thickly with dread. A dream in which she, dressed in white skirts and a red cloak, was snatched up by her hair from the easel she was working at in a small room in the Museo del Prado, painting a copy of a triptych by Hieronymus Bosch, snatched up by a man with mad staring eyes and his lips pulled back in a rictus, who'd floated in through a window, snatched up and then dragged out of the Museo, through the air over Madrid, and out of the city, over the countryside about, passing strange scenes below, a small town through whose crowded streets was being led, sitting on the back of an ass, a woman, with her hands tied, chin held up by a wooden yoke, stripped to the waist and wearing a tall conical hat painted with garish designs, while the rabble jeered at her, then on and past the town and over a forest of dark firs, where the girl, the great artist's daughter, saw a withered crone and a voluptuous young woman, both naked, flying by, riding on a broom between their thighs, then further on the forest gave way to a blighted country where little grew and a hulking beast, with the body of a lion, but the head of a rat, lay sickening, feeble, and spewing corpses in a ditch, and then they saw ahead a mountain shaped like an anvil, with a citadel atop, and suddenly soldiers with red plumes in their black shakos were shooting with rifles at her and the man who hauled her through the air, and one of the bullets struck the man, puncturing his belly and letting the air out of him, and he dropped her, and she fell down and landed in a mire, sinking to her knees, which knocked the wind out of her, and when she got her breath back, and the whistling faded from her ears, she heard a wheezy music and looking up saw, close by her, a veiled woman in a chair playing a concertina and, surrounding her in a ring, a mob, dressed in drab, leering and touching themselves under their clothing, and she realised she clutched a pitchfork in her hands, and that before her was a giant vulture, standing up with its wings spread wide and terror and pleading in its eyes. She made to stab the bird, but always, before she pronged it, she started up shaking and slick with sweat. Whenever she awoke she had the strange feeling owls and cats had been crowding around her bed, just the moment before, and she saw always a shadow moving on the walls of her bed chamber, the shadow of a goat with gimlet horns, standing on its hind legs, and clad in a black cloak.

The young woman knew the imagery of her recurring dream was drawn from her godfather's, her father's, work and felt obscurely he meant to warn her about something through it, but could not make out what it was. But she knew it was important—that one night the tines of her fork would sink into the vulture's flesh, and the day that followed would be terrible. She knew she needed to find out what her father was trying to tell her before then. The dream enervated her and she grew sicker each day. And more hopeless.

The young woman, not wishing to wake respectable people sleeping peacefully in their beds, crept quietly up the wide curving stairs of the stately neoclassical building, with their ornate balustrade, to the apartment on the third floor where the warlock awaited her. She let herself in. Outside it was a cool autumn night, but within the apartment was a fug—a fire blazed somewhere, she could hear it crackling, and the air was laced with the smoke of burning resins and herbs, heady and fragrant, like incense, but tinged with corruption. She loosened her mantilla. Standing in the dark hall, she called out, but there was no response. Then, seeing flaring light under one of the doors, she pushed it open and went through. She found herself in the apartment's grand salon. The fire she had earlier heard roared in the grate of a fireplace with carven marble pilasters—one, Cernunnos with stag's antlers and myrtle coiling from his open mouth, and the other, a beautiful dryad emerging dreamily from the trunk of an oak. The only other source of light was a brazier burning pitch, and the illumination in the room was glaring but fitful, red, hellish. The spare furnishings—a low coffee table, a drinks cabinet, fronted with etched glass, a chaise-longue, a loveseat, and two armchairs upholstered in red leather—had been pushed to the edges of the space, up against the wall-hangings, which mostly depicted tableaux drawn from common life—a fish market, barques at anchor in a harbour, a vineyard on a steep hillside—though there was one scene from the life of Jesus, an unusual subject, the Exorcism of Legion, shown after Christ has cast the demons out of the afflicted man and into the herd of swine. The wild staring eyes of the hogs as they bolted, bristles raised along their backs, towards a cliff edge, discomfited the girl.

The pungent reek wreathed the room, rising to the high ceilings, with their rococo cornices and frescoes of fauns and nymphs dancing with abandon. It fumed from a censer swung on a chain by a man who wore a collarless blue serge coat, a humble working man's garment, over a pair of green breeches, embroidered with gold thread, of very fine quality and workmanship. The man dressed in this odd, mismatched, and rather quaint get-up had the face of an anchorite, lined, raw boned, and weather beaten, a face that belied his great wealth and the luxurious dissipation of his life. His grizzled hair was cropped very short, and he wore a skullcap at a sardonic angle.

The girl nodded to him. "Don José."

He smiled at her. "Rosario. So good to see you again." His voice was hoarse, but warm. Smoke furled about his face.

"Thank you. I didn't know where to turn."

He hung the censer on a brass stand in the corner of the room, then crossed over to her, took her hand, and bowed to kiss it. "Those prints will be more than adequate recompense."

She cringed away, snatched back her hand, and hugged the portfolio to her chest. "We didn't discuss that!"

He shrugged. "Those are my terms. If you want to be free of the nightmare, well then . . . "

She glared at him for a time, shaking her head. He stood there, looking up at the cavorting nymphs and fauns. Then the girl spat, "Why here? Why drag me back here?"

"His spirit remains here, of course."

"Close to his bones?"

"Close to the place of his passing."

"And why will it come when we call it?"

The warlock did not answer, but merely moved aside, and gestured to his right. Near to the edge of the cleared space, to the left of the door, there was something on the floor under a cloth the colour of blood.

"What's that?"

He grinned, then crossed over, beckoned her to join him. She did so and he swept away the cloth with a flourish like that of a torero with his *capote de brega*. Beneath, sitting on a hassock, dark wool stuffed with horsehair, was a massy skull. It was whole, save that its jawbone was gone.

The girl gasped and the blood drained from her already sallow face. She went white as tripe.

"You stole his skull?"

"How do you know it?"

"That imposing brow. Those lumps that indicate the development of the faculties of imitation, secretiveness, and destructiveness. Yes, I'd know it anywhere, that skull."

The warlock nodded. Then the girl, peering closer, saw a hole just behind the sutures running over the top of the cranium. She hunkered down and looked at it more closely. It was small, neat, much like the borings deathwatch beetles make in the timbers of old buildings.

She looked up at the warlock. "Have you drilled into it? Why would you?"

He bent over. "I have not. That's old." He pointed. "Look how the edges are yellowed as the rest."

"Someone did this to my father while he was laid out in the mausoleum? Why?"

Straightening, he looked at her, shrugged. "I'd hazard it was bored before he died, actually. But how and why, I cannot say."

She stood again, nodded. "How will the skull aid in finding out what is happening to me?"

"We'll ask it."

"Ask a skull?" She stared at him, incredulous.

"Or rather, we'll ask your father. Let him speak through his mortal remains, and through his work," he said. "Through the prints you've brought."

The warlock explained to the girl how the ritual would work. They'd lay out all eighty-three prints of the series in the girl's portfolio face down on the floor. Then she'd roll the artist's skull across them. The prints on which the skull came to rest would be turned over and the warlock would read the images for omens.

"The necessary preparations have been made," he concluded. "This is how the great man's spirit will speak to you."

"But won't we wake any sleepers in the apartment below?"

"What an odd concern. But no. The man who lives down there is stone deaf. He was an artillery captain, lost his hearing during the Belgian campaign when a mortar blew up near him. He won't hear a thing."

The young woman nodded and handed over the portfolio.

The warlock shuffled and laid the prints out, face down, in a pattern whose significance was obscure. The young woman stood to one side, watching on. She wondered whether she'd been foolish to trust him, but she hadn't known what else to do. All the friends in whom she'd confided had dismissed her nightmares as merely a mark of her ailment, rather than its cause, had advised her to seek medical counsel. But all the while she'd been getting sicker and sicker. She'd written to the warlock in desperation, and his reply had convinced her he knew of the nature of dreams, of how they can open up onto sublime or terrible vistas of reality. So she'd come despite her misgivings. She saw she'd been right not to trust him entirely, but thought the loss of the prints a fair price for the relief his rite promised.

When the warlock was done, the white squares of the prints' backs formed a shape something like the pallid carcass of some abyssal monster washed up on the foreshore. The girl felt queasy to look on it.

"Now it is your turn," he said to her. "Take up the skull, and I will make an incantation over you, and you must then roll it across the prints. Wherever it lands I will turn over that image and read for you its meaning. We will need to do this several times. In this way, the skull, or rather your father's spirit, will tell of what is to come, of what will happen to you."

So they began. The girl took the skull in her hands and stood cradling it, while the warlock, who'd taken up the censer again, swagged her in cloying and sickening fumes and barked a guttural formula in a language she didn't recognise. Then she rolled the skull. It rattled over the uneven boards, the knots in the wood, across the prints, before coming to rest on one somewhere in the middle of the pattern the warlock had set out. He crossed to it, nudged it aside with his foot, then picked up and turned over the print it had landed on. He motioned to the girl to join him. She went. The print was number nine in the sequence, a print with the words "*No quieren*" written underneath the image.

He studied it a moment, then began to speak. "How might we read this? The soldier in the fur hat makes an attempt on the virtue of the girl in white, but she fights back, clawing at his face. The woman behind will stab him, plunge her knife into his back. She is fierce, determined. You must stand strong, Rosario, and help will come, perhaps from an unexpected quarter. And what's that in the background? A war machine of some kind?"

The girl shook her head. "It's a waterwheel. Look at the reflections in the water."

"Ah yes, so it is. That's important. The wheel symbolises the cyclical nature of life. That everything is always changing while staying the same. Water is ever flowing. Acceptance is necessary, but you must also resist."

The warlock then put the print back down, still face up, and directed the girl to take up the skull again and retreat to the edge of the space. Once more he mumbled his occult formula and wreathed the girl in sweet foul smoke. Again she rolled the skull.

This time the print landed on was thirty-seven, captioned, "*Esto es peor.*"

"A man's naked carcass impaled on the branch of a burnt tree. The arms hacked off. That title. There is worse coming your way. But what might that worse be?"

The print was gruesome. The girl shuddered.

"Look at the face of the corpse," the warlock went on. "Slack. That mouth gaping. A skin mask no one wears. Maybe to say that what you might lose is your essence. That you'll be left hollowed out . . . "

And so they went on like that, the warlock pronouncing his mystical refrains over the girl, she rolling her father's skull over the prints, and he interpreting the images it came to rest on. And if it fell on one of the face-up prints, already consulted, the girl would simply roll again.

The next print was sixty-eight, which had the caption, "*Que locura!*"

"This makes sense of my reading of the previous image. Look there at the collection of antic masks piled up around a chamber pot. Slack masks that look on the bared arse of a friar squatting to shit after his evening meal. Those who witness the exposed anus of the numinous are hollowed out. And look over here. Devout paintings and sculptures jumbled about, with a mannequin or puppet in a dress in their midst. Are you to be a puppet of those forces? And look at the spoon the squatting friar still clutches. The cosmos is voracious."

Seventy-four. "*Esto es lo peor!*—Here you can see religion working with the wolfish to dictate terms to the dispossessed and brutalised. The wolf with the scroll, sitting up, writing, shows that beasts can take the aspect of men, just as men can that of beasts."

Seventy-two. "*Las resultas*—Look here at the vampire bat battening on this corpse. Look at its mad staring eyes. Are they not the eyes of the artist, your father? The meaning here is clear."

Seven. "*Que valor!*—A brave woman with long dark hair, wearing a white dress, clambering over bodies to man a cannon, to defend a garrison. That could be you, if only you were brave enough, touching the taper to the fuse. And wheels again, attached to the gun carriage. It's obvious what that signifies."

Seventy-nine. "*Murió la Verdad*—Look! Look at the close resemblance between you and this Truth, lying bare breasted in the dirt, light still shining, but fading, surrounded by hypocrites and the blind, and mourned only by her sister Justice, who clutches her head in despair, her scales, strings tangled, at her side. Notice that the bishop standing over you, wearing his mitre, has your father's face."

The girl peered close and saw it was true.

"This is our last roll," the warlock said then. "The last print we'll consult."

She threw the skull a little harder this time, and it tumbled clattering to stop on a print at the farthest edge of the monstrous shape on the floor of the room in that apartment in the old quarter of Bordeaux. The prints turned over looked as if cankers had formed on the tallow hide of the leviathan. Or eyes opened in it. Together the young woman and the warlock crossed to look.

"Eighty," he said. "*Si resucitará*—The coincidence of this turning up now. It shows we have been on the right track."

She nodded.

"This is you as you will be soon if you don't act," he continued. "Dead. Your light only a glimmer. Surrounded by creatures of the night. Monsters and beasts. While a masked figure by your feet clubs with a heavy cudgel something held in his hand. That figure, with a hood concealing his features, is again your father, the great artist, cause of your affliction, but also, though the hopeful caption for this image is surely sardonic, your possible saviour. And he smashes with a club something that looks a great deal like a skull!"

As he finished his volley the warlock swung the censer, giving off another waft of noxious smoke. The young woman, caught up by his words, lifted her booted foot to stomp on her father's skull, to shatter it and release herself from his malign hold. But then, looking up, she saw the terror in the eyes of the pigs running towards the cliff edge in the tapestry, and she recalled her father's kindness, how he'd often taken her on his knee when she was a child, while he painted, and how, when he was dying, she'd read to him from Cervantes, whose work had always made the great artist so happy. And her foot glanced off the skull, rather than coming down square on it, as she'd meant, and instead of being smashed, it just spun off a little way.

The warlock opened his mouth to berate, but before he could, the skull, lying on its side, still rocking back and forth a little, began to speak.

"In my forty-sixth year, late in seventeen ninety-two, I fell ill. All the winter through I suffered agonies and was many times on the brink of death. But I survived, though I'd never really recover. Something had burrowed into me, lodged itself in my brain."

The girl and the warlock stood listening, both agape. The brazier had gone out and the fire burnt low, and in the trembling light the Gadarene swine on the wall seemed to rush pell-mell to their deaths.

"Some have called that thing genius," the skull went on. "But it was hell. Don José is covetous of it and lured you here, Rosario, daughter, knowing somehow that only you could call it forth. That was a wretched, a foul . . ."

The voice of the skull, the voice of the great artist, had been fading, and now dropped to a soft murmur. At the same time the girl and the warlock, gawping, saw something black, sheeny crawling from the hole bored in the crown of the skull, though it was hard to make anything out in the gloom. And then the thing was gone in a flicker of elytra and there was a low whining in the room.

The warlock stood staring, body slack as if sinews unstrung. The girl wrestled the censer from him and swung it at his head, clubbed him to the ground. Coals tumbled onto his coat and onto the prints spread about, and a blaze sprang up swift. She turned and ran, leaving him lying there amid the flames. As she fled down the stairs of the apartment building, she heard that buzzing again and felt a pang at the back of her head as if an insect had stung her there.

She sickened on the journey back from Bordeaux. Just after passing through Saint-Jean-de-Luz she fell into an ague, sweating and shivering in her corner of the coach. Her handmaiden nursed her as best she could, and there chanced to be a doctor joining them in San Sebastián, who administered a purgative and drafts from a flask of fever remedy. With their ministrations, and the good care of the keepers of the inns she was carried into on the route, deranged and screaming about Black Devourers and the Great He-Goat, she pulled through, though she was tottering on wasted legs when she finally climbed down from the coach in Madrid.

She'd learnt to paint at the knee of her father, the great artist, and had always had an aptitude for it, an aptitude that had got her work at the court he'd so hated. But from that time on she felt that genius in her which was like a living death. Her father had given in to it, but she fought for dear life, no matter its tricks. She continued as a copyist, and sketched and painted her own work, for which she was acclaimed, but she kept her subjects light, portraits and domestic scenes, ignored the screaming in her hindbrain, the throbbing of her pituitary. Later she was appointed drawing tutor to the child queen, Isabella. She lived well, but the strain took its toll.

One day, in the sweltering summer of 1843, she left the palace and was caught up by a throng of agitators. She saw a young man crushed underfoot by the rabble, his blood on the cobbles. Later, after she'd made it back to her studio, the thing in her brain made her paint the scene, the cruel baying masks of the mob, the young man pulped beneath their boots. Then she fell into a swoon.

On rousing, with a great effort of will she was able to burn that canvas to ashes in the grate of her fireplace. But something finally gave out. She died on the floor of her studio, blood leaking from her mouth, before a copy of *Las Meninas* she'd been making. She was only twenty-eight.

III. A Chance Encounter in Barnsbury

One afternoon, late last summer, a close sticky day with a sky the flat grey of spoiled fish, I was walking through London's Barnsbury, cutting from St. Pancras, where my train had set me down, to a pub in Dalston where I was meeting friends. As I walked, I was turning over in my head Ambrose's talk about sorcery, sanctity, and sin from the "Prologue" to "The White People", thinking on saints, sinners, and ecstasy, and on the look I had seen once on the face of a painted martyr in a church in Bayonne. I'm sure many of you know Barnsbury—a region of smart Georgian townhouses and well-kept private squares. But there are still, in the midst of all that affluence, odd pockets of squalor—terraces with flaking paintwork and railings cankered with rust. I was passing by one of these shabby rows, when I happened to look down to a basement flat and my eye was snagged by something in the window. I stopped and peered. On the sill, leaning up against a grimy pane, was a book whose cover illustration—a malevolent goblin sat cross-legged, ringed by toadstools—was very familiar.

As I stared, shocked by the coincidence, feeling as if I had invoked the volume, the door to the flat opened and an elderly man shuffled out. Bald, with a grizzled patchy beard, gaunt, almost fleshless. Scruffily dressed in a tweed jacket gone hairy, an Oxford shirt open at the neck, and a pair of threadbare corduroy trousers. He didn't notice me at first, was fixed on fumbling his door closed and locking it with an old-fashioned brass key with stubby wards. But, starting up the stairs to the pavement, he saw me gawking and smiled hesitantly.

"Sorry," I said. "I happened to glance over and see your *House of Souls* as I passed. Didn't mean to stare."

He squinted at me a moment, wary—his sunken eyes were rheumy and grey—and I thought he was perhaps going to retreat back into his flat.

"It's a first edition, isn't it?" I pressed. "That Sime image is so unsettling."

The man stood mute a little while, staring at me, right hand gripping the wrought iron balustrade. I was just about to shake my head and walk on, when he shrugged and said, "Have you an interest in Machen, then?"

A hoarse croak, as if he'd not spoken in a long time.

I nodded. "I have."

"Well, perhaps you'd like to come in and see the book? It's something of a special copy."

I pondered this a moment. "I don't want to keep you."

"It's no bother. I was just heading out to the post office." He patted the pocket of his jacket and I could see an envelope jutting from it. "But it will keep." He turned and unlocked his door again, held it open for me. "Do go in."

After hesitating just a moment, seeing no harm in it, I entered. I came into a short hallway. To the left, through an open door, I saw a kitchen, *The House of Souls* propped up on the windowsill, above a decrepit gas oven. The old man, after grabbing the volume, ushered me through to a room at the back of the flat. A study, with a heavy mahogany desk and several bookcases, all filled with old books. The long-pile carpet and the flock paper on the walls were dark red. The atmosphere was oppressive; the must of the books was in the air, but also a dank cellar smell, and both were overlaid by a cloying note, as of incense. There was a bay window at the back, and outside was an overgrown garden, the trees and shrubs straggling yet rank.

The old man gestured to a Queen Anne wing chair with worn green upholstery. "Please, do sit."

I perched nervously on the edge of the chair.

"I had the book in the front window as a signal, you see," he said, pacing back and forth before me. "For someone who hasn't showed. But you saw it instead. Would you like to take a look?"

I nodded, and he handed it down to me. "Turn to the title page."

I did and saw, opposite the Sime frontispiece, which was hazed behind tissue paper, a dedication in a sprawling hand: "To the Barnsbury Hermit, Coleridge of our profane modern era," it read. "With fond recollections of our many conversations about literature and the ecstatic. Ever your poor Boswell." Beneath was a spidery signature I knew.

I looked up at the old man. "Who was the dedicatee?" But I hadn't needed to ask. I realised then that the paper on the walls, of a deep and heavy crimson, almost black, was the same Machen had described.

He laughed, took the book back from me, and put it down on the desk. I felt as if I had wandered into a dream.

I didn't therefore ask how he was still living, but instead, "Have you kept up your literary studies?"

"I have," he replied. "I continue to encounter the quality of ecstasy in all sorts of works, often in those places where others might not expect it. And I still find that many of the books considered most literary lack it, whatever their other merits might be."

I nodded, then was struck by a notion. "What about Machen's aesthetics? Did he ever discuss them with you?"

"Not really. He was interested in my ideas, and they clearly chimed with his, but he kept his cards close to his chest when it came to discussing his own work."

Just then a great pale bird lurched, beating its wings, over the wall, and alighted in the branches of a sickly beech in the garden. It perched fluttering there. I thought maybe it was only a newspaper, borne on gusts, but then it spread its wings, flapped them twice, and whooped into the violet sky.

"But," the Hermit continued, not apparently noticing I'd been distracted, "he was obviously quite as interested in that quality of ecstasy as I am, and I do have a sense, based on his writings, of his approach. But here's a tale that might shed some light. It was the last time I saw Machen in fact. Probably in the second half of the nineteen-twenties. Not that we fell out, though I was irked he wrote about our encounters as if he'd fictionalised me, but simply that when he left London, we rather lost touch. He'd invited me over to a shindig at his place in St. John's Wood. I don't recall who was in attendance, some minor literary luminaries I suppose. But I do remember we were made to play that game of Machen's invention, Dog and Duck, rolling balding tennis balls along the paths in his garden.

"And Machen served a punch at the event, named in honour of the sport. Deceptively mellifluous, but in truth highly potent. All the guests became drunk, but in a light and agreeable way. In the highest of spirits. The game and the difficulty of it, you had to put curve on your ball, get it to sweep round the path, a near impossible feat, became the source of much hilarity.

"The punch was served out of a bowl of bluish-green glass inlaid with silver leaf. At one point I was standing with Machen at the punch table, as he ladled out slugs for the guests, and asked him, I think, what the secret of his writing was. He winked at me, flicked the bowl with a forefinger so it rang low and sweet, and said, 'The Cauldron of Rebirth.'

"That stuck with me," the Hermit went on. "I thought about it a lot afterwards. *Y Pair Dadeni* appears in the Mabinogion. It's a magical cauldron able to revive the dead. Machen, as I'm sure you know, in his writings on the Grail romances, suggests that some relic of Celtic sacramental tradition was fused with pagan magical cauldrons and the Chalice of the Eucharist, to give rise to the popular conception of the Sangraal as a cup. Thinking on Machen's invocation and also of the idea he and I discussed many times of the writer of fine literature as a kind of hierophant, I felt as if I had discovered a key of some kind to his work. But it eluded me then, and continues to elude me."

The Hermit, who had gone on with his pacing before me, gesticulating, turned then, pulled out from behind the desk a mahogany chair with an ornately-carved back, and sat down facing me. Outside the light was fading—more time had apparently passed than I'd realised. My friends would be missing me, and there would doubtless be messages from them on my phone. But, still agog, as if at the sight of a statue of some olden saint come to life, I wanted to hear more. So I prodded. "What do you make of Machen's style? Of his prose?"

"Well," the Hermit said, leaning forward with his elbows on his knees, and steepling his fingers. "As many have noted, there could be said to be three phases to his writing. The first is very distinct. As he writes in the introduction to this volume," here he took up and waved at me *The House of Souls*, "his first works are written in the ornate English of the early part of the seventeenth century. In the late eighteen-eighties he abandons this for a *fin-de-siècle* style, modern, yet decadent, rich in symbolism and imagery. This is sustained throughout the eighteen-nineties, his most fertile period, and reaches its apotheosis in *The Hill of Dreams* and the sketches of *Ornaments in Jade*. The subsequent shift in his approach is much more subtle, a gentle turn towards a starker, more journalistic tone. The second phase of Machen's writing is generally held to be the richer, but I feel the drying out of the prose of the late work to be equally, or perhaps even more potent."

"But don't you think," I put in, "that through symbol and suggestion, the work of the eighteen-nineties reveals to us great mysteries perhaps absent from later stories?"

"I think," the Hermit replied, "that the *fin-de-siècle* work attempts to mimic the ecstatic moment, but is doomed to failure. The veil cannot truly be lifted in that way, by fiction masquerading as liturgy, and Machen realises this. What he does instead, increasingly, with some missteps along the way, is embed the numinous in the stuff of the mundane, aggregate details, on their own prosaic, but cumulatively strange, that tear the paper of the page and let things in through the rents. Of course, the subtle and musical style is still there, but employed more sparingly, and is perhaps even more luminous for that. Think of a story like 'Opening the Door', whose central events are told baldly, but which accretes a strangeness in the accounts the Reverend Secretan Jones gives of the tricks memory, or some other force, plays on him. Think of how it builds to the moment when 'three children playing some game or other', in the passage behind the Reverend's house are revealed as 'horrible, stunted little creatures', and the plain prose is freighted with suggestion." He paused, tugged on his right earlobe. "I like to think some of that approach came from our conversations."

The Hermit then got up and crossed to his bookcase, tugged out a copy of *The Cosy Room*, stood leafing through it while I watched on.

"Here we are," he said, when he'd found the page he was after. "The final passage of 'N' seems to me to sum up the approach of Machen's late phase. When Arnold says, 'I believe that there is a *perichoresis*, an interpenetration,' I think Machen is telling us about the interweaving of the numinous and the mundane it has been his project to illuminate. This moment also gives us an example of the literary technique he has settled on to do it, especially when he follows that line with the transcendently strange, 'It is possible, indeed, that we three are now sitting among desolate rocks, by bitter streams . . . And with what companions?' "

The Hermit closed the volume and put it down on his desk. It was now nearly dark without and very dim within. He was a looming shadow. Gloom pooling in his eye sockets made of his skull a death's head. I shifted in the armchair.

"Or that's my feeling anyway. We talked a lot of Rabelais, he and I, when we met to discuss literary matters, and it was the mixture in that odd Frenchman's odd books of the sacerdotal and the scatological he found most compelling. And he loved his taverns for their curious blend of reverence and bawdiness. In the alchemical crucible base metals are transmuted into noble ones."

The Hermit sat back down in his chair and sighed. I had the feeling the interview was at an end. But as I was about to say something, thank him for his insights, he spoke again.

"There was some truth in that story, 'N', you know? The fairy house on the hill, I could show it to you, if you'd like? We're not far from Stoke Newington here."

Part of me did wish that, but I told him politely, "No," and went on to join my friends.

With Scourges, with Flowering Sprigs

That Friday morning Kalina woke before it was light, shivering though she was swaddled in a thick sleeping bag. It was only mid-October, but already winter had bared its teeth. Zlatko lay wrapped up beside her, grunting and farting. He looked placid and content, as he always did, asleep and awake. Nothing fretted him. Once, years before, Kalina had loved that; for a long time now it had just irked her.

After wriggling out of her cocoon, she pulled a blanket round her shoulders, unzipped the tent, and went outside to put some water on the Primus for coffee. It was still early, but if she got to the care home where she worked before her supervisor she'd be able to pilfer a bit of breakfast from the trays laid out by the caterers for the residents; they'd run out of bread and eggs at the camp, and there was nothing to eat but tinned beans, and she hated tinned beans. While the water heated up, she spooned coffee and sugar into her mug and looked about her. Three tents, bright fabric spattered with mud, pitched at the heart of a small clearing in a copse on a hill a mile or so north of Luton. Five of them had come over from Varna that summer, Kalina and Zlatko, another couple, Bogdan and Svetlana, and a friend of Zlatko's, Stanko, who had lank hair and was a bit of a creep, often ogling the two women. The previous year there'd been a bigger group and they'd lived in a small house, and, though it had been cramped, they'd been sleeping four to a room, it had been fun, friendly and lively. It had been before Bogdan met Svetlana. Kalina and he'd had an affair, under Zlatko's nose. For a couple of months she'd felt alive. She'd avoided Bogdan back in Bulgaria that winter. But it was a torment to have him so near again and to not be able to touch him, to hold him.

Zlatko had not been happy about the cost of renting, so had decided they'd camp this year. He was working again as a baggage handler at the airport, as was Stanko. Bogdan had a job as an Amazon delivery driver. The home Kalina worked at was residential care for old people with dementia; she was qualified as a nurse. Apart from a few weeks at a cosmetics shop at the start of the summer, a job she'd been fired from, Svetlana had not been able to get work, had lain around the campsite griping all day. Kalina resented her and the way the men indulged her moods. But at least now the weather had turned she could no longer slob about in her underwear.

And the weather really had turned. Kalina was freezing even with the blanket round her shoulders. There was dew on the tents, glistering beads. She hoped the cold would mean they'd soon have to go home; they'd already stayed longer than they'd planned.

The water boiled, Kalina poured some into her mug, stirred till the granules dissolved. Then, as she hunkered there, hands cupped around her steaming mug, sipping the hot, thick coffee, she thought about the dream she'd woken from, whose filmy web was wrapped still about her head.

She'd been wandering around the main villa of a place called the Quiet Nest Palace, a grand residence in Balchik, a resort on the Black Sea coast not far north of Varna. It'd been built as a summer home for Queen Marie of

Romania between the wars. The villa was white stucco, a mixture of Art Deco and quaint medievalism. It had a minaret. Now it was a museum. Kalina had visited it several times as a child, knew the layout. But in her dream, she couldn't find her way about. There was chamber after chamber, all sparsely though opulently furnished. A grand bathroom with a marble tub. Then, where there shouldn't have been one, a flight of stairs. Kalina remained at its foot, peering up into gloom. Where could the steps lead? She thought there might be a slight greying of the dark far above. A window letting in a greasy light through some smeary pane? Or the glimmer of a nest of glow-worms? She pondered climbing to find out. But then thought of the dangers. A rotted-out tread. A dancing bear goaded savage by the pain of the ring through its nose. A slimy man with a dull rusty blade; squirrels with quick sharp teeth; a bloated toad with wattles and a poison sac. An old woman bundled up in rags hunched over a hurdy-gurdy, waiting to strike up an eerie buzzing melody. The dread was thick.

But Kalina climbed anyway. After some way there was a dogleg, and she rounded it to find, at the top of the stairs, Queen Marie standing rheumy eyed in a niche, cradling in her arms, like a Madonna cradling a Christ child in a roadside shrine, a dead lamb, its throat slit and wool matted with gore.

Queen Marie saw Kalina approaching, nodded her head, smiled wan. She wore her auburn locks piled on top of her head, a cornflower satin dress with puffy sleeves, and strings of pearls around her neck and in her hair. She dropped the dead lamb, and it hit the floorboards with a wet smack. Then she had a notebook in her hands. And began to read from it, peering intently at Kalina the while.

Her voice was soft, so soft, barely there at all. But behind it was an angry thrum like a riled nest of wasps. She had a slight accent. Kalina, straining to hear what she was saying, caught just fragments.

" . . . seethed in . . . a curse trembled . . . they that had of the horse you burnt the devils and burrowed painted wooden free of parings . . . angry sea marrow from the dead grandmother's spat-on pottage. You hollowed proclaimed you for stewing and foul cat, but the end, up for wasn't . . . days, driving cores, threaded of your arms. Kept yours, but muttered wardings . . . a beautiful them, hissed wished was the plump herb of nestled in the long teeth . . . clipped your dew from rite and legs, your hair liver, your riddled bones slurped wept and your arms . . . boy sickening . . . your guts, into your scalp, bound to the wights ragged to sank. You locked nails, cut the sacrifice and lock a mob. They it with spite . . . her books. Old bone, like from your hair . . . your sweet curls, your blood . . . with scourges, flowering sprigs, learnt the flesh."

Then the dead lamb got tottering to its feet, bleated and mewed, and repeated over and over like a refrain, in a deep, hoarse voice, wound gaping beneath the working of its jaw: "With scourges, flowering sprigs, learnt the flesh."

Kalina had awakened then.

She gulped hot coffee. From near at hand, she heard the chittering call of a nightjar. Just then Stanko unzipped his tent and stepped out, stretched and yawned. The vest and boxer shorts he wore were stained and yellowing. He grinned at Kalina.

"Morning," he said. "No one else up yet?"

"Not yet," Kalina replied, shrinking back from sweat stink and garlic-sausage breath. She felt acutely aware she wasn't wearing a bra under her t-shirt and pulled her blanket more tightly about her.

Stanko squatted down next to the Primus, sparked the flame, held his hands out to it. "Cold, isn't it?"

"Don't waste the gas. Put some clothes on."

"All right," he said, turning out the stove.

He stood. Just then there was the sound of fumbling from Bogdan's and Svetlana's tent, and a breathy moan from Svetlana.

Stanko leered at Kalina. She got up, turned away, and walked out of the clearing, through the trees and to the edge of the copse, stood looking across grey fog swirling in the fields at the lights of Luton a little way off. After a short while, she heard Stanko coming up behind her.

"Go away," she said, without turning round.

She felt him lay his hand gently on her shoulder, shrugged it off, turned. Stanko had put on his overalls and high-vis jacket. He was looking at her with genuine concern.

"Look," he said. "I know you don't like me, but really, I'm worried about you. You seem so down."

Kalina sneered. "I'm fine."

Stanko frowned. "You don't seem fine. I've seen the way you look at him."

"At who?"

Stanko scratched his head. "She has nice tits and everything, but you know you're so much more beautiful."

Kalina sighed and pushed past him, hard. Walked back towards the camp. He hissed after her, "Don't be such a bitch."

It was not a good day. It was sweltering inside the home, and Kalina very quickly sweated through her nylon uniform shirt. When she opened a window to let in some fresh air, one of the old men in her care scolded her, kept bawling about how cold he was, about how he'd catch a chill. Another resident lost control of her bowels, and Kalina had to clean her up. Then Kalina's manager reprimanded her, in front of other carers, for how she'd made a bed—it was an excuse, it was nothing at all. Her eyes pricked, but she just managed to hold back the tears. She wept bitterly in a toilet cubicle later, though.

So that evening, when she went to the Romanian corner shop she and Zlatko wired their earnings home from, after she'd been to the bank to withdraw her week's pay, Kalina decided not to send the usual amount. She kept a little more back, just enough for a couple of pints of beer and a packet of crisps. She was craving a cold lager, the tang and fizz of it. She knew Zlatko would find out, that he wouldn't be happy, and that he'd be disappointed rather than angry, and that that would irritate her so much, but just then she didn't care.

She took her cash and went to a pub just up the road, an old boozer called the Bricklayers Arms, the Brickies to the locals, a place with sporting memorabilia on the walls, a TV for showing the football, two or three fruit and quiz machines.

It was pretty dead inside, only a handful of regulars sipping desultorily at beers, and Kalina was glad—she didn't want bustle. So she went up to the bar, ordered a pint and some crisps from the barmaid, a chirpy brunette, and took them over to a table in the corner of the back room, away from the other drinkers—she didn't want to fall into strained chat. She took a big gulp of her lager, sighed, then tore open the packet of crisps, ate one. They were wild thyme and rosemary flavour—she'd bought them thinking of how those herbs grew all along the Black Sea coast, their scent heady in summer.

She wasn't sure about the crisps, they were a bit too salty, didn't really taste of much, a bit chemically, synthetic, but the beer was just what she needed, cold and bitter. She sank down in her chair, gazed at the images churning on the screen of a quiz machine, thought of nothing.

She'd just gone up to the bar, got herself a second pint, sat back down, when someone came into the pub. She couldn't see through to the front room from where she was sitting, but heard the girl behind the bar say, "Alright, Pearl?" She didn't catch the response, but a minute or two later an older woman walked into the back room holding a glass of red wine in her hand. She was striking looking, stood tall and upright, moved with grace. She was wearing a gorgeous vintage dress, dark green, beaded, with straps, which fell straight to the knee. Round her neck was a fox stole, the muzzle biting down on one of the hind legs, and she had on pale-rose leather gloves. She looked about her, then took a seat at the empty table next to Kalina's.

Kalina didn't want to stare, though couldn't help but glance askance. The woman, Pearl, sat there, sipping her wine, eyes glazed and distant, head very erect on her long pale neck. Kalina saw that she was actually quite elderly, hair thinning, skin papery and liver spotted. But still, she was beautiful.

A few minutes later someone else entered the pub. Had a conversation with the barmaid while ordering a pint of cider. A woman. Kalina didn't catch much of what was said, but heard her say something derogatory about "the Muslims". Then saw a look of panic come into Pearl's eyes. The old woman began breathing slow and shallow. Then with trembling fingers scrabbled in her clutchbag, before, with a murmur of relief, pulling out a matchbox, a large one, Bryant and May Cook's matches, which seemed ancient, design faded, card worn soft. Pearl set this on the table beside her glass, placed her left hand on it. Then took another sip of her wine.

At that moment Kalina smelt, over the reek of stale beer rising from the carpets and the faint acridity of stale smoke still lingering in the soft furnishings ten years after the ban, over Pearl's rose fragrance and the whiff of disinfectant coming from the toilets, another smell, one that reminded her of home. Wild rosemary and thyme, the savour of it. Like the crisps should have tasted. She looked around for the source, but could see nothing. She took another swig of her beer.

Then there came a muffled screech, lasting a moment, then silence, then a screech again. Kalina was puzzled, wondered if it was an odd ringtone. But after a moment she realised what it was. She peered at Pearl and, as she did, saw the matchbox shift a little under the old woman's hand.

She blurted, without thinking, "Is there a cicada in that box?"

Pearl looked over. She squinted at Kalina, then smiled.

"That's a lovely accent. Where are you from, dear?" Her voice had a soft, if nasal timbre, and a lilting cadence.

"Varna."

"That's in Bulgaria, isn't it?" Pearl asked, cocking her head.

"Yes, on the Black Sea coast."

Pearl nodded. "How lovely! And what brings you to Luton?"

"Just working here for a few months to earn some money. We're sending most of it back to our families."

"And what's your name?"

"Kalina."

Clapping her hands softly together, Pearl exclaimed, "Oh, that's a beautiful name! Mine's Patricia. But everyone calls me Pearl." She took a sip of wine. "Would you care to join me?" She gestured at the empty chair beside her.

There was a warmth, a kindness about the eyes. So Kalina took her pint and went to sit with her.

They talked for a bit about the weather, about the cold snap, then about the pub. Pearl was a regular, had been for years. She asked Kalina what it was she did, and it turned out Pearl had a friend who lived in the home where Kalina worked, and they talked about that, the poor management, the drive to save money, the neglect of the residents. Then Pearl told Kalina she was a sculptor, abstract modern pieces hewn from stone or wood.

"Don't work much in stone these days though, don't have the strength." She took a phone out of her bag. "Can I show you?"

Kalina nodded.

Pearl swiped through some shots of intricately carved forms—whorls, spirals, some adorned with gold leaf or copper wire. They looked alien, like deep sea creatures Kalina thought.

"These are just ornaments," Pearl said. "I miss the days of working on large-scale pieces. It was so satisfying! But I'm far too old for that now."

"You don't look too old," Kalina said.

Pearl laughed. "Oh, you are a sweetheart! But I'm nearly a hundred!"

Kalina squinted at her—she seemed so spritely.

"Yes. Born at the end of the First World War. But you asked about my matchbox. Would you like to hear the story of it?"

Kalina nodded.

"Well, it's old. It was made for me by an anarchist, and sorcerer, in nineteen thirty-seven, in Catalonia." She smiled. "But would you like another drink? My treat."

Kalina nodded. "If that's okay? A lager?"

Pearl went up to the bar, fetched a pint for Kalina, a glass of wine for herself. Then, once sat down again, she began to tell of the time she spent in Spain, during the Civil War.

"I was a nurse with the POUM. We were the goodies, fighting Franco's fascist Nationals. After some brief training in Barcelona, I was sent to the front line in west Catalonia to join the PBS, the Percy Bysshe Shelley Battalion. Only there about six months. But because it was mostly dreary hanging about with only very sporadic bouts of fighting, it seemed to drag on forever."

Pearl told Kalina about the tedium, the fitful bursts of danger. About the trenches and dugouts strung along both sides of the line. The awful claggy mud. She explained how most of the time all that was exchanged between the positions of her battalion and those of the fascists were desultory insults. There were only two brief, if brutal, skirmishes while she was there, with some killed and wounded; most of the injuries she treated were accidental: the ancient rifles the militia were issued with had the bad habits of going off if dropped or of exploding in the hands when fired, and there were often incidents with "bombs", the crude and dangerous hand grenades the soldiers used.

The worst thing, Pearl told Kalina, was the stink. Behind each position, on both sides, there was a festering midden of food waste, rusty tins, and shit. The reek was high and cloying, made you retch. You never got used to it.

Pearl was at the front from mid-January till the end of June. She told Kalina how at first the cold was awful, how it was almost impossible to get warm, how they took in desperation to burning olive oil in sardine tins and fires of gorse, wild rosemary and thyme, which flared up and were ash in minutes. How it was a relief when spring came, bringing with it warmer weather, though the rains turned the trenches and dugouts to sumps.

"The strangest thing about the place that April," Pearl said, "was how dead the land was. The hillsides were bare, apart from a very few scrubby thickets, and the only animals I saw, that weren't pack mules or cavalry horses, were the rats that scurried everywhere. There weren't even any birds in the sky, save the occasional lone buzzard, circling. Once, a young German soldier shot one of these down and we made a stew of it. But the meat was rank and greasy."

Kalina grimaced, took a swig of beer.

"Then summer came," Pearl went on, "and the heat sapped us and sharpened the stench to where it became near impossible to breathe."

"It all sounds terrible," said Kalina.

"It was, dear. The only moments of beauty were the sunrises. I'd read Homer as a teenager, but had never quite appreciated that epithet of his about the 'rosy-fingered dawn' till I saw daybreak there." She looked at Kalina. "Have you read Homer, dear?"

Kalina nodded. "I really wanted to study classical literature. But my family wished for me to take up something more practical, so I went into nursing. I like it, though I'd prefer to work in a hospital than a care home. I shouldn't complain, though. In Bulgaria, I've been struggling to get a job at all. You have to know the right people, know who to bribe."

Pearl reached out and stroked Kalina's arm. "I'm sorry. Life is very hard nowadays."

Kalina shrugged. "It's harder still in Bulgaria. So much corruption. So much poverty."

Pearl pursed her lips, nodded.

It was still quiet in the pub, though the Friday after-work crowd were starting to come in. Kalina reflected on how pleasant it was to sit, drink, and have a friendly conversation, get away from the tensions of the camp. She drifted slightly. Then realised Pearl was speaking to her again.

"In the end, we could no longer hold our part of the line. The Nationals received a supply of new weapons, several machine guns among them. With our antique rifles it would have been a slaughter had we stayed there. So we were given the order to fall back. To return to Barcelona.

"When we got there, we found things in a sad way. The egalitarian ideal had failed. There was fighting in the streets, communists against anarchists. One of the first things I saw stepping off the train was a poster. On it was a cartoon of a shadowy figure wearing a mask marked with the hammer and sickle, a mask that was slipping to show, underneath, a hideous twisted face branded with the swastika. It was supposed to represent the POUM. They were trying to paint us as fascist sympathisers. Things were fraught. If I hadn't had this, well . . . " She tapped the matchbox. It had been quiet while she'd been talking of the war, but then it chirruped loudly again.

"So, what is it?" Kalina asked.

"Let me tell you."

Pearl explained how, when her battalion withdrew, they had to make their way cross-country some distance, before they could get on a train to take them back to the city. A band of fascists tracked them, sniping from a distance. On the second day one of the other nurses, a young German girl called Bettina, took a bullet through her left lung and died coughing blood, out on a sere hillside, leant up against the trunk of a lone pine. Several others of Pearl's company were wounded.

On their trek, they passed many signs of rite and magic. A ram's head impaled on a post. A lime tree swagged with strings of dried peppers. Black Madonnas in niches in stones by the side of the paths, including one that was devouring her son, as Saturn is in Goya's famous painting.

Then, on the third day, they rendezvoused with a local anarchist brigade.

"The meeting place was the bowl of an extinct volcano. A small medieval chapel down in the crater. We thought we'd thrown our pursuers off the scent, but we couldn't be sure. Our comrades greeted us with a meal, one of the best I'd had in a long while. They'd cooked lentils in gourds buried in a silage heap, something they did whenever they wanted to avoid tell-tale smoke or firewood ran low. The heat from the rotting mulch was enough you see."

Kalina made a face.

"Sounds disgusting, I know," Pearl said. "But I promise you it was delicious. And there was wine too."

They ate well, caroused a little, though quietly, and then, it being warm, bivouacked out in the open. The air was clean, scented with pine, and rosemary and thyme. It was one of the best night's sleep Pearl had had in a long time. But the sentries sounded the alarm a little before dawn, the coming sun a smear of blood in the sky to the east. They'd spotted the fires of the fascists, not far off. Even with his knowledge of the local terrain, the leader of the anarchist brigade, Juan, a man in his mid-fifties, with a craggy but kind face, felt it was unlikely they'd be able to outrun the Nationals without leaving their wounded behind.

So, following some deliberation amongst the commanders, a decision was taken to try some folk magic. The word went round. When Pearl heard, she was sceptical and concerned, but still went with some of the others to see the rite carried out.

"They had," Pearl told Kalina, "a large black bull in a pen, up on the lip of the crater. We climbed up. When we got there, Juan, who it seemed was a sorcerer as well as an anarchist, drowsed the beast by wafting a burning bundle of flowering rosemary and thyme under its nose. Then, whilst it was slumbered, others climbed into the pen with it. They pinned bundled sprigs of flowering rosemary and thyme to its flanks, flowers blue, pink, and white. Blood dripped, pooled beneath the beast's hooves. They bound Roman candles to its horns, tied squibs to its tail, then stood back. Juan intoned a few phrases I didn't catch, in Catalan I think, then taking out a box of matches, lit the tapers of the fireworks, loosed the tie securing the gate of the pen, and stepped back."

The bull, roused, roared, pawed the ground, reared and plunged, then broke from the pen and crashed off into the brush. Those watching saw the stars of the Roman candles shooting up, above the treetops, as the beast ran down the hillside and off towards the fascist camp, its bellows fading into the distance.

"What happened?" Kalina asked.

It was well into the evening by then, and the pub was quite full. She knew Zlatko would be wondering where she was. She didn't care.

"I don't know," Pearl replied. "It was a miracle a forest fire wasn't sparked, it had been dry for so long. As for the Nationals on our tail, we heard no more of them."

She had, she said, asked Juan what the rite had been. He'd explained there was a kind of warding in rosemary and thyme, especially if used when in flower and sparked by the right incantations.

"That night," Pearl told Kalina, "he made, for a few of us of the PBS, personal talismans using the same magic. A cicada in a match box, with sprigs of flowering rosemary and thyme tied about it. The box must never be opened, but as you can hear, the cicada impossibly still lives, eighty years later."

Kalina squinted at Pearl. Pearl smiled wry, and with a slight challenge, at Kalina. "But perhaps you don't believe me."

"No, I think I do? In Bulgaria we have tales about the power of those herbs. When I was small, there was a boy who wouldn't share his toy with me, a painted horse. I bound flowering sprigs of rosemary and thyme to a finger bone I dug up in the village cemetery. With a lock of my dead grandmother's hair which I'd kept. She was a witch."

Pearl frowned at her. "Really?"

"Yes. The boy grew sick. Everyone knew the curse was my fault. I was a bad child. They punished me. The boy was all right in the end, but no one would be my friend after that."

Pearl took a sip of her wine. It was quite crowded by then, even in the back room, and noisy, so they were leaning into each other to hear.

"Oh, my dear," the old woman said. "I'm sure it wasn't your fault. That sounds like a cruel way to treat a child."

Kalina shrugged.

The two of them chatted a bit more about other, more mundane things. The conversation turned to where Kalina was living, and she told Pearl about the camp outside of town. Pearl was horrified.

"You can't live like that, dear. Not with this cold weather we're having. I can offer you a room. Come live with me for a bit."

Kalina shook her head.

"I wouldn't charge you," Pearl said. "Honestly, it would just be lovely to have someone stay."

"That's so kind of you. But I can't leave the others. Besides it's just for a couple more weeks, then we're going back."

"Are you sure, dear?"

Kalina nodded.

Pearl only stayed another ten minutes or so, finishing up her drink. "Kalina, dear," she said as she got to her feet, "it was so good to meet you. But I must be off now. I'm a little tipsy if I'm honest." She put her hand on Kalina's arm, smiled. "Do take care of yourself, and I hope I'll see you again sometime. And let me know if you reconsider my offer."

She walked out. Kalina waved. Then sat finishing the last of her beer. It was only when she got up to go herself, she noticed Pearl had left the matchbox behind. She looked at it a moment, then pocketed it and went out into the cold and damp.

Kalina told herself she'd taken the matchbox so she could track Pearl down, get it back to her. But over the next days she made no effort to do so. She kept the box on her at all times, in her handbag, in a pocket. Now and then the cicada chirruped.

And things got better. Zlatko had not been angry with her when she'd returned late that evening from the Brickies, smelling of beer, and he seemed generally less aloof. Stanko backed off. Bogdan and Svetlana fought. Kalina's manager treated her with greater kindness, and the care home's residents were less demanding, more grateful. Those few days were amongst the happiest she'd ever known. Not thrilling, like the weeks of her affair with Bogdan the previous year, but contented.

But one morning, just three days before they were due to fly back to Bulgaria, after Kalina had woken to her phone alarm, yawned, and stretched, she reached under her pillow to find the box wasn't there. Zlatko had left early for the airport. She rummaged about, throwing pillows, sleeping bags, clothing around, but did not turn it up. She wondered if Zlatko or one of the others had taken it, but how they could have done so without waking her, she didn't know. In the end, she had to go to work without it.

That day, her shift finished mid-afternoon. When she got off, she decided to have a wander round Luton before heading back to the camp.

She heard the din of the mob before she saw them. She was walking through Bury Park, down a shopping street lined with halal butchers', grocers', fabric shops, takeaways, barbers'. A vibrant part of town. But there were oddly few people on the street. Then, from around the corner, Kalina heard a racket of angry shouts, chanting. A rabble baying, with one voice, "A Christian country for Christian people." And Kalina had a vision of a strange island, somewhere in regions hyperborean, where spindle-shanked and sickly folk, with skin so pale as to be translucent, scraped and grovelled before gory crucifixes and sang bizarre melancholy hymns. But rounding the corner, the first thing she saw was an orange woman with mauve hair, face twisted with ugly hate, carrying a white plastic cross. She had on a green badged cap, and there were others with her, men mostly, unhealthy looking, tattooed, wearing the same. They were rowing with locals. Near at hand, a woman in a hijab was patiently explaining to a middle-aged man with a face the colour and texture of glazier's putty the difference between the headscarf she was wearing and a burka, and why she chose to cover her hair. Kalina could see that the man wasn't taking any of it in; his mouth had a rubbery set to it.

She walked past. The woman with the brightly dyed hair was arguing with a young man in an apron who stood in the door of a butcher's.

"Jealous, innit," said the man, "that we're taking over."

The woman's voice was like the squawking of a sea fowl. "You're not taking over."

"Yeah, mate."

"No, you're not. This is still a Christian land. We're taking it back."

"It's as much ours as it is yours."

"Yeah? And look what you've done to it." She pointed at Kalina, who was just then skirting the tangle. "Women scared to walk about in their own country."

Kalina stopped and turned to her. "This isn't my country."

"Oh," said the woman. "Where are you from then?"

"Bulgaria."

"That's still a Christian country though, right?"

Kalina looked up at the Arabic script in white on red above the halal chicken shop next to the butcher's.

"Officially. But we're all still pagans. At heart."

"But you wouldn't want to see your country overrun with mosques and Sharia law, would you?" The woman strove to contain her rage, but spittle flecked her lips.

"What happened to you?" Kalina asked. "Why are you so angry?"

"This isn't about race."

"I didn't mention race."

"This isn't about race, I'm a Christian."

She was brandishing her cross and staring wild eyed at Kalina, like a saint facing down a demon in a medieval icon.

"When," asked Kalina, "did you last read the New Testament?"

The woman squinted. "Why?"

"Because this isn't the kind of thing Christ was supposed to have been about."

"What would you know about it? You're not Christian, or you'd side with us."

"I'm not Christian. I told you, I'm a pagan. Though I don't believe in anything, not really. But you're not Christian either. That's my point."

The butcher grinned, winked.

The woman thrust her cross at Kalina. "You come over here and take jobs from decent English folk. Don't you feel ashamed?"

Just then Kalina saw Pearl, among some stragglers at the back of the march. She looked weary and broken down, far older than when Kalina had chatted with her in the Brickies, was being pushed along in a wheelchair.

"I feel ashamed. But not for that."

The woman opened her mouth to reply, but before she could say anything further, Kalina crossed to Pearl. She wasn't dressed glamorously, as she had been before, but wore an old stained floral-pattern frock. Her hair was greasy, tangled and straggly. She also wore one of the absurd badged caps, though balanced askew on her head, as if placed there by someone else.

"Pearl?" Kalina said, approaching.

The old woman looked up at her, peered blearily.

"Who are you?"

"Kalina." She crouched down in front of the chair. "Don't you remember, we met in the pub a couple of weeks ago? You told me about when you fought in the Spanish Civil War."

The woman pushing the chair looked at her. "Pearl ain't fought in the Spanish Civil War." She was puffing away at a stinking cheap cigarette.

Kalina ignored her. "How are you, Pearl? Are you okay? Why are you here?"

Pearl shrugged.

Kalina took her hand. "Pearl, you fought against fascists before. Don't march with them now."

Pearl glared at her. "You took something from me."

"I did and I'm sorry. I don't know where it is now, but I'll find it and get it back to you."

Just then the woman with bright hair came up behind Kalina and shoved her to the pavement.

"You're as bad as these Muslims, you know that? Taking jobs from decent British people. Leave Pearl alone. Go back to Bulgaria, you're not wanted here."

An elderly man, with a long beard, wearing a thawb, came up behind Kalina, offered his arm, helped her to her feet. She thanked him, looked at the woman.

"I will. I mean, I hate it there, but I hate it here more."

She turned, strode away. As she did, she heard Pearl call after her, but kept walking.

Agitated, Kalina paced about for hours before she made her way back to the camp, and it was already dark by the time she got there. It was a starless night, a rack of thick cloud scudding overhead, only rare glimpses of a foundering moon, pallid, bloated. Entering the copse, she heard groaning. The ground beneath her feet was churned to mud. She stopped, took out her mobile, and turned on its torch. The beam flashed out and lit on something. Pearl's matchbox, trampled in the filth. Kalina went down on hunkers to peer at it. Shook out the contents. Flowering sprigs of rosemary and thyme. But no crushed, perhaps desiccated cicada. Instead the herbs were bound to a yellowing bone with what looked like human hair.

Kalina stood. Listened. Low moans and a kind of pathetic whimpering. She already knew what she'd find in the clearing, so turned aside and walked on, down the side of the knoll and across the fields, towards a swathe of horizon where only a few scattered lights showed.

She trekked across fields, mostly pasture and corn stubble, for what seemed hours. Then she turned her ankle badly on a furrow, fell to her knees. She sat there a while, rubbing the tender joint. It panged and she was worried she'd not be able to walk on it. At some point she looked up and saw Queen Marie looming over her—pale slack face, wattled neck hung with pearls, sad eyes, beaded dress. The Queen was sat astride a bull with bundles of flowering rosemary and thyme pinned to its flanks, Roman candles bound to its horns, squibs tied to its tail, all firing and crackling. But the beast was calm, looked placidly down at Kalina with its great brown eyes.

Queen Marie smiled. "With scourges," she said. So gently. But with a buzzing undertone. "With flowering sprigs."

And Kalina nodded.

Let It Be a Blood Ape on the Prowl . . .

his antic text was passed to me a good few years ago now, by a friend, Laila, who knew of my interest in such things. One evening in an alleyway in Camden, behind the restaurant she was then working at, next to the large kitchen bin, she came across a ram's skull with involute horns, which was swagged with fruit and vegetable peelings and looked, in Laila's words, "like some pagan fetish". Threaded through the empty orbits was a strip of paper, almost like a length of tickertape, on which, in a tiny meticulous hand, was written what seems an invocation of sorts. Of all the texts I've found or been given, this one, though it suggests nothing directly uncanny, is perhaps the one that disturbs me most:

Let it be a blood ape on the prowl and a stooping screech owl, let it have a tapir's snout, a hagfish's grisly gape, a fox's mealy muzzle, a goat's breath and grizzled beard, a sea devil's lure, a vulture's ruff and tonsure, a platypus's venomous spur, a lobster's claw, a badger's paw, give it a toad's throat sac, an armadillo's plated back, the mandibles of a stag beetle, a turkey's snood, carbuncle, and wattle, a hog's bristles and wild eye, the bottle-green sheen of a blowfly, and flesh soft, pallid like a grub's, give it a warthog's tusks, a narwhal's braided horn, and the tottering gait of a foal new born, let it have a rat's tail, a man o' war's scourges, a goat's lustful urges, a cock like a ram's, a weasel's sneer, an echidna's spines, let it whine like a hyaena, whoop like a gibbon, yowl like a mandrake, growl like a bear, let it live in air, in water, on land, and let it wait in the dark to gnaw out his pineal gland.

Under the Sign of the Black Raven

s told, I have for some time been collecting strange texts, in particular those unsettling artefacts which describe fantastic events in such a way as to seem more *account* than *story*. I thrill to the shock of the uncanny they give rise to, though I'm aware most are in all likelihood mere fictions designed to evoke precisely that shudder. Occasionally though, I happen across one which cannot easily be dismissed as fabrication. This is the tale of one such text and the terrible events it gave rise to.

In 2004, a friend of mine, well, an acquaintance really, Martin Camblin, a scholar of Early Modern English drama, was sent to examine some annotations a private collector had discovered in a copy of the third quarto of Kyd's *The Spanish Tragedy*, which, or so the collector thought, provided new information pertaining to the authorship of the 1602 additions to the play. In fact the marginalia were clearly a much later forgery and of little interest. However, Martin did find, tucked into the book, folded into quarters, something that intrigued him—a handbill advertising what sounded a bizarre spectacle:

Under the Sign of the *Black Raven, Southwarke,* during the periode of the Froſt, and the Fair on the frozen *Thames,* is to be ſhown (by *her Majeſties* Order) an Horrible and Prodigious Sight, a Faerie Child, chang'd in the Nurſing for an Infant born in *Oxford* of the body of *Rebecca Cartwright*. Though it has the ſeeming of a Babe Aged no more than three Months, is ſcarce the bigneſs of a Cat, it is learn'd in Diſcourſe, as if Threeſcore Years old. It divines the Future with Biblical Lots, and its Prognoſtications are exceeding accurate in all Particulars. In Demeanour, it is largely Grave, though ſometimes it jeſts moſt filthy. By ſetting it againſt the Sun, or holding Candles behind it, the whole Anatomy of the Body may be ſeen. It is mostly quiet, but when Fear moves it, wails like a Mandrake. It does not ſuck at the Breaſts of Woman, but twice each day drinks down a quart of Rooſter blood. It hath never been ſhewn, ſave to ſome Perſons of Quality. If any Perſon has a deſire to see it at their own Houſes, we are ready to wait upon them any Hour of the Day.

Likewiſe a merry Ape from *Bengal*, that dances, plays on the Tambour, and drinks Spirits. Alſo a ſtrange Mallard from *Norwich*, having no wings, but Three proper Legs, and Two Fundaments, both it makes uſe of at One time.

Vivant Rex & Regina
Anno Domini 1608

Handbills advertising similar freakish attractions at sixteenth and seventeenth century London fairs being commonplace, the collector had considered the flyer of little interest, an insignificant document used as a bookmark, had not even opened it out. Martin though, was fascinated by the genre and unfolded the handbill to examine it more closely. In doing so, he discovered on the back a short handwritten text:

I was wronge. That thing is not the Fruite of my loins nor of anie of womankinde. The Others died moste bloudie. Why It lets me live on, I knowe not. It tormentes me. It plaies Cat and Mouse. I hear it scritching on the panelling of the Library Door. I fear It awaits Its Wyrde kin. Wherefore does It keep me trapp'd heere like an Animal in a Trappe? I pray Our Lord will keep me safe, but I feare e'en He has no poweere o'er that Strange kinde. Readeere, heede thee my Warning, the Folke are Reale.

The collector merely shrugged when Martin pointed out the odd note, dismissed it as "doggerel". Martin, horribly fascinated, asked him if he would be prepared to part with the handbill, and he agreed to do so, for a modest sum.

Intrigued by his find, Martin for a few months spent much of his spare time in research, hoping to discover something to cast light on the dark enigma. At some point during this period, knowing my interest in such things, he showed me the handbill, asked my opinion of it. I told him that, though the handbill itself was certainly real, I thought the note some later fakery. He enquired why; I shrugged.

He glared at me. "The hand looks authentic enough."

"Oh, come on," I replied. "That's easy to imitate. And even if it is genuine, then it's an early seventeenth century prank, or some delusional ramblings, perhaps of a woman badly affected by what we'd now call postpartum depression."

"Maybe," Martin said. "But I'm not so sure."

Martin's investigations into the strange handbill turned up nothing. But then, in late 2006, entirely by chance, while researching witch trials in early Jacobean London, he found among an archive of worn seventeenth-century broadsides one that told a tale that struck him cold:

THE MOST VILE AND BLOODY MVRHTERS COMMITTED BY A VVITCH of *Highgate*, called *Rachael Camlet*, who was executed at Tyburn the 16th of Februarie laſt paſt. 1608.

LONDON Printed for William Firebrand and Iohn Wright, and are to be ſold at Chriſts Church dore. 1608.

On the 16th of Februarie laſt paſt a young woman *Rachael Camlet* of *Highgate* most worthily ſuffered death for Witchery and Black Murder. The harlot pleaded Innocence at her Arraignement, but the Opinione of the Court was of her Guilt, and ſhe was Convicted and Sentenced to be Hanged.

Witneſſes related to the Court that *Rachael* was founde, in Januarie this Year, by a Neighboure, who hearing a Deviliſh Tumulte entered the Houſe of *Rachaels* Husbande, *Walter Camlet*, a Mercere. The Neighboure found *Rachael* in the Library of that Houſe, infenſible, weltering in the bloode of her Husbande, *Walter*, and of their three Servantes. The Neighboure, ſtricken with horror at what he ſaw, called for aſſiſtance. Others were alſo diſtreſſed. There weere cleare Signs of Witchery and foulneſs and the Murders were moſt vile.

Rachael was taken to the Village Lock-up, for her Incarceration. When ſhe came againe to herſelf, ſhe raved about murderous Goode Folke. The manie who ſaw her in her cell ſpoke of Diabolic Poſſeſſion.

At the Triall the Court was told, by *Walters* Mother, *Marjorie Camlet*, how *Rachael* had committed Adulterie with a fallen Prieſt, during one of her Husbandes long trade voyages, and got with child. *Walter*, a compaſſionate Man, returning to finde his Wife ſwolt, did not caſt her out, but let her ſtay on with him, at his Houſe. After the birth, during *Rachaels* Confinemente, the Child was given to an Orphanage, and *Walter*, a goode man, ſuffered his wife to ſtaye on with him.

Theere was one who ſpoke in defenſe of *Rachael*, a *Mary Pepperhill*, friend of the accuſed, a looſe woman certainly, and mayhap another Witch. She ſtated ſhe had been at the Froſt Faire on the *Thames* with *Rachael* the weeke before the murders, and that they had ſeene a Faerie Child theere, and that *Rachael* had become excited, certaine the Changeling was in ſooth the Child her Husband had taken from her, ſwore to get it back. She thought *Rachael* had acted on this Oathe, and that the Charlatans ſhewing the Changeling might be behinde the Murders. *Marys* teſtimony was diſcredited though, by her railing againſt the virtuous *Walter* and *Marjorie*, whom ſhe called Inceſtuous.

The Court did not pauſe before declaring *Rachaels* Guilte.

A curiouſe Appendix was provided by Locals of *Highgate*. It was tolde how Something was Wrong with the Houſe of *Camlet* after theſe Happenings, Something moſt Dreadful and terrible Strange, with the Proportions or the Shadowes, and no man could abide the place. Hence, in March, it was burn'd to the grounde by diſtract Villagers.

For some time after discovering the newssheet, Martin continued his enquiries. He learnt nothing further, so far as I'm aware.

In the summer of 2007, I lost contact with him. I learnt, during the winter of that year, from mutual friends, that no one had seen or heard from him for some months, not even his family. Then, on the 13th March 2008, during a hailstorm, I happened to look out the window and saw him outside my building, huddled beneath an old oak. I went to the front door of the block, called him over, took him up to my flat. He told me he'd been waiting for me, then began raving about the "Folk" and eldritch terrors, said he was going to destroy the "cursed handbill". I asked him if, instead, he would be prepared to sell it to me. A look of cunning fleeted across his face and he agreed, naming a small price.

He went away, returning about an hour later with the flyer and a photocopy of the broadside he'd found. I paid him and he left again. The next day he rang me and, frantic, snivelling, begged me to burn the handbill. When I asked him why I should, he abruptly hung up.

Three weeks later, Martin came again to my building. It was late. This time he pressed the buzzer for my flat. When I answered, we spoke on the intercom. He begged me to come to the door of the block. There was a hitch in his voice and he sounded close to sobs.

I went down. Opening the front door to see him huddled, cowering, in the porch, I was shocked; he looked ravaged: one eye blacked, swollen shut, face scratched, knuckles bruised, several teeth knocked out, blood down his shirt front. There was something feral about him too.

He'd been mugged, he told me, badly beaten. I urged him to go to hospital, but he wouldn't. He just wanted to borrow some money. I took him to a cash machine, got some out for him. Baring his teeth in thanks, he took it from me, then turned, loped away.

I've not seen him since. Afterward I found out he'd attacked a young woman, a post-graduate student he'd been pestering for months, after getting her into his office on a pretext, one evening when the building was quiet. Earlier on the night he came to my flat. Her injuries were severe. Apparently she was so distressed she wouldn't speak about what had happened, had barely spoken at all since. I don't know what happened to her. I think she left London suddenly.

Two days later I received a voicemail from Martin. Incoherent ranting about the handbill, the "Folk". "They love a shambles," he yelled twice. Then, whining into his phone, "Meant no particular malice, though." He stifled a frenzied laugh. "Our screams. Our screams. Just thought we were having fun, I think."

I deleted the message. Later it occurred to me I should have played it to the police maybe. But I didn't.

There are two brief epilogues to this tale that shed no more light, only murk. In the summer of 2009, I was involved in a project studying the earliest "corantos", or printed newssheets, circulated in Britain. In one, from May 1621, I found a brief item reporting the deaths of a pair of swindlers:

> Two Men were beaten to Death in Februarie this Year, by the vexed folk of the Citie of *Norwich* for Charlatanrie. The Offenſe was the diſplaying for money of a Changeling, which was but an ordinary Human Infant thieved from an Orphanage that

they made to appear to ſpeak by a kind of caſting of the voice, perhaps related to the Gaſtromanſie or Ventriloquie of Witches. This Deception they had been practiſing for manie years.

Then about four months later, ascending the escalator at Southwark underground station, I found a folded piece of paper in the pocket of my overcoat, put there, I suppose, by someone under the cover of the press of the crowd on the tube. Some kind of prank. On it was scrawled some bizarre verse:

> We rend your flesh, we are the Fay,
> We break your bones, we are the Fay,
> We spill your blood, we are the Fay,
> You are the Fey, you are our prey.

I've no idea as to the truth of what happened, or if I take a risk sharing this story now. But after finding that note in rhyming iambic tetrameter in my coat pocket, I crumpled up the handbill and burnt it in an ashtray on my desk, wafting the wispy smoke out the window with the first book I laid my hands on from the piles there, which happened to be a facsimile copy of Arthur Machen's *The House of Souls*.

The Purblind Bards

I found this text quite recently, written out on a piece of lined notepaper that had been folded into a wad and jutted from between two bricks, where the mortar had been scraped out, of a low wall just round the corner from where I live. Perhaps it's just a prose poem, left there so someone would find it, but to me it has the feel of something shoved through from another place:

When I was a child, sometimes, not often, a bard would come into town, gather a throng about them in the market square, and pour stories of sites mythic, like Old Street or Elephant, Somers Town or Ladbroke Grove, into our gaping ears. These were souls who'd ventured into the sweltering interior, the foetid guts, wormed down the city's gullet, and made it out. Made it out, but only just. Riddled with disease, encrusted with cankers, with scabies, abscesses, and fungal lesions. With sight failing, eyes shrivelled by sunlight glaring off glass and steel. With straggly lank hair, which would keep falling in stringy locks over their eyes and which they would keep pushing back—the gesture of a maniac or illuminé. With long suppurating sores on their flanks, thighs, and calves, where strips of flesh had been carved, jerky for some corporate gunslinger. They wandered from place to place, weak eyes rheumy and poignant, like the eyes of a doe or an anchorite, plying their tales, bursts of brutality and dark eroticism for jaded provincefolk. I don't know what happened to them, but they don't come around anymore, haven't for years. And for us here, the city itself seems now like nothing more than a wondrous and terrible dream. It might be that's all it ever was.

And Yet Speaketh

"I've sammed up coals in Barnsley pits . . ."

He sighed—he'd lost his place. Looking up from the article, an academic piece about sensationalism in the newspapers of the late-Victorian period, Tristram saw that the train was passing by a small industrial estate: factories, builders' merchants, a yard full of stacked pallets, piles seemingly teetering, near collapse. They were somewhere just outside Hatfield and crawling along—it was Sunday, there was work being done on the line near Potters Bar, it would be slow going till they were clear of the area.

"With muck up to my knee . . ."

Tristram was on his way back from Barnsley, his childhood home, a trip to see his father, who'd had a couple of health scares. It had been the Easter holiday period so he'd not had any teaching or administrative duties for the London university where he worked as a lecturer in English Literature, and had been able to get away for a couple of weeks.

"I've sammed up coals in Barnsley pits with muck up to my knee . . ."

It was this snatch of lyric, sung in a bone-weary quaver, which, stuck in his head, was keeping him from focusing on his books and papers. He was worried his concentration would be spoilt for days. It didn't particularly matter, he'd no deadlines looming, but as he'd just taken a longish break from his research, he was eager to get back to it.

The train was just then passing a furniture warehouse that backed onto the railway line, and Tristram saw, amid the vivid tags splashed across the brick wall, some graffiti in a dull reddish-brown paint, obviously done, not with a spray can, but with a brush. It was hard to make out, but, peering, Tristram read:

Cocka doodle dooe,
Peggy hath loft her tonge.

Tristram's notice was caught, not just by the bizarre, antiquated spelling, the long "s", but by a freakish coincidence. He'd been commissioned to write a scholarly, but popular volume on late-Victorian newspaper reports of anomalous and paranormal phenomena. While researching this, a few weeks previously, he'd come across a report from 1876, in *The Illustrated Police News*, of the abduction, mutilation, and murder of a child in the county of Hertfordshire. The circumstances were singular, though it's hard to know the extent to which they'd been exaggerated by the paper. It seemed that, in April of 1874, a young girl had gone missing from a small charitable orphanage in the Hertfordshire countryside, not far from Hatfield. Her body was found a few days later, in a ditch near the village of Fenwold. She'd been dressed in the smock she'd been wearing when last seen, though her skirts were in tatters and mottled with green, as if she'd been dragged through underbrush. The front of her garments had been stiff with blood; her tongue had been cut out at the root. But it wasn't blood loss or infection that had killed her; the back of her head had been caved in with a rock. The culprits had never been found. The writer of the article had imagined an occult element to the killing, dreamed up a rite honouring Beelzebub, in which the tongue had been offered up as a tribute to that demon, given to flies to blow maggots in, a scene the artist illustrated with lurid gusto.

The girl's name had been Mary, not Peggy, but Tristram wondered if the graffiti referred to that long ago crime (though the odd orthography hinted at an earlier period). Perhaps kept alive in local memory, though it was otherwise little remembered. Whatever, it was strange and unsettled him.

Just then, the train went by another line of scrawl, this painted on a panel of a slat fence. It read: "Sing to the tune of Effex good night." A little way beyond this, Tristram saw a small huddle of rail engineers, all wearing garish orange tabards. A few of them had mallets in their hands and were lashing out with them. As the train passed by, Tristram tried to get a look at what it was they were striking, but he couldn't really see. He thought he glimpsed tawny and black feathers flying, a flash of red, had the unsettling impression the workmen were beating the brains out of a flock of chickens they had penned between them. But of course that couldn't be. He was just imagining it. And then the train left the engineers behind.

It approached a tunnel. On the brickwork by the entrance, Tristram saw some more graffiti, a stanza of verse, again daubed in that dull red paint, again written in an archaic style:

Come gather thou, come gather here,
And make thy hearts like unto wood,
For if to my tale thou give ear,
Thou wilt hear of wonder and blood.

Tristram had a light teaching load that semester, which was in any case winding up, so was able to spend much of the following week at the British Library, sitting at the desk he favoured in the reading rooms there. But as he'd feared, he didn't make much progress, found it hard to keep his mind on his research. And it wasn't the weird graffiti, or the engineers with their hammers that distracted him. It was that grim splinter of folk song, the line from "The Dalesman's Litany". It had lodged in his brain.

"I've sammed up coals in Barnsley pits with muck up to my knee . . . "

And he kept thinking back on his trip to see his father, Augustus, the previous week. It had been the first time he'd been up north, gone home, in some years.

When he'd first arrived into Barnsley train station, got off the train, and stood on the platform a moment, he'd been surprised by how fresh and clean the air seemed; it had been warm and close in London, hazy with pollution, as it always was. He'd left the station, walked out into the odd mix of foursquare sandstone grandeur and ugly modernity that characterises Barnsley town centre. On the walk to his father's place, the house he grew up in, it had been bright, sunny, and the rows of brick terraced cottages had cheered him. The friendliness of the place, so different from London's chill, had struck him; folk had nodded and greeted him when he'd passed by, a dog walker had stopped and asked if he needed directions. But he didn't need directions, he knew those streets, had spent his childhood and teenage years first running them, playing games with his friends, then sloping about, smoking and drinking, or skateboarding.

But a couple of days into Tristram's stay, the weather had turned, grown grey, and the town had seemed to close in on him, to stifle him. Then he'd remembered why he'd left.

When Augustus answered the door to Tristram's knock, he coughed, a hacking cough, then squinted out. He was a small wiry man, muscles like knots in whipcord, and showed no sign of age or frailty, though his face had grown drawn and haggard since last Tristram had seen him.

"Son," he said. "You've been working too hard in library. Does thou ever get out? In sun? Thou looks pasty as the underbelly of a flounder."

He reached out and tousled Tristram's sparse hair, as if he were still a child, not a grown man, and a broad-shouldered, balding, heavily bearded man at that.

"Hi Dad," Tristram said.

Augustus spoke in the old dialect, for all that he was too young really to do so, spoke like someone a generation older than he was. It was an affectation and a snub to the South that had closed his beloved mines. He hated that Tristram had abandoned the North, first to study at a redbrick with a good reputation in the Midlands, then to make his home in London, the traitorous capital.

Augustus had made up the bed in Tristram's old childhood bedroom, now the spare room. When Tristram came down to the kitchen, having put his things up there, he found his father had made a pot of tea.

"Tea?" Tristram said. "I don't drink tea."

"Well, lad, you should."

Augustus got down a tin of chocolate biscuits from a cupboard, and the two of them, father and son, sat at the table in companionable silence, hands wrapped around mugs, slurping their teas, occasionally dunking a biscuit.

Tristram lay in in the mornings, reading books taken down from the shelves that lined the walls of his old room, childhood favourites, Alan Garner and Susan

Cooper, and gazing down out of the window at a small patch of waste ground beyond the fence at the bottom of the garden. Towards the end of the Second World War, a lone incendiary bomb, dropped by a German plane off course and needing to rid itself of the last of its payload, had struck and razed the small factory occupying the site. The land had never afterwards been built upon, had been abandoned to riotous scrub. Often, when Tristram was a young boy, he'd squeezed through a gap in the fence and wandered through the tall grasses, nettles, brambles, and stunted alders that had grown and still grew there, chatting with friendly figments, striking out with brittle stalks of dead cow parsley at dark ones.

In the afternoons, on dry days and in light mizzle, Tristram and Augustus would walk around Barnsley, to the ruins of Monk Bretton Priory, or take a drive out into the surrounding country for a tramp. Augustus was still fairly hale, despite the black lung that had made his breathing shallow and laboured for the past twenty years. But when the rainfall was heavier, his ailment would trouble him more, and he'd hack and cough, and they'd stay in and watch old black and white comedies on Augustus's ancient TV set: Charlie Chaplin, Fatty Arbuckle, the Three Stooges, the Marx Brothers, Laurel and Hardy, the Keystone Cops, and, Augustus's favourite, Buster Keaton. Then they'd eat tea: a stew, a hotpot, a curry, or a lamb shank. The food was always delicious; Augustus was a really good cook. Then they'd stay up into the night drinking Yorkshire bitter and blended Scotch, and playing board games, from classics like *Scrabble*, *Monopoly*, and *Risk*, to lesser-known favourites of Tristram's childhood, *Lost Valley of the Dinosaurs*, *221B Baker Street*, *Escape from Atlantis*, and *Spy Ring*. And they'd listen to LPs on Augustus's record player.

One night, Tristram, exhausted by a long trudge out on the moors, went to bed before his father, leaving Augustus sitting up, drinking and listening to old folk albums. Tristram fell asleep straight away. But he woke up a few hours later, in the middle of the night, and realised he could still hear music from downstairs. Worried, he went down. The door of the front room was ajar. Peering through the gap, he saw his father, sitting in his armchair, drinking whisky. The song playing was "The Dalesman's Litany", in Tim Hart and Maddy Prior's version. Augustus was silently weeping, tears running down his face. Tristram stood there a moment, on the threshold, unnoticed, heard that line, in Hart's wavery keen. Then he crept back upstairs, went back to bed.

Augustus had worked at the Barnsley Main pit till he'd been laid off in the late '80s, for agitation and supporting union action, and had afterwards had to work as a jobbing labourer. He'd never really struggled to find work, as he was friendly and people trusted him, but he'd always regretted the loss of a trade he'd enjoyed and taken pride in, for all that it had left him with lungs full of coal dust.

Tristram had been born soon after Augustus had been sacked. While his mother, Julia, was pregnant with him, she'd found a lump in her left breast. Tests showed it was a tumour, malignant, but she'd refused treatment, lest it harm the baby, till after she'd given birth. By then, though, it had been too late, the cancer had riddled her, and she'd died when Tristram was only four months old.

Augustus had not named Tristram till he was five months. When, five or six years later, young Tristram had asked, after being mocked at school for his odd name, why he'd been given it, Augustus had winked, and taken him on his knee.

"Here, lad, is my theory. My name, Augustus, is supposed to mean glory to anyone who has it. Well, it hasn't to me. Mine's been a hard life, as thou know." He sighed, but then grinned. "Hark at me. A reet mardy sod." He tickled Tristram's belly. The boy squirmed away. "Anyroad, I were thinking on how thou might throw off bad luck that's seemed to follow me. But then, aha!" Here Augustus clouted the side of his head with his hand. "It buffeted me on skull. If I give thee an awful name, one that's said to bring bad luck, happen opposite will be."

And so it had largely proved. Tristram had done well at school, got into a good university, got funding for further study after. In fact, he'd suffered no real disappointments in life. Save one.

On the Thursday of the week after he'd come back from Barnsley, Tristram met Nadia in the evening. She'd also been researching in the British Library, so they met in the foyer, and wandered to a pub a couple of streets away, in Somers Town, for a drink. It was a nice enough place, and handy, if a bit garish, music a little too loud, which was a shame, as it could have been really snug: it was an old boozer, with dark oak panelling on the walls, and leadlight windows. Tristram got them both a pint, ale for him, cider for Nadia, and they found a small table in a quiet corner. It had been a while since they'd last seen each other; Geoff, Nadia's husband, had been transferred for six months with his job to a post in a Wall Street firm, and she'd gone with him. So they spent a bit of time catching up—Nadia telling Tristram about New York, he telling her about his trip to see his father, about a bit of travelling he'd done in northern Italy.

Then they began talking about their research. Nadia was working on a book about accounts of magic and miracles in Britain in the sixteenth and seventeenth centuries, when the culture was shifting from a world based on supernatural principles to one governed by scientific rationality, but people were still being hanged for witchcraft and divine acts were still believed in.

"It's a fascinating period. Our modern, 'Enlightened' " —the quote marks traced in the air by her fingers, the capital letter suggested by intonation—"worldview was in its nascency, still slopping around in its birth fluids, caul atop its head, umbilical cord probably wrapped around—"

Tristram had hit her on the head with a beermat.

"What?" Nadia frowned, pursed her lips.

Tristram laughed. "I feared you were going to get lost forever in the purple-prose arabesques of that image."

"Oh yeah," Nadia said, and snorted. " 'Cause you're really one to talk."

Staring at her blankly, Tristram shrugged. Nadia shook her fist at him.

"Anyway," he said, "you were saying, it's a fascinating period, blah, blah, et cetera."

"Fuck you, Tristram," Nadia said, laughing. "Yes, it is fascinating actually. You can see so many of our contemporary attitudes in it, but there was a general belief in, not just religion, but in all kinds of other-worldly happenings, and these things are not shocking or strange or noteworthy as they are in later periods of interest in the supernatural, but just part of day-to-day life."

Nadia was flapping her hands about, getting excited, breath quickening, talking too loud. A young couple on a neighbouring table, in a romantic huddle, clutching hands, looked over, faintly irritated.

"The quotidian round," Tristram said, portentous.

"Quite," said Nadia, then let out her pent up breath in a rush. She lifted her pint. The beermat it was resting on came with it, stuck to the bottom. The cider was chill, and dew was beading on the outside of the glass. From time to time a drop, swollen and heavy, trembled, then ran in a rivulet down the side of the pint, and the beermat was damp. Nadia plucked it from the bottom of her glass, smiled, and threw it down on the table. Then she took a long swig of the cider. Tristram watched all this and felt a pang in his chest.

They chatted some more, Tristram telling Nadia a little about some of the bizarre late-Victorian newspaper stories he'd unearthed, had another pint. Then Tristram proposed they have something to eat. Nadia didn't fancy pub food, she'd had it once that week already, so they discussed other options, and eventually settled on a Szechuan restaurant just over the road, which Nadia had eaten in once before and claimed was excellent.

They crossed to the place, got a table, and ordered drinks, beer for Tristram, glass of red wine for Nadia. They started looking at the menu. Then Nadia's phone chimed and buzzed. She took it out of her bag, peered at it, sighed, muttered, "Fuck's sake."

"What is it?" Tristram asked.

"Oh, nothing. Just that Geoff had promised he'd be home later, but now he's saying he's got to work all night. Second time this week."

"Sorry," Tristram said.

"Ah, it's fine, only I was looking forward to seeing him. He's been working through the night so often recently . . . I should have known better than to marry a merchant banker."

"Should've married a fellow academic. We never have to work through the night."

He'd meant it as a joke, but couldn't keep the wistfulness from his voice.

There was a moment of awkwardness, then Nadia picked up her menu, stared intently at it.

"Right," she said. "What shall we have?"

They ordered fairly adventurously from the regional specialities: dandan noodles, mapo doufo, a tripe hotpot with sweet potato noodles, braised ducks' tongues with fermented chilli bean paste. The food, when it came, was great, tasty and authentic, given heat by chillies and Szechuan peppercorns. The only dish they didn't particularly like was the ducks' tongues; they had a fatty texture and tasted rancid, something the spiciness of the sauce they were served in couldn't mask. To eat them you had to slide the pinguid flesh off a central sliver of cartilage. It was unappetising, and as a result, after they'd finished the rest of their meal, the tongues still sat on the table, warming over a couple of tea lights in a small silver chafing dish.

"I guess we should ask them to take that away," Tristram said.

Nadia nodded slowly, but she wasn't really listening. She was gazing at the tongues. She took a sip from her wine glass, then leant over to reach down to where her bag sat on the floor. She began rooting through it for something. After she'd rummaged a short time, without apparently laying her hands on what she wanted, she hefted her bag, a capacious brown leather sack, bulging, overstrained, worn and battered, onto her lap, continued her hunt. She began taking things out and piling them on the table in front of her as she delved: her purse, wired earbuds tangled in a knot, a couple of exhibition guides, a small makeup bag, a banana, spoiled and black, a hoop earring, several loose tampons . . . Tristram looked on, quizzical.

Then she found what she'd been looking for: a small notebook with a picture of one of Louis Wain's hallucinatory cats on the cover. She pushed her thick black hair behind her ears, opened the jotter, and pointed to something she'd scrawled there in pencil. Tristram peered at it, Nadia had dreadful handwriting, then made out:

1606, 13 Octobris: Entred for his Copie under the hand of Mafter Whyte, A ballet of the Murther of A boy of 3 yeres of Age whose fifter had her tong[u]e also Cut out and yet fpeaketh.

Tristram looked up at Nadia. "That's weird."

"Strange, isn't it?"

Frowning, Tristram said, "That's not what I meant exactly. Actually, well . . . No, you tell me about this first." He prodded the scribble in the notebook.

"Well," she said, "the Worshipful Company of Stationers recorded, in a register, for a fee, the titles of printed works in the sixteenth and seventeenth centuries."

"So?"

"So that's an entry recording a broadside ballad telling of a real life crime."

"What's the story of the ballad, of the 'murther'?"

Nadia grimaced and wrinkled up her nose, a habit of hers when she was about to explain something she thought fascinating, a habit Tristram found endearing.

"Well, the ballad itself has been lost, apart from that record. No trace of it exists."

"Oh," said Tristram. "Disappointing. I was looking forward to a gory tale of child murder and the cutting out of tongues."

"Hah! Actually you're in luck, for though the ballad is not known, two pamphlets, prose accounts, of the incident have survived. There are discrepancies between them, but by and large they agree. The story's actually quite famous. One of the accounts contains the rhyme, 'Cock a doodle doo, Peggy has lost her shoe,' as the first thing the girl says when . . . "

She trailed off, blinked, then smiled. "Well, I shan't wreck the story, but yes, it's the first place those verses are recorded, so it crops up in a few histories of folk song and children's rhymes. But the full bizarre and bloody tale is often not given, or if it is, it's garbled."

"So what happened?" Tristram asked.

"Well, there was this family who lived somewhere called Devonshey Hundred in Essex, a loving couple, Anthony and Elizabeth James, two kids, boy and a girl, named after their parents, though the girl was known as Besse, on whom they dote, you know, perfect set up for a tragedy . . . "

So, of course, the idyll was shattered by a gang of brigands, who, falling upon the family at a time when all their servants were off at the county fair, ransacked the house, butchered the parents, divided the spoils, and scattered.

"One of the broadsides gives some quite gory details," Nadia said. "According to that account, Elizabeth James was pregnant again at the time of the murder, and the villain who made away with her, the only woman among the thieves, did so by cutting open her belly, becoming, as the text describes her, a 'tragical midwife'."

The robbers realised they couldn't leave the children to bear witness to their crimes, but, sated with blood, couldn't bring themselves to kill them. So three of the brigands, including the murderous harlot, were tasked with taking the children away. They rode through the night and the day following, as if a family out to visit relations, the children in panniers slung over one of their horses, and at dusk arrived in Bishop's Hatfield in Hartfordshire, where they took a room for the night in an inn owned by a man called Dell. Dell being blind and infirm; the house was run by his wife Annis.

The brigands began to sup mead and wine, and to discuss what they should do with the two children. At a loss, they asked their hostess, Annis, for counsel, showed her their riches, and promised her a share if she would help them. Annis pondered, but only briefly, then advised them to slit the boy's throat and cut out the girl's tongue. This was settled upon. The villains toasted their fiendish pact, then fell to drinking in earnest.

"While they got plastered," Nadia went on, "the pamphlet tells us the little girl, Besse, was sitting in the room with them, watching on. A horrible detail, if you think how scared she must have been."

Tristram nodded.

"Anthony wandered down into the street, where he was seen by a number of villagers, including a tailor, who, intrigued by his fashionable coat, took a pattern of it."

Then, having dined with the children, the miscreants went to bed. They got up in the middle of the night, roused Anthony and Besse, told them their mother and father were near, took them downstairs. Annis and her son George waited there. One of the rogues took Anthony out into the inn's yard, dragged him behind a big stack of firewood, stopped his mouth with cow dung, threw him to the ground, and slashed his throat ear to ear.

George was then tasked with guiding the evildoers towards a pond about a mile off, that local lore told was bottomless, and into which they could sink the body.

The boy's carcass was bound to a stake with rope, and the company set off, George ahead, holding a pikestaff, the two male thieves behind, with the body, and, in the rear, the murderess, who led Besse by the hand. The harlot was heartless, encouraging the girl on by telling her her brother and father and mother waited for her ahead. Then, as they neared the pond, she told the girl to sit on a stile, bade her stick out her tongue, grabbed hold of it, wrestled open the child's jaws with her thumbs, took her knife, and cut the tongue out at the root. The girl moaned, gargling blood, but the woman held the knife to her throat and threatened to slit that as she had slit her tongue. Then she made Besse bear her severed tongue in her apron on to the pond.

When they arrived there, the villains cast Anthony's body in, and made Besse throw her tongue in after. Then they returned to the inn.

The next morning, the murderers gave a share of their spoils to Annis, then left, taking Besse with them. About half a mile out of town, they came across a beggar. They gave him a piece of money to take the mute girl off their hands, then rode off. The beggar soon abandoned the child, and she wandered lost in Hatfield Wood a time, before some locals took pity on her, gave her some food.

She spent some days roaming the countryside, before fetching up in London, where she ended up begging at the door of a barber-surgeon, making pitiful signs to her mouth. He opened up her jaws, saw the cause of her suffering, a dreadful abscess where her tongue had been cut out. Being a kindly man, he took her in and treated the infection. Then, when the wound was healed, he sent her on her way. She roved London and Essex for four years, keeping life and limb together by begging for scraps of food.

"One of the accounts," said Nadia, "tells that whenever anyone spoke to Besse during this time, all she could do was hoarsely mutter, 'Moka, moka.' "

" 'Moka, moka'?" Tristram asked.

"Yes. It's the little details that make the case so fascinating. It's also told that when any kind people gave her something to eat, because she had no tongue to help her to swallow, after she'd chewed the food, she had to pull out the skin of her throat with her fingers and gulp it down."

Meanwhile, Anthony's body was discovered by some hunters' dogs, just three weeks after it was cast into the pond. It was taken to the coroner and displayed for the town to identify. By his distinctive green coat, and his red hair, the boy was recognised as the same who had been seen at Dell's inn a few weeks before. Suspicion fell on Annis, for her husband was not only blind, but known to be mild, and she was called before the local justice. But she denied she knew the child, claimed too many people passed through her house for her to recall all that had lodged there. Many were suspicious of her, including the judge, but nothing could be proved, so she was let go, though she was bound over from assize to assize for four years.

"Then," Nadia went on, "when that four years was nearly up, the crime nearly forgotten, and Annis soon to be dismissed by the court, Besse returned to Hatfield."

On the third day she was in town, she happened across Dell's inn and stood before it crying bitter tears and miming her brother's murder: pointing to the woodstack, stopping her mouth, throwing herself down, drawing her finger across her throat. Suspicion was once again roused against Annis Dell. The justices took the girl in, learned her name by calling her different names till she responded to Elizabeth, then showed her several pieces of clothing, including the dead boy's coat, and seeing her reaction to the garment, a vehement passion, became convinced she was his sister.

She was then given to be looked after by the town. But still nothing could be proved against Annis Dell.

Sometime the following spring, Besse was playing in a park with the daughter of the kind goodwife who had housed her, when hard by them a cockerel began to crow. The goodwife's daughter mocked the rooster's call, singing, "Cock a doodle doo, Peggy hath lost her shoe." She then turned to Besse and said, "Besse canst thou not also do?" And to goodwife's daughter's surprise, Besse sang the rhyme.

Staggered, the goodwife's daughter ran back to the village crying, "The dumb girl Besse can speak, the dumb girl Besse can speak!" And all the town gathered to see the girl without a tongue, who could nevertheless talk. And Besse began immediately to tell all about the murders and to condemn Annis Dell.

Over the next few days, the justices of the peace interrogated the girl, trying to catch her out in a lie. They tempted her with riches and threatened her with infernal flame, telling her that if any should be falsely hanged on account of her testimony, she would go straight to hell.

"And, and this is really bizarre," Nadia said excitedly, "one of the justices even put on a horned devil mask, and jumped out of a bush at Besse, terrified her, and made menaces. And she still stuck to her story." Nadia flicked through her notebook, found what she was looking for. "Besse would say, 'Good gaffer Devil does not hurt me, I speak nothing but truth, and what the thing within me instructeth me to speak.' "

"Hah!" said Tristram. "That's amazing. And this is all contained in the prose account of the murder?"

"One of them, yes. It's quite long."

"Well, how does it all end? Is justice served?"

"I'm coming to that."

Annis Dell and her son George were called to trial when the assizes were next held at nearby Hartford. They pleaded not guilty. The girl, Besse, gave evidence against them saying that since God had lent her speech by a miracle, she would with that inspired breath follow the law of them and have their bloods lawfully, who stole away her brother. Annis persisted in her denials, and, as she had a reputation for honesty and the good treatment of travellers, many still believed her. But then some credible persons of Hatfield gave testimony against her, avowing that blind Dell, by then passed away from his various infirmities, with whom Annis had lived in unhappy matrimony, had often been heard to say, "Thou mayst rise a while, but a day will come when thy villainies and murthers will appear, when thy fall shall be low enough." This was enough to convince the jury, who gave a guilty verdict. The judge, when passing sentence, asked George and Annis to look into themselves, and consider how near they were to their graves, and reflect on how their crimes had been revealed by God Himself through a miracle, and to give up the others involved in their bloody actions. But nothing apparently prevailing to mollify their obdurate hearts, they simply replied, "Since the law hath cast us, we desire to die."

"I suspect though," said Nadia, "they actually didn't know where the robbers and murderers had gone. It's strange to me that there was apparently no distinction made, in the early seventeenth century, between giving advice, for a fee, to murderers, and committing murder yourself. Neither of the accounts say that Annis or George had anything to do with the actual killing. But they were still sentenced to be hanged as murderers. While awaiting death, in jail, George supposedly asked his mother to reveal to the world the true extent of his guilt, but she refused, saying, 'Son be contented, take thy death patiently, it is now too late, I have spoken what I will.' So resolved to death, he spent the time remaining in prayer and in the singing of psalms, and was pitied on the scaffold while Annis was pilloried and booed."

"Fascinating," Tristram said. "I wonder how the girl was really able to begin talking again?"

Nadia shrugged. "I read somewhere that a lot of people who had their tongues cut out at that time were able to relearn speech. The job was mostly botched and there was usually a stub of the tongue left. But who knows? Maybe it was a miracle?"

The waiting staff had not bothered them while Nadia was telling her story, so the dish of ducks' tongues still sat on the table. The tea lights had gone out, and the sauce was beginning to congeal. Tristram took a swig of his beer, then grabbed a tongue with his chopsticks and waggled it at Nadia.

"Or perhaps she had a mystic duck's tongue transplanted into her mouth?"

"Jesus," Nadia said. "Put that down." But she was grinning. "I don't know. People took magic very seriously then. One of the accounts also tells the story of a woman who was hanged at the same time as the Dells. She was accused of using witchcraft to bring about sickness and death. Men, women, infants, and cattle were afflicted."

"Does it say how she did it?"

"When they searched her house they found this chest. In it were the scattered bones of the skeletons of a man and woman, hanks of hair, of all different colours, and a parchment, folded up very small."

Nadia paused, took a sip of wine, smiled at Tristram. "Now this is really cool. When they unfolded the parchment, they found there was a life-size heart painted in the middle, and round the outside, connected to the heart by tendrils, were representations of different bits of the human anatomy. The witch claimed, with the aid of the bones, hair, and the spirits that attended on her, to be able to inflict pain on any part of a person, by pricking that place on her parchment with a needle. To kill, she simply needed to jab the heart."

"So like a Voodoo doll?"

"Action at a distance. That's the principle of all magic really, isn't it?"

"Diction at an asstance."

"Shut up, Tristram."

"Sorry. That really is interesting."

"I know. There's also an amusing bit at the end which tells the story of how the witch was finally apprehended. By a local drunk. Apparently he called her ugly in an inn. Very inventively."

"What sort of thing?"

Nadia consulted her notebook again. "Well, he asked her to look the other way, saying he couldn't abide her nose. Or, he said, she could turn her face the wrong side outward, so it might look like raw flesh for flies to blow maggots in."

"That's pretty mean."

"I know. I think he deserved what happened to him."

"Which was?"

Nadia looked again at her notes. "The witch said to him that he might throw in his drink apace, but that he would not find it so easy coming out. The drunkard joked, saying that it would come out beneath, and that the witch might have some of it, and that he hoped it would poison her, but it did not come out, and the drunk grew swollen and distended, and in great pain, and with a dreadful rumbling in his belly. He was only cured by tracking the witch down and scratching her face, after which he hauled her off to the law."

Tristram chuckled. "I didn't realise research into seventeenth century murder ballads could be so fun."

"Yep. There's lots of crazy stuff. How about you? Tell me more about these sensationalising Victorian newspapers."

Just then their waiter came over and took away the ducks' tongues. Tristram noticed the restaurant had mostly emptied out. He glanced at his watch. It was getting late. He called to the waiter as he was walking off, asked for the bill. Then he turned to Nadia.

"Do you want one more, back over the road?"

Nadia looked at her phone, pursed her lips, then smiled. "Go on then. But just a swift half."

Once they'd paid up at the restaurant and were settled in the pub again, now quieter, half empty, the music turned down, Tristram told Nadia some more about his research.

"It can also be quite entertaining. Some of those late Victorian tabloid stories are pretty mad, especially the paranormal ones."

Nadia nodded. Tristram went on. "But the event I'm looking into at the moment is just tragic, if strange. And, and this is what I was saying was weird earlier, it took place near Hatfield, and involves a tongue being cut out."

Tristram told Nadia about the orphan girl's murder, got his tablet out and showed her the photo he'd taken of *The Police Illustrated News* article.

Nadia paled. "Fuck," she mouthed, then drained most of her half at one gulp.

Suddenly they were both sombre. Tristram wished he'd not mentioned the coincidence. He'd thought it was merely uncanny, now he saw it was sinister.

Nadia stood. "Fancy a brandy or something for the road?"

"Yes. Whisky would be good."

"Sure."

Nadia went up to the bar and came back with their drinks. They sat sipping the spirits in a slightly fraught silence. Then Nadia's phone chimed and buzzed again. She looked at it, scowled.

"Fuck's sake," she muttered.

"Alright?" Tristram asked.

"Yes," Nadia said. Then she sighed. "Well sort of."

"What? What is it?"

"Geoff and I were going to get away this weekend. A nice country break. I'd been looking forward to it."

"And?"

"And that was him, cancelling. Apparently he's got to go on a colleague's stag do now. Who organises a stag do at less than a week's notice?" Nadia pursed her lips.

Tristram shrugged. "Shotgun wedding?"

"It's just that line of work. They're all dicks."

Tristram hid his smirk by taking a sip of his beer. Then he had a thought.

"If you're free then, do you fancy a walk in Hatfield on Saturday? I've been meaning to go up there, see where this murder took place. And we could see the scene of your 'murther' too?"

Nadia smiled. "All right. Sounds good. But I want to end up at a country pub."

"Sure. We can do that."

Tristram and Nadia had met at university. They were on different courses—Nadia was studying French, and Tristram, Philosophy and Literature—but they were in the same seminar for an optional module on Symbolism and Decadence. From the very first session they sat together and got on really well. They were reading French texts in the original, and Tristram struggled a bit with the language, so Nadia helped him out, and he explained some of the cultural and contextual frames to her. They became good friends, often went out together. Nadia's family were Muslim, though not strict, and she, though she claimed to believe, followed few of the tenets, did not cover her hair, drank, even ate pork.

She had full dark lips, a light down above the upper, large brown eyes, thick eyebrows, a sweep of glossy hair. Tristram had fallen in lust with these things at first sight, fell in love with her when first they conversed, but waited six months before asking her out. They were at a gig with some friends when he did. Nadia had stopped smiling. Grimaced. She hadn't thought he saw her like that. They were such good friends, wouldn't it be stupid to risk their friendship? And, with finality, her family weren't that strict, but they would never let her see someone who wasn't a Muslim. Tristram was crestfallen. He drank heavily that night, and over the next days. But he really wanted to stay friends with Nadia, and after a few weeks things between them returned pretty much to the way they'd been before.

On graduating, both Tristram and Nadia decided they wanted to continue their studies. Tristram chose to stay on where he was to undertake his master's, while Nadia moved to London for hers. They kept in touch. Then after a few months, in the spring term, Tristram went down to visit Nadia. She met him off the train. There was a man with her. Physically he couldn't have been more different from Tristram; where Tristram was short, stocky, swarthy, with a thick beard and thinning hair, he was tall, slender, athletic, blond, clean shaven. Nadia introduced him. Geoff. He wore a light blue shirt, open at the neck, grey flannel trousers, oxblood boat shoes. Tristram wore skinny jeans, skate shoes, hoodie. Absently, he tugged at his beard.

The three of them went for drinks and food near the station. Things were strained, though Tristram felt he was doing his best to be friendly. Nadia and Geoff had met at a club in the West End. Geoff was a bit older. He was a merchant banker, worked in the City. It wasn't just in looks that he and Tristram were opposites—Geoff came from a background of privilege, his father was a diplomat of some kind, and he'd been public-school educated, had studied at Oxford. His cocksure swagger was in stark contrast to Tristram's diffidence, his plummy tones, to Tristram's gravelly South Yorkshire accent.

Tristram cut his visit short that time, making up an excuse about an assignment that needed writing, but he never gave any outward sign of his hurt, and he and Nadia stayed friends. He even grew to like Geoff well enough over time, though he always thought him a bit brash and hollow. When Nadia and Geoff got married, Tristram was Nadia's maid of honour. It was a great joke, especially with his full beard and sparse head of hair.

Because he looked "hard", people were always trying to start a fight with Tristram; he usually managed to talk his way out of trouble though, and when he didn't he'd take the blows and not strike back. He was gentle in his manner, always helped people with heavy bags, lent a hand carrying prams up and down steps, gave directions to tourists. But since adolescence he'd always been troubled by strong urges to hurt himself and others, to throw himself off that cliff or tower, jab that fork through the soft meat of his cheek, welt that pregnant woman's bump, push that little girl in front of the train, set fire to that old man in the wheelchair, to grope, maim, kill. He dwelt on these urges. They distressed him. He was terrified that he might act on one, against his will.

He'd been in counselling for this. His therapist had told him it was quite normal, that a lot of people felt those kinds of things often, that it was actually a sign of a healthy moral sense. But he was not reassured. Still felt that under a thin veneer of socialisation, he was some kind of brute.

Tristram and Nadia met at Finsbury Park station fairly early on that Saturday to catch the train to Hatfield. It was one of those spring mornings when the sun is strong behind a haze of cloud, and it was warm and rather close. They met outside the station, by the ticket machines. They hugged, picked up returns, headed up to the platform. As they walked up the stairs, Nadia kept up a breathless monologue about the research she'd done the previous evening into the location of Bishop's Hatfield village. It seemed it no longer existed, had presumably been subsumed into Hatfield town at some point. But there was a school called Bishop's Hatfield, a girls' school, and she supposed it might well be on the site of the old village. Tristram nodded. Nadia began to explain she'd taken a look at the school on the street view of an online map, but Tristram interrupted, told her to hold that thought, said he just needed to use the station loo and grab some breakfast before they headed out. Nadia had eaten, but asked for a cup of tea.

Inside the toilet, it was gloomy, and there was a bad smell of mingled piss, shit, and disinfectant. Standing at a urinal, Tristram saw, scrawled in felt tip on the flaking paint above, amid the usual lewd jokes, offers of sex, terrace chants, and crude sketches of big-breasted female torsos and spurting cocks, a very odd rhyme:

> But as old Sefoftris faw fortune,
> In a carts ceafelefs turning wheel,
> So fates wax and wane as the moon,
> And one who ftood, is made to kneel.

Tristram pondered its meaning as he relieved himself, but he could make nothing of it. He'd no idea who "old Sesostris" was, for one. He made a mental note to look it up later.

He then popped into the café on the platform to buy a croissant and a coffee for himself, tea for Nadia, went back over to where she stood. Their train was delayed by five minutes. While they were waiting, Nadia told Tristram about what could be seen of Bishop's Hatfield Girls' School and its surrounds on the streetview.

"It's on a fairly main road, there's nothing much around it really, another school, a venture scout hut. It must have been the end of a school day when the camera car drove past. There are parents waiting in parked cars, gaggles of girls in uniform on the playground and just inside the gates."

Tristram nodded, took a bite of his croissant.

"Well," Nadia went on, "something in the image really unsettled me. Most of the girls waiting are in pairs or clusters, but there's one standing on her own. It doesn't look like she's in uniform, like the rest, though it's hard to tell, because not just her face, as normal, but her whole body that is blurry, as if she was jigging about when the photo was taken. But it looks like she's wearing some kind of smock and apron."

Tristram finished chewing, swallowed. "That is weird."

Nadia sipped at her tea, then took out her phone, found a picture in her gallery. "Look, I took a screenshot, see?"

Tristram took the phone from her, enlarged the image. "Where am I looking?"

"Over to right, in front of the netball post."

"Oh yes, I see."

Nadia peered at Tristram. "Strange, huh?"

"Not that strange. You get loads of weird glitches in these street views."

"I guess, but . . . " She trailed off.

"But what?"

"Oh, I don't know."

Just then their train pulled into the platform. Tristram handed Nadia back her phone. They got on board and found a seat. What Tristram didn't tell Nadia, what he thought about a lot after, was that it had looked to him like the blurry girl was sticking out her tongue.

On the way out of London, the train passed Victorian terraces of red brick, modern blocks of flats of steel and glass, a sewage treatment plant, some half-full gasholders, and Alexandra Palace up on a hill, its rose window a single eye glaring down at the city, its transmission mast a bony finger stuck up to point or gesture obscenely. It was hot on the train, the air blowing in through the open windows stirring the fug, but not bringing any cool. Across from

Tristram and Nadia sat a middle-aged black woman in a loose fitting dress with a bright floral print, who was fanning herself with a copy of *The Watchtower*, and an old man, with unhealthy grey skin and a wispy beard, who had a fold-up bicycle between his legs, and who had kept on, in spite of the heat, his fluorescent jacket and cycling helmet. He was reading from a piece of paper torn from a reporter's notebook, mouthing the words, as if he were an actor learning his lines. Tristram watched furtively, trying to read his lips. It wasn't easy, but he made out an odd, disconnected phrase here and there: "Quoth she, I'll perform thy petition, and ripped up the mother's belly"; "With last breaths, before death sever, rolled their eyes, lifted up their hands, and bid each other, farewell ever"; and, "Bedabbled with their parents' blood, boy weeping, girl, face black with rage." Tristram guessed they might be lines from an Elizabethan or Jacobean revenge tragedy. Nadia must have caught something of this too, as she began to talk about *The Witch of Edmonton*, the famous tragicomedy of 1621.

After they'd passed by Alexandra Palace, much of the rest of the way out of London was through deep cuttings, and nothing could be seen from the windows save for scrub growing on the banks. Then the train entered a series of long tunnels and the stink of diesel was thick in the carriage. When they emerged the other side, it was into open country: a quaint white house on a grassy hillock, horses in a field, stands of poplar and birch. Everyone in the carriage stopped talking as if some spell had been cast. Nadia, who'd been telling of the pamphlet that had inspired the writing of *The Witch of Edmonton*, broke off to look out, leaning over Tristram, who was sat in the window seat, to get a better view. Strands of her long thick hair tickled his face, and he brushed them away.

After they'd stopped at Potters Bar, Tristram kept a look out for more of the strange verse he'd seen on his way back from Barnsley the weekend before. The train was going quite fast, so he couldn't make any of the graffiti out, but it slowed coming into Hatfield, and he saw some painted on a garden fence. It read:

The boy wore a coſtly greene coate,
With nine skirts as was new faſhion,
Seeing him, a tailor took note,
Made a meaſure of the pattern.

Tristram pondered a moment, but could not make much of this.

On walking out of Hatfield station, Tristram and Nadia first saw, on the other side of a main road, the wrought iron gates of Hatfield House, with, in front, an imposing statue of some grandee—bald and bearded, wearing a cravat and frogged greatcoat, and, to one side, a red-brick lodge, steeply gabled. But Tristram had looked up Bishop's Hatfield Girls' School using the map function of his phone, and their way lay in the other direction, back over the railway tracks. They crossed them using a pedestrian footbridge. The stairs up reeked of piss, the hidden spot beneath them clearly used by drinkers caught short on the way home late at night. Nadia wrinkled, then pinched her nose. Tristram followed behind. When they were in the middle of the bridge they heard a dopplering two-tone horn, and an express train rushed up from the south, beneath them, and through the station.

"There was a crash here, wasn't there, a few years back?" Nadia said.

Tristram nodded. "Yes, that's right. Not many died, but it was serious. Lots of people were injured. There was another crash here in Victorian times. Unlucky spot."

They went on. The sun had burnt off most of the haze, and it was getting quite warm. Nadia stopped to take off her baggy sweatshirt, shoved it in her bag. Underneath, she wore a plain white vest. Static from the sweatshirt left wisps of her hair floating around her head, catching the sunlight, like a nimbus. There was a light sheen of sweat on her forehead. She looked very beautiful. Tristram wondered again why he continued to torment himself, why he didn't just allow their friendship to fade.

They walked down a hill through a quiet industrial estate. Then Nadia recoiled from something on the verge by the side of the road, grabbed hold of Tristram's arm. He looked over. A dead pigeon lay on the grass like an offering. Its head had been torn off, was missing, its chest laid open. Its innards bulged wetly, mauve and tallow. The carcass thrummed with blowflies and wasps. One of the dead bird's wings flapped dully in the breeze from time to time, and when it did the insects rose in a billow and moiled about before settling again.

"Yuck." Nadia mimed retching.

"Must've been a cat," said Tristram. "Or a fox."

Nadia peered at him. "Tristram, it's a pigeon."

Tristram was nonplussed. He was about to say something, when Nadia cut him off, grabbing his arm again, shaking him, grinning in his face. "A joke, you idiot. Jesus." Then she looked back at the dead pigeon. "That's really gross. Come on, let's go."

They walked on. A little farther down the hill they passed by a flyer taped to a lamp post. At first Tristram thought it might be a lost pet poster, but drawing nearer he saw that the image at the top of the flyer was actually a woodcut depicting a pile of logs, towards which a young boy was being dragged roughly by a man. Both wore archaic clothing. Below the woodcut was a four-line stanza:

> The brute ſtopt the boys mouth with dung,
> And dragg'd him behind a Woodſtacke,
> Then down on the hard earth him ſlung,
> As he were rubbiſh in a ſack.

Tristram shook his head, and kept walking by.

Nadia, who'd spotted him looking at the paper, asked, "What was that?"

"Nothing," he replied.

"Lost pet?"

"Yeah."

"Glad I didn't see it. Always makes me sad."

They soon came to a junction with a wider road. Tristram's map told them to turn right. They walked along. The road was lined with a mix of modern housing and the odd much older building. Some of these even had timber frames and thatched roofs. Then Nadia pointed out a sail boat mouldering under a beech tree.

"I wonder why that's been left there? No lakes round here big enough to sail on that I know of."

Tristram shrugged. He did not point out to her what she seemed not to have seen: the graffiti on the wall behind the dinghy. It read:

> Then they ſat down upon a Stile,
> Whore bad Wench her tonge to ſtick out,
> The Girle obeyed, Harpy did ſmile,
> Then cut the tonge out at the root.

A short distance further on, Tristram's map told them to take a left onto a road called Brain Close. They walked down it a way through a 1970s council estate. To their right, a dingy concrete tower block rose up. There were soft drinks cans, crisp packets, and chocolate wrappers, in the gutters, on the front lawns. Then the road narrowed, and of a sudden they were on a country lane bowered by beech, hazel, and oak. It was a relief to be shaded from the sun, which had grown quite hot. There were hedges on either side, of hawthorn and dogwood. The trunks of the trees were twined with ivy, and bindweed was woven through the hedges, its white trumpet flowers lacing the air with a cloying scent. There was no rubbish, no rubbish at all.

Nadia smiled. "This is amazing! Who would've known this was here?"

On either side there were wooden gates in the hedgerow. Beautiful old timber-clad houses painted cream could just be glimpsed.

Before long the lane became a path, and then came out into a meadow, a copse of beech, elm, and conifer a little way off, clouds like teased wool in the sky, the warbling call of a bird.

"Beautiful!" Nadia said. "The air's perfect."

She took a deep breath in through her nose. Tristram, flustered, had to turn away.

And then they were out on another main road, by Bishop's Hatfield Girls' School. They wandered about a bit, looking at the school, at the Venture Scout hut opposite it, but they saw nothing unusual. So they began to walk up the road, towards the centre of the town. A group of the elderly on mobility scooters went by, going at some speed. Tristram didn't really get a good look at them, they were gone too quickly, but he had the impression of hollow eye sockets, sparse hair sprouting from carbuncled scalps, skin fine as tracing paper stretched over brittle bones. And a high thin keening, a verse of song sung:

Only hoarſely could ſhe mutter,
When any one ſpake to her,
And *Moka, moka* utter,
Inſtead of any anſwer.

Tristram and Nadia soon came to a roundabout, round which traffic was flying. They went down into an underpass. After a short walk through a tiled corridor, they emerged into an open sunken area, with rose bushes dotted here and there, some benches at the centre. On one of the benches, was a cockerel, an impressive brute, with orange, green, and black feathers, a keen beak, a stiff comb, full dangling wattles, and a wicked glint in his eye. He strutted about on the bench, glaring the while at Nadia, then threw back his head and crowed, loud and long.

Nadia turned to Tristram, winked, then sang at the cockerel, "Cock a doodle doo, Peggy has lost her shoe!"

The bird flew at her, pecking and scrabbling with its claws. She tried to fend it off, but it wasn't till Tristram kicked it that it flew away again, back to its perch on the bench. It had scratched Nadia's hands and forearms, drawn blood.

"Fuck," Tristram said. "Are you okay?"

Nadia watched the cockerel warily. "I'm okay. Bloody thing."

"Do you need to see a doctor?"

"No, I'm fine. I'm up to date with my tetanus. I'm not worried."

Tristram frowned. "Well, if you're sure?"

"Yep. Let's keep on."

They left through another underpass. There was some graffiti on the tiles in this one. It read:

And when foode charity would beſtow,
The Girle would ſtrain, chew to a pulpe,
Then, lacking tonge to helpe her ſwallow,
Pull out the skin of her throat and gulpe.

They walked on past.

They soon arrived in Hatfield Market Square, an ugly modern shopping centre. It was run down, many of the shops were closed, windows boarded up. One shop seemed, from its window display, to sell only kits of military planes, tanks, and artillery, and figurines of British animals, in human postures and wearing old-fashioned clothing, a badger in a tweed jacket, horn-rimmed spectacles perched on its nose, smoking a pipe, a bat in twinset and pearls, popular children's toys of a time before smart phones, tablets, and consoles. The models were posed so it looked as if they'd been frozen in the midst of a brutal skirmish, one the wildlife folk were winning.

In the centre of the square there was a small garden, a patch of grass, some shrubs, a dwarf willow tree, but the plants were sere, and the ground littered with takeaway cartons, crisp packets, bottles, and cans. Two boys and a girl, all around nine or ten, sat on a bench, passing a plastic bottle between them. They were dressed in the fashions of an earlier era: the girl wore a floral-print pinafore dress and a ribbon in her hair, the boys, short trousers, blazers, shirts, and bowties. The girl was very pale, had smears of raspberry and chocolate sauce about her mouth, and matted and tangled thick brown hair. The two boys were also unwashed and unkempt. One had very light blond hair and a ruddy complexion, the other, black hair and dusky skin. Spotting Tristram and Nadia, the girl called to them.

"Oi! Hey! Come over 'ere!"

They crossed to the bench. Nearing they saw that the bottle the children were swigging from was strong cider, and that they were unsteady, swaying, their eyes glazed.

"Are you alright?" Nadia asked.

"Are *you* alright?" the black boy parroted back at her.

"Are you drunk?" said Tristram.

"Are *you* drunk?" the wan girl came back, then stuck out her tongue.

"Do your parents know what you're up to?" Nadia said.

"Do *your* parents know what you're up to?" the fair boy said, leering. The black boy and the pale girl began to cackle.

Nadia shook her head, and turned to walk away.

"Wait!" the girl cried.

Nadia turned back. "What is it?"

The girl looked up at her and said, very sweetly, "Got a fag?"

Nadia tut-tutted and walked off. Tristram remained a moment staring at the children, before following after.

Then one of the boys called out, "Looking for Bishop's Hatfield, innit?"

Tristram and Nadia stopped, looked back.

"We've found it, thanks," Nadia said.

"Nah mate," the girl scoffed. "Int where the school is. It's somewhere else, small place called Fenwold."

"Shit," Tristram whispered to Nadia. "That's the place where the Victorian orphan was found with her tongue cut out."

Nadia peered at him, then looked back at the girl. "How did you know we were looking for Bishop's Hatfield?"

The girl shrugged. "You just look the type, yeah."

"How do you know that's where it is?" Tristram asked.

"Just do," the girl said.

"Are you sure?"

The girl flew into a tantrum. "Shut it! Shut your stupid ugly face!" Then stomped off, stood a little distance away, staring down at the toes of her black patent-leather buckled shoes in a sulk.

Tristram was taken aback. Turned to the blond boy. "I didn't mean to upset her. It's just that we'd really like to find that place."

The boy leered. "Don't worry 'bout her. She'll get over it. Only that bishop's been bugging her, innit. Dirty ol' creeper."

"Bishop?"

"Look, don't bother, bruv," the black boy cut in. "But Fenwold's the place you want. Reckon they changed the name to try and stop that bishop hanging round."

Tristram was going to ask something further, but just then the fair boy grinned broadly, threw back his head, and began crowing like a cockerel. Very loud.

So Tristram and Nadia walked away. "That was awful," Nadia said. "Those poor kids."

Tristram nodded, but he was preoccupied. "Seriously," he said. "We should go there. What do you think?"

Nadia shrugged. "Alright? I guess?"

"Let's get a cab." Tristram pointed at the office of a minicab firm on the other side of the square. They started walking towards it. Behind them, the little girl was singing while one of the boys beatboxed in accompaniment. The girl had a good voice, lilting and pure. She sang:

The other child ran home amazed,
Crying the dumb Beſſe can ſpeak,

Drawn into wonder the town gathered,
All wanting to fee the freak.

The dispatcher in the minicab office was a man in late middle age. He sat hunched at his computer, wearing an earpiece and mic, staring blearily at the screen. When Tristram and Nadia entered, an electronic bell rang above the door, and he looked up. He ran his left hand though the sparse strands of lank grey hair stuck to his scalp. In his right, he held a cigarette, between thumb and forefinger, ember tucked into his palm. The office reeked of stale smoke, and the wallpaper and calendars hung on the walls, one of cats in yoga poses and one of teapots, were stained tobacco dun. As were the tips of the man's fingers, and his neat white moustache was mottled with it. He stared at Tristram and Nadia a moment, looking them over, eyes narrowed. His face was the flat grey of spoilt fish, save the nose and cheeks, which were red, stitched with broken veins. He took a sip from a mug, cleared his throat, and spoke. He slurred his words ever so slightly.

"Cab is it?"

"Yeah," Tristram responded. "That'd be good."

"Where's it you're going?"

"Fenwold."

"I see now. Well."

The dispatcher let his words hang in the air, looked Tristram and Nadia up and down again, took another sip from his mug.

"Well," Tristram said. "Can you get us a taxi?"

"She's very pretty," the dispatcher said to Tristram, indicating Nadia with a nod of the head. "You're a lucky man."

Nadia sighed. Tristram reddened, clenched his teeth.

"Look, can you get us a cab or not?"

"Now, now," the dispatcher said. "Just a minute."

He tapped away at his keyboard, mumbled something incoherent into his mic. Then looked up at Tristram and Nadia. "On its way. Be here directly. Go and wait out front."

When Tristram and Nadia got into the back of the cab, the driver looked at them in the rear view mirror. "Fenwold, is it?"

"That's right," Nadia said. "Do you know how far it is?"

"Shouldn't be more than ten, fifteen minutes."

"Great, thanks."

The driver set off. "Sorry about the noise," he said over his shoulder.

Tristram and Nadia noticed then that there was glossolalia over metallic whines coming from the car's speakers.

"I recognise this," Tristram said. "I know what it is."

"It's bloody awful, is what it is," said the driver. "But I'm on hold to an airline company, and I need to stay on the line."

"Okay, no worries," Nadia said.

"Luciano Berio's 'Visage'," Tristram said in a low voice, leaning in to Nadia. "I actually really like it."

Just then there was a roar and three low-rider motor trikes went past, ridden by men in leathers, wearing open-face helmets and goggles. Each had a patch sewn to the back of his jacket with the words, "And Yet Speaketh", embroidered on.

"That's weird," Tristram muttered to himself. He turned to Nadia, but she was looking the other way, had missed the bikers. The Berio piece had wound up to a crescendo of howling, crazed laugher, sobbing, and static crashes.

"Jesus," said the driver. "I hope they answer soon."

He caught Tristram's eye in the rear-view mirror.

"What it is is, my mother-in-law, well she ain't got long left. Cancer."

Tristram and Nadia expressed their condolences. The taxi had left the town behind, and was driving along a road between grassy verges, hedgerows and fields on one side, woodland on the other.

"Thanks," the driver said. "We were all supposed to be going on holiday, see. Had our flights booked. So I phones up this morning to cancel hers, the mother-in-law's, and the woman I'm speaking to, when I tells her why I'm having to cancel, says, 'I can give you the number of a witch. She could do a spell.' I was on speaker phone, so the wife heard an' all."

He glared at Tristram in the rear-view mirror. Tristram, realising a response was called for, said, "Right."

"Exactly. Totally inappropriate. So I'm phoning back to speak to a manager, make a complaint. Which is why I've got to stay on hold."

The taxi dropped them at the centre of a picturesque village, opposite a pub called the Comb and Wattle. On the sign were a pair of gamecocks in a pit striking out at each other with their spurs. Ironically, the birds lacked both combs and wattles, having been dubbed and cropped, as gamecock generally are. Nadia paid the driver, and he drove off. His call to the airline was still on hold, the Berio at an ague pitch: bitter prophecies, tender maledictions, whispered imprecations, bellowed insinuations, bone-thrumming noise. Tristram stood looking at the pub. The sun was now blazing down, and it had become uncomfortably warm in the taxi.

"Open, I think," he said to Nadia. "Fancy a half before we have a wander? You did say you wanted to end up in a country pub."

"Yes," she replied. "That'd be good. And perhaps we can come back after. If it's nice."

Inside, Nadia took a seat at a table in a bay window at the front of the pub while Tristram went up to the bar to order a couple of half pints of ale. The Comb and Wattle was a typical old country boozer, exposed stone and wooden beams, a big fireplace with an iron grate, horse brasses, corn dollies, and antique farming tools on the walls. A rusty harrow hung from the ceiling. There was strangely, out of place, an old photocopier in one corner. One other customer, an old man, sat slumped on a stool at the counter. He had a shock of white hair, a grizzled beard, a kind face. He peered through half-moon spectacles at a crossword puzzle in a newspaper he had open on the bar, drank a dark beer from a dimpled mug. He nodded, friendly, at Tristram, and Tristram nodded back.

The bar was staffed by a young woman with curly brown hair and dimpled cheeks. She smiled at Tristram.

"What'll it be?"

Tristram ordered. While the woman was pulling the halves, he asked if she knew if the village had had any other names before Fenwold.

She paused in drawing the beer, looked at Tristram strangely. "As far as I know, it's always been Fenwold. Why do you ask?" She was smiling, sounded breezy, but her eyes were cold, hard.

"Never heard of Bishop's Hatfield?" Tristram asked.

"I can't say as I have," the barmaid said. "And I've lived here all my life. 'Cept, no, it's a school isn't it?" She was still smiling, but had a white-knuckle grip on both the handpump and the handle of the pint glass.

The old man sat at the bar cleared his throat. "Actually—"

But the barmaid cut him off. "Now, Leonard, you know no one's interested in your stories. Leave the man alone, he's just come in to enjoy a half with his girlfriend." She turned to Tristram. "She is your girlfriend, isn't she?"

Tristram opened his mouth to respond, but just then Leonard stirred himself. "Beth," he said to the barmaid, "How many—"

But she cut him off. "Now Leonard," she said, sternly, as if talking to a badly behaved child. "These nice people don't want to listen to your nonsense. The rest of us put up with it because we're locals, but they've come up from London."

"Well, I've had enough of it!" He slurred his words slightly, and his voice quavered with anger. "Quite, quite enough."

He stood, swayed there a moment, unsteady on his feet, then his shoulders fell, and he sighed and sat back down again. He took a long swallow of his beer, wiped froth from his moustache with the back of his forearm, and turned back to his crossword.

The barmaid, Beth, rolled her eyes at Tristram, tapped her temple, then put the two half pints down on the bar.

"That'll be four pound eighty-four."

Tristram took out his wallet, handed over a note. As the barmaid was giving him his change, she said, "She really is stunning."

Tristram was slightly taken aback. "Yes," he stammered. "She is."

"Enjoy your beer."

He carried the halves over, sat down next to Nadia. He noticed Leonard looking in their direction, but when he caught the old man's eye, he turned away. Tristram took a sip of his ale.

"That was weird."

"What was?" Nadia asked.

"Oh nothing. Just an odd atmosphere. The old guy's pretty drunk."

"Look what I found on the windowsill," Nadia said, holding out a folded sheet of paper. "This really is strange."

"What is it?"

"Take a look."

Tristram took the sheet, unfolded it. On it was a woodcut of a man in a devil mask with horns jumping out of a bush to scare a young girl. Under this strange print were two stanzas of verse:

But to her ſtory ſhe held faſt,
Euen when threatened with peſtilence,
The Diuell and hellfire blaſt,
Or tempted with wealth immenſe.

To euery question did ſhe reply,
Blandiſhed or in fear of hell,
I muſt not lye, I muſt not lye,
I haue that within bids me truth tell.

"What do you make of that?" Nadia asked.

"I don't know," Tristram replied. "But you're right, it is odd."

While they supped their ales, they chatted, about various things. Then at one point Tristram realised Nadia wasn't listening to him any more, but stared glumly into her beer.

"You all right?" he asked.

She immediately cheered. "Yes, fine! Sorry, I was miles away. But I'm having so much fun today, thanks for this. You really are a good friend." She gave him a bright smile.

Tristram took a long draught of his beer, finished it off. As Nadia still had more than half of hers left, he went up to the bar to get himself another.

Once they'd finished their drinks, Tristram and Nadia left the pub, thanking the barmaid, who nodded at them. Leonard watched them leave with a tight smile on his face, then went back to his crossword. They wandered down Fenwold's main street, down a hill. Most of the houses were old, whitewashed masonry, stout oak beams, and thatched roofs, and the newer buildings had been designed sympathetically to harmonise. Tristram and Nadia didn't see many people, an elderly woman walking her dog, a small yappy thing, a builder up on a ladder fixing some guttering. Within a few minutes, they were on the edge of the village; it was a small place.

They looked about them. To their left, across a meadow, was the village church, a Norman construction of flint and sandstone, with chequered patterning on the gables and squat tower. There was a stile in the wall and beyond, a footpath leading past the churchyard. Tristram looked at the map on his phone and realised the path would take them out on a loop and then back round to the other side of the village. They decided to take it.

The path led them past the end of the graveyard. They stopped, leant on the low stone wall, and looked at the memorials there. Most were plain headstones, many older, of weathered sandstone, inscriptions hard to make out, some newer, black marble with gilt lettering. There was a low spreading yew, gnarled limbs, dark green needles. Nadia pointed to it.

"They can live a long time, yew trees. Over a thousand years in some cases. It's quite likely this tree was standing when Besse James spoke though she had no tongue."

Tristram turned to her. "Wow," he said, sarcastic. "That is just *so* profound."

Nadia grimaced and thumped him on the shoulder.

"Ow! That wasn't necessary."

"Yes it was." She thumped him again.

He tried to trip her, but she dodged, then turned and sprinted, laughing, down a hill, through a meadow strewn with small yellow and white flowers. He ran after, tried to grab her. They ended up tangled together, lying on the floor, panting and laughing.

Tristram stood up first, offered a hand to Nadia.

"Dick," she said, smiling, then took his hand. He helped her to her feet.

They walked on, through a copse. It was nice and cool in the shade of the beech, birch, and elm foliage. The path brought them out next to a pond fringed by reeds. They stood, looking out over the water, at the cornfield beyond, and at a pair of kestrels gyring and hovering overhead. Then one of the falcons stooped down and flapped back up from the corn stalks, a small creature, perhaps a vole or shrew, dangling from its talons.

"Poor thing," Nadia said.

"It's just the way of nature though, isn't it?" said Tristram. "The strong will prey on the weak?"

As he said that, there was a gurgle from the pond, as if something had disturbed the sediment, and some bubbles rose up, broke the surface. There was a stench, and both Tristram and Nadia gagged, then, covering their mouths and noses, went on past the pond, and followed the path up a hill, back towards the village.

On the edge of Fenwold, they passed a ramshackle old hut. There was something sinister about it, and they hurried by. Just beyond, they came across a group of young children, five of them. They were on a small patch of open ground off to one side of the road, in the middle of which there was a chicken run. Unlike the children they'd seen in Hatfield Market Square, these kids were dressed in modern clothing: jeans and T-shirts. They were poking long sticks through the wire netting of the pen, trying to goad the big cockerel who strutted there, amid his hens. From time to time he would fly at the children and crow, and they would taunt him by singing, "Cock a doodle doo, Peggy has lost her shoe."

Tristram and Nadia leant on the low wall at the edge of the bare patch, and Nadia called out, "Where did you learn that rhyme?"

The children turned to face her. They began pointing at their mouths, signing that they could not speak.

"But we just heard you singing," Nadia said.

One of the boys in the group, who was a little taller, and perhaps the leader, stuck up his middle fingers. The rest began scooping up gravel from the ground and hurling it at Nadia and Tristram. They backed off and went on their way.

"What the hell was that all about?" Nadia asked.

"I've no idea," said Tristram.

They walked on a bit mazed, unaware of their surroundings. And soon reached the centre of the village again. It was late afternoon; the sun had begun its descent towards the horizon. They went back into the pub. They were worn out and disorientated, the antic experiences of the day finally catching up with them. The place was still empty of patrons, save Leonard, still sat at the bar. While Nadia and Tristram had been walking, he'd obviously had a few more pints, was even more slumped on his stool. Beth stood as before, behind the bar; she waved to them when they came in. Nadia crossed to the same table they'd sat at earlier, while Tristram went over to order some drinks.

"Two halves of ale," he said to Beth, pointing to the handpump.

She looked at him quizzically. "Why don't you just have a pint?"

"We both want a half."

"We?" Beth said, cocking her head and pursing her lips.

"Huh?"

Tristram turned to look for Nadia, but the pub was empty. "She must've gone to the toilet." He turned back, smiled at Beth.

"You feeling all right?" she said. "You came in on your own. I watched you."

"No, I came in with my friend. The one who was with me earlier."

Beth took a step back, folded her arms, squinted at Tristram. "You were on your own before, too."

"What?"

"About three hours ago, you came in here, on your own, drank a couple of pints, left. Seemed normal then. Didn't he Leonard?"

The old man looked up. Gazed at Tristram with rheumy eyes. He nodded.

"See?" said Beth.

Tristram started shaking his head, pulling at his lower lip with his thumb and forefinger. "No, I came in with Nadia, my friend. You said she was stunning. Don't you remember?"

"I don't know what you're on about. But if you want to stay in here, perhaps you'd best have a soft drink."

So Tristram ended up sitting back at the table in the bay window, a pint of cola in front of him. He took out his mobile phone, but it was out of battery—he'd run it down using the maps to navigate.

The pub slowly filled up around him. At some point Beth was replaced behind the bar by an older man who wore a short-sleeved shirt and had a tattoo of a cockerel on his bicep, and whom Tristram assumed to be the publican, and Tristram went up to order a beer. The man peered at him, but served him.

No one bothered Tristram as he sat there into the evening, slowly getting very drunk. He felt hollow, he didn't really know how he felt. At one point, he overheard a woman sitting near him saying to her companion, "What're you doing? Don't do that." And had a vivid memory of asking Nadia how Geoff's stag do was going, and her face crumpling, and her telling him how she'd called Geoff's mobile that morning before setting out to Finsbury Park station and it had been answered by a woman who'd told her, when she'd asked, that Geoff was in the shower and they'd just had a great fuck thanks, before hanging up. And Nadia had begun to sob, and Tristram had hugged her, to comfort her, for the longest time, and had then tried to kiss her, but she'd pushed him away. Remembering this, Tristram gulped down half a pint in one, and felt better.

Later, Tristram got hungry and ate a burger from the pub kitchen. He was reeling drunk, but he didn't stop throwing back beer. Two old men joined him at his table, but after casting a glance in his direction, ignored him. They were drinking half-and-halfs of bitter and pale. They sat quietly for a while, then one of them fetched a cribbage set and a deck of cards from the bar. The set was like a box with the scoring board on the lid and the pegs inside, and when one of the old men opened it, Tristram saw, as if it were before him, a wooden chest, lid raised, with inside it yellowed bones, two skulls, hanks of hair, a folded parchment. He shook his head to clear it.

The pub had mostly emptied out by the time the publican rang the bell for last orders. Tristram, full from all the beer, had switched to Whisky Macs and was nursing a large one, sipping it, enjoying the burn of the drink in his throat. With dusk, the weather had turned squally—thick low clouds wracked across the full moon, scuds of rain spattered the Comb and Wattle's windows—and he regretted the fact he was dressed only in shorts and a T-shirt. The pub swam about him.

Then the publican left the bar unattended a moment, went back into the kitchen. Leonard, who was still at his place, lurched up, staggered over, and handed Tristram a copy of the pub's menu, before stumbling back to his stool, turning away.

Tristram looked down at the menu. Leonard had drawn and written on the back. At the top, he'd sketched out something that looked like a seventeenth-century woodcut depicting a young girl and an older woman standing either side of a fire, over which the woman held a crucible containing something that looked like a large slug. Underneath, he'd scrawled:

So to the Gaole they were conueyed,
To wait upon the gallows tree.
There Iohane Harrison alſo ſtayed,
Awaiting hanging for witchery.

She had brought mis'ry to many,
Through her power of inflicting,
In ioynt, ſynnow, or place any,
On the body, pain tormenting.

Many were by her hand ſtricken,
Her ſpirits had cauſed men, women,
Children & cattell to ſicken,
Suffer violent pangs & then,

To wither away and then die.
It was by a Fuddle-caps,
She was apprehended finally.
She had given him clap,

After he croſſt her with ſcuruy Ieſts,
So he hunted her all night long,
Till finally he made his arreſt,
And to ye towne dragged her along.

Another priſoner heard ſome talk,
Between the *Dels* and this Hagge,
To ſet it down though, we do balk,
As it may be a lye and a brag.

But what the priſoner did tell,
Is that the Witch fleered at *Dels* wife,
When ſhe was thrown into her celle,
Annis said, what Crone, you wiſh for ſtryfe?

The Hagge ſneered, You ſhould not ſtryfe with me,
With arts Diuellish and black,
So ſhe could with her words condemn thee,
I gave that poore Childe her tonge back.

You did, cried *Dels* Wife, why? For Iuſtice?
Nay, for the law I care not one fig,
Quoth the Witch, you have giuen offence,
By killing my imp, Whirligig.

Annis recalled the act and wailed,
For ſhe had kill'd the cat for ſport,
So ſhe ranted and ſhe railed,
And curs'd what ſhe had fooliſh wrought.

How did ye do it? quoth *Dels* wife,
You may ſay as we are all to die.
I baptiſed my Witchs knife,
In infants bloode, quoth the Harpy.

Found a wand'ring Childe and tooke her tonge,
Then aided by my *Iucubi*,
The Diuell, my charts & my bones,
Performed an awful rite whereby,

That tongeless Wench again might ſpeak.
She is now become a dread thing,
Poſſeſſt forevermore by fiends bleak,
And by pangs of hunger in Spring.

Thus the hag concluded her tale.
Annis gnaſhed her teeth and ſhe ſwore,
Curs'd the Witch while they bided in Gaole,
At times, at others did implore.

The Crone waited calme ſometimes laughing.
Dels Sonne meanwhile ſpent his days,
In weeping, wringing his hands, praying,
And ſinging pſalms to the Lords praiſe.

With other figns he repented,
And did true contrition fhow,
So he only was lamented,
When the three went to the gallows.

After reading this, Tristram downed the rest of his Whisky Mac, turned the menu over. There he saw, one of the lunchtime options, "Tongue sandwich". And he had a vision of a human tongue, raw, bloody at the root where it had been severed, laid out in a silver chafing dish. And then heard a sound, like "Moka, moka", saw someone pulling out the skin of her throat with her fingers, and heard gulping. Heard wordless howling and spluttering. Heard himself say, "I'm sorry. I'm so sorry."

Then the publican rang the bell again and bellowed, "Right, that's time. Come on, everyone out. I've got a bed to go to."

And Tristram got up from the table and left the pub, walking out into the dark and the foul weather.

The Yellow Book

"Dorian Gray had been poisoned by a book. There were moments when he looked on evil simply as a mode through which he could realise his conception of the beautiful."

– Oscar Wilde

About five years ago, Beth and I were at a dinner party with some old university friends and their partners. Beth and I had been part of the same crowd back at the provincial redbrick we'd attended, though we'd not got together till a few years later, and often caught up with the people we'd hung around with then. The hosts, Michael and Lorenzo, had prepared a tasty supper, which had been eaten with relish, the wine was flowing, candles in holders on the table were the only sources of light, there was something suitably sedate on the stereo, Gorecki's "Third" I think it was, and the mood had therefore waxed rather nostalgic and maudlin, a yearning for lost days of youth—we were all in our late-thirties, and for some of us they seemed rather long ago. We were telling the same old stories when Crispin, who was the only one of us who'd gone into the city, where he'd done really rather well for himself, snorted.

"Blah, blah, blah. Fucking hell. Broken record. You saps."

We all groaned. We knew Crispin. He liked to rant after a few glasses of wine.

"Only a few months ago," he went on, "I had a stag do in Amsterdam, a colleague's, that ended up in a real fucking bacchanal."

He was about to launch into a story I at least had heard before, which involved quantities of booze and drugs, several prostitutes, one arrest, and a near-drowning in a canal, when John broke in. John was Beth's friend Julia's partner. Julia had gone to university with the rest of us, but was shy, and apart from Beth, who'd lived with her, I guess we didn't know her all that well, though Beth always got her invited to these gatherings, and she invariably came along. John, we hardly knew at all, though he and Julia had been together nearly a couple of years and had been out quite a few times with us. But that was unsurprising really, given that most of our conversations revolved around reminiscences of old times or obscure in-jokes at which we'd fall about laughing, often before the punchline had even been reached. But even so, he seemed particularly diffident, if nice, I thought. Like Crispin, he did something in high finance, but unlike Crispin, was withdrawn and serious. He had a thick beard and rheumy sad eyes. His voice was soft, low, and hoarse, and you really had to pay attention when he was speaking, especially if other people were talking at the same time. I thought he and Julia were well-suited—I'd always thought her a bit mousy if I'm honest. And she'd been single for so long before she'd met him. Beth kept saying how lovely it was to see her happy for a change.

Anyway, it was a surprise when John spoke up. "I went on my friend Sebastian's stag about three years ago now. That *genuinely* ended up in a bacchanal . . . " He trailed off, grimaced, then grinned, looked round the table at us.

Crispin bristled, but I kicked him under the table, and he grumbled and sat back in his chair. Protective of Julia, Beth had been wanting us to get to know John a bit better and was quite beaming at his taking the floor. Julia though, peered at him.

"Who's Sebastian? You've never mentioned him."

"We lost touch because of what happened. But perhaps . . . " Again he trailed off.

"No, go on, tell us," Beth said. "We want to hear now."

Julia smiled, tilted her head at John.

"All right." He took a long swig of his wine and went on. "So anyway, the stag do was in Norfolk. The stag, and many of his friends, had been to university in Norwich. So had I in fact, though not at the same time. The others were spending a couple of days on a narrowboat on the Broads, but I'd something on at work, could only get up for the big Saturday night on the town."

John told us how he'd taken a train to Norwich from Liverpool Street station on a warm day in late spring, taken a midday train so he'd have time to potter about a bit before he met the others, revisit the days when he'd lived there. He was going to stay the night on the barge, but knowing he'd have no opportunity to wash the following morning, hadn't bothered with an overnight bag or a change of clothes—all he had with him was a canvas bag, carried over his shoulder, with a few essentials in, sunglasses, umbrella, that sort of thing. He was looking forward to a night out—he'd been working really hard and had had to entertain clients in his free time, and the stress had been getting to him; he'd not slept well for weeks, troubled by dreams in which he leapt off high structures—tower blocks, suspension bridges, electricity pylons—with wire nooses knotted around his neck.

After arriving at Norwich train station, he wandered the town, finding little had changed since his time there, and after a bit ended up in a secondhand bookshop in Tombland he'd spent many happy hours looking round back then. As he entered, a bell over the door chimed, and the cashier, who was sat behind the till, a man in middle age who wore horn-rimmed half-moon spectacles, looked up and nodded at him. Inside, the shop was a boggling maze of shelving laden with books. John began to negotiate the cramped and twisting ways, browsing the stock. He'd no real intention of buying anything, but cast his eyes over the spines lest a title intrigue him. There were few other customers, but from time to time he had to squeeze past someone or was jostled as he bent to peer at a book. Then, in the theology section, an elbow caught him in the ribs, and turning to glare he saw a striking young woman, with green eyes, a wave of reddish-brown hair, and a stippling of freckles across the bridge of her nose. She mouthed an apology, grinned sheepishly, and John, charmed, returned her smile before turning back to the shelves.

It was further down the same aisle he came across it. The yellow of its spine made it stand out from the dull greens, browns, and reds of the other volumes. The words written there in cursive, almost a scribble, caught his attention: *Day's Horse Descend.* He wondered what they could mean. So he reached out and took the book from the shelf. He looked at the front of the dust jacket. There was that odd title once more, again in a script that resembled a scrawl, black against the jaundiced wrapper, and below, a name printed in blackletter, "Hendrick Van der Decken". There was no illustration or anything like that. John turned the book in his hands to look at the back.

"Well," he said, looking round the table, "I read the description there. The book was a collection of prose poetry by a late nineteenth-century French decadent, Gilbert Moreau. Van der Decken was a pen name, taken from the captain of the legendary *Flying Dutchman* in magazine stories. Moreau had been a friend of Lautréamont's. Apparently Wilde read the book." John shifted in his chair and took a sip of his wine. "I was intrigued. So I opened it, found a price on the flyleaf which seemed reasonable, and took it up to the counter."

The bookseller had squinted over the top of his glasses at John. "I didn't know I'd a copy of this in stock. What do you know about it?"

"Nothing. Just caught my eye. Thought it looked interesting."

"Oh, it is. Strange book. Not many people have heard of it now. It's got a bit of an odd reputation. Hardly any copies were printed. Published at the author's expense. I think most of them ended up in the Seine."

John nodded.

"And this was the first and only translation into English. Nineteen sixty-seven. Again a small run. Anonymous translator, press no one's ever heard of. Never been reprinted. Oh yes, it's a strange one all right."

He rang the book up on the till, and John paid. The bookseller put *Day's Horse Descend* into a brown paper bag and handed it to John, who dropped it into his tote and left. As he pulled open the door, setting off the chime again, he turned to look back into the shop. He saw the beautiful redhead standing at the mezzanine balustrade, leaning her elbows on it, and grinning down at him. He smiled back, a little awkwardly, then went outside.

He walked down the street a short way and found a bench with a view of the cathedral spire. The sun had breached the clouds, so he got out his sunglasses and put them on. Then he took *Day's Horse Descend* out of his bag, opened it to the translator's introduction.

John looked round at us. "I can still recall a few details from that introduction. Supposedly, and I really like this, Moreau wrote slowly, and mostly at night, while throwing knives at a picture he'd tacked up of Diderot, whom he hated."

"When did he live?" Lorenzo asked.

"Like Lautréamont, he died during the siege of Paris. I think he was about thirty then, I don't remember the exact year of his birth. Around Christmas time, eighteen seventy, a gargoyle fell from the walls of a church, struck him down."

I looked over at John. "You said Wilde read the book?"

"Well, that may have been pure conjecture on the part of the translator. But they claimed in their introduction that an earlier draft of *Dorian Gray* existed in which the yellow book Lord Henry sends Dorian was clearly intended to be Moreau's, and that it wasn't till around the time of the final draft that it was switched for a work modelled on Huysmans's *À rebours*. No idea if that's really true though."

"So, what's the meaning of the odd title?" Beth asked.

John took a swig of wine, then wiped droplets from his moustache with the back of his hand. "The English, *Day's Horse Descend*, was Moreau's original title. A pun in French, though I can't remember on what."

"Ah," said Beth.

"Anyway," John went on, "just as I'd finished reading the introduction, and was about to turn the page and start on the poems, my mobile buzzed in my jeans' pocket."

John took his phone out, looked down at the screen. A message from one of the stags to say they were about ten minutes or so from the pub where they were gathering. John shut the book, slid it back into its brown paper wrapper, put it in his canvas bag. As he did so, he thought that, knowing Sebastian and his friends, knowing how the night was likely to go, he'd be lucky if he still had the bag come the morning. Then got to his feet and headed to meet the others.

But by some stunning fluke, John's bag was still over his shoulder as he reeled through the mist just before dawn the following day, staggering along the river path outside Wroxham, where the stags had moored their barge. Still with all his stuff in, including *Day's Horse Descend*. He was using the torch of his mobile to light his way, and there was a diffuse nimbus about him as he stumbled along. Finally he sighted the boat, recognising it by the stag who lay face down on the roof, snoring fit to rouse the dead.

John hopped on board and walked the length of the boat to see if anyone else was still awake, but they were all passed out, strewn throughout the barge. He felt too wired from what he'd taken to even contemplate sleep. So he sat down on a folding chair in the bow, and looked about him at the mess. The small area of deck was littered with bottles and cans, cigarette and spliff ends, a couple of pornographic magazines. His eyes alighted on a plate in a corner, on the white dusting on it. He crossed over, took the dish up, moistened his right index finger, ran it across the plate, then put it to his mouth, licked off the powder that clung to it. A shudder went through him. But it wasn't enough—he craved more. Then he remembered the plastic baggie of stuff he'd stolen from the stripper's flat. Taking it from his pocket, he tipped a small mound of the powder onto the dish, chopped out a couple of lines with a credit card, snorted them with a rolled-up fiver.

He sat back and waited. After a short while a kind of elation welled within him and he sighed.

At that moment the sun sent its first wavering tendrils of light over the horizon and they shone on the calm surface of the river and caressed John's face and heavy limbs and he felt warmth and joy build. He took a cigarette from his pack, lit it, sucked deep, before letting the smoke spill from his mouth with a sigh. He thought about the night and grinned. It had been shambolic, but lots of fun. Moments flashed back to him as he sat there smoking. Meeting the others in the sunny garden of the pub, having a few beers. The grisly spectacle of one of the other stags tearing off the head of the roast suckling pig they'd eaten there, poking his fingers into it, making it speak. He'd been pretty good at throwing his voice, and the effect had been uncanny. The first bump of coke John had snorted, off the webbing between his thumb and forefinger, after they'd finished the meal. That had perked him up and got him looking forward to the night's debauch.

After that things were hazier. A strip club. A private table at a night club, on a balcony overlooking the place, with vodka, whisky, beers, and mixers on ice. Fizzing sparklers stuck in the ice bucket, their afterimage dancing about the club. Giving the toilet attendant a twenty pound note to turn a blind eye to powder snorted and dabbed in cubicles. The terrible music, the dancefloor a sweaty, heaving morass of people in trashy clothes. Slurred attempts to talk to women in the smoking area.

And sharper, running through, the image of a beautiful girl with reddish-brown hair, green eyes, and freckles.

John had been sitting in a booth in the strip club, having a good time, but still feeling a bit awkward, not by then drunk or high enough to overcome his natural reticence, not quite ready to take part in the antics of the others, who were already lairy. He cast occasional embarrassed glances at the strippers, but mostly stared down at his beer, chatted to the stags who drifted over to him from time to time. Then, when the rest of the party were all over by the stage, whooping as the stag was humiliated by two of the girls, he even got bored enough to take *Day's Horse Descend* out of his bag and begin to flip through it, desultorily. But before he'd settled on a poem to read, he heard a voice at his elbow.

"Mind if I join you?"

Looking round, John saw crouched beside him the woman who'd jostled him in the Tombland bookshop. She wore a fussy yet scanty set of underwear, in the same green as her eyes. Flushing, John saw she was freckled all over.

"No, that's fine," he stammered. "But I'm really sorry, I won't want a private dance or anything like that."

"That's all right," the redhead said. "We can just chat. Perhaps you could buy me a drink? A tipple at the start of my shift is always welcome."

"Sure," John said. "What would you like?"

"An absinthe would be great. Tell them it's for me and they'll give you a sugar cube, spoon, and jug of water. They know how I like it."

"Okay." John stood, started for the bar. Then turned back. "Oh, what's your name?"

"Sibyl."

John frowned at her.

"What can I say? Old-fashioned parents."

When John returned from the bar with the drinks on a tray, his a whisky, Sibyl had taken off her shoes and tucked her bare legs up under her on the red velour couch. She smiled at John as he set the tray down and sat next to her, then went about louching her drink, stirring in the sugar. Her eyes glittered.

"I love the way it turns cloudy like that!" she said, more to herself than anything.

"Do you mind if I take some of that water for my whisky?" John asked. "If you're done with it?"

"Help yourself," Sibyl said, shuffling closer to him. "I love this stuff," she said, taking up her glass. "The Green Fairy."

She took a sip, then grinned at John. She had long canines that touched her red-painted lower lip when she smiled.

"I quite like the idea of it," he said. "The decadence. But the taste? Not so much."

"I like it. But I *love* the idea of it. I'm studying Art History, and it's the Symbolists I like best. Klimt and Rops and Moreau. Moreau especially."

"Actually," John said, "you look a bit like his Salomé."

She turned to him, rolled her eyes. "Seriously?"

John thought a bit. Then shrugged. "Yeah. Sorry." Then, remembering *Day's Horse Descend*, which he'd put down on the table, pointed at it, said, "You know, I bought this at the bookshop earlier. It's by another Moreau, a poet."

She raised her eyebrows, laughed. "Ah, so you do remember me from the bookshop."

John stuttered, "Well, I . . . "

Sibyl nudged him with her elbow, laughed. "I'm only teasing. So, who's this other Moreau?"

John told her a little of what he'd learned from the introduction, and afterwards they both talked about the late nineteenth century and how they wished they could have lived then.

Then Sibyl said, "It's my turn on stage soon. I need to go get ready. Come over and watch me? I'm afraid it won't be as classy as the 'Dance of the Seven Veils'. But at least they don't make me use the pole anymore."

"Why not?"

"Health and safety. Honestly, I was a liability!"

John laughed. "Sure, I'll come watch."

Sibyl buckled her heels, then stood.

"Oh, and thanks for the absinthe!"

She took up her glass and drained the syrupy dregs at a gulp before going backstage. John waited for the lights to dim and for her to come on, but just then one of the other stags came up to him.

"We need to go. We're late for our reservation at the club, and apparently they'll give our table away if we don't show up soon."

"Okay, sure."

"Having a good time over here, by the way?"

"Yeah, all right. Can I stay a few minutes?"

"No. We've got to go. Come on."

As they were leaving the strip club, the lights in the place dimmed and a spot was shone at the stage. John hung back, but a stag grabbed him—"Are you pissed? Come along!"—and dragged him into the street. It had turned chilly, and John did up the buttons of his jacket.

Much later on, in the nightclub, there she was again, weaving towards John across the crammed dance floor. By that stage, he was pretty much wrecked. Sibyl was dressed in a strappy dress which had a kind of metallic sheen to it. They danced together for a bit, then she took his hand and led him out of the crush. Before he left the club, he found out from one of the other stags where they'd moored the barge, how to get there, wrote it down on a scrap of paper, put it in his wallet. Then went with Sibyl back to her flat. Arriving, they went straight into the bedroom.

A little while later, John was woken from a drowse by the snick of a key turning in a lock, the sound of the flat's front door opening. There was a dim light from the bare low-wattage bulb hanging from the ceiling rose. Sibyl, who'd heard the noise too, sat bolt upright, then, when there came a jangle, as of a bunch of keys being put down on a table, jumped out of the bed, grabbed a T-shirt from a heap of clothes on a chair, wriggled into it, and, with an urgent look on her face, gestured under the bed.

John rubbed his bleary eyes, then, seeing how serious Sibyl was, got up and lay down on his front, wormed into the dark space beneath the frame.

Sibyl threw his underwear, shirt, jeans, jacket, boots, and bag under the bed with him. He heard the bedroom door open then shut again. He writhed into his clothes in the cramped space, then lay there staring up at the stained underside of the mattress through the slats of the wooden bedstead. Earlier he'd noticed a birdcage in the corner of the bedroom. Now he could hear its captive fluttering frantic against the bars.

He lay and listened, over the noise of the caged bird's throes, to the muffled conversation in the corridor outside.

"Babe," he heard Sibyl say. "You're home early."

"Yeah," came a gruff voice. "Job finished sooner than expected, didn't it."

It was dusty under the bed and John's eyes itched, and his nose was twitching, and he feared he might sneeze.

"Oh, that's great."

"Yeah. Got any food in? I'm starving."

"Got some bread."

"That all? Fucking hell. Well, toast will have to do I suppose."

The voices moved away, grew fainter, and John could no longer make out what was said. He lay there, waiting. Then he noticed something tucked between one of the slats and the mattress, reached up and pulled it out. It was a baggie of white powder. Right, he thought, I should at least have something for my trouble, and pocketed it.

Then he heard the door of the bedroom creak open, and Sibyl hiss, "Get out, now!" He rolled from under the bed, stood, snatched up his boots and bag, and padded, in his socks, on the balls of his feet, out of the room. At the other end of the corridor he saw Sibyl silhouetted in a doorway, and beyond her, sat on a shabby couch, smoking and eating toast, a young man he supposed was her boyfriend. John crept to the front door, opened and closed it behind him, as quietly as he could, and then fled, down the stairs, only pausing at their foot to pull on his boots before going out of the building, into the cool night air. At the end of the street, before rounding the corner, he turned to look back. He saw Sibyl's flat immediately—the light was on and the curtains open. She and her boyfriend were embracing in the window, stark against the bright light. The curtains of the apartment above were also open. Though that room was in darkness, John could just make out someone standing there. He had the clammy feeling he was stared at. Peering, he saw eyes, glinting. A figure that seemed misshapen somehow. Neck too long. Then a pair of huge wings beating in the gloom. Of course it was just a dressing gown or something, but John still turned and ran.

He waited in line at a minicab rank in the centre of town. When he got in he asked the driver to take him to Wroxham, to the river there.

John paused then and took a long swig from his wine glass. It felt like he'd been going on for a while, but actually, when I glanced at my watch, it seemed little time had passed. Julia stared at him in dismay, and Beth was glaring angrily, her fists clenched, her cheeks pink, but seemingly unable to say anything. John was apparently unaware.

Then Crispin spoke up. "That it, mate? Or is there more?"

John turned to him. "There's more."

"Well, go on then."

So John, after another swallow of wine, did.

As he sat there on the deck of the barge, smoking, facing out across the river, looking into the thicket that came down almost to the river's edge on the other side, looking at the small birds flitting between the branches, piping and twittering, the sun warm on his face, that sense of well-being sluicing through him, he reached into his bag, took out *Day's Horse Descend*, and began to read the poems. He knows he got through about half the book sitting there then, but he couldn't remember much at all of what he read, save for a couple of the poems' titles, "The Turnip and the Bearded Swan", "The Leviathan in the Wood Grain", and that it made him feel the interconnectedness of all things—of the trees and the scrub, of the birds, of everything from the knot of elver squirming in the shadow of the bank a little way upstream, to the scattering of stars that could still be faintly seen in the west of the lightening sky.

But then blood dripped fatly from John's nostril, spattered the page of the book, and broke his reverie. He tilted his head, pinched the bridge of his nose, tasted a salt tang at the back of his throat.

He realised then how much time had passed while he'd been reading. Overhead, the sun was now far above the horizon. He heard the boom of a bittern.

He was dabbing at the star of blood on the leaf of the book with a tissue from his bag, blotting it, when he heard a sound, and turning saw Sebastian coming out of the cabin, yawning and rubbing his eyes.

"Morning," said Sebastian. "How's it going? Don't tell me you've not slept at all."

"I haven't," John replied, shutting the book. "Got here a couple of hours ago, but wasn't tired, so I've just been reading."

"You must be knackered."

John shook his head. "Nope. Still pretty wired, so . . . "

Sebastian crossed over and sat on the gunwale facing John. He looked at the book. "What's that?"

"Just a book I picked up in a secondhand bookshop before I met you all yesterday. A translation of a collection by a French poet. Decadent stuff."

Sebastian peered at him. "Decadent?"

"You know. Late nineteenth century. Themes of sin and ecstasy. That kind of thing."

"Ah, okay. Talking of sin and ecstasy, what did you get up to last night? You left the club with one of the strippers, right?"

John tugged on his beard. "Well, we went back to hers. A bit later her boyfriend showed up, and I had to sneak out."

"Well, nice work."

"Hmm."

John took out his cigarettes, offered one to Sebastian, pulled another from the packet for himself. They lit up, then sat in silence, puffing away. The warmth of the sun was a balm. A breeze had got up, and the rays skittered on the river's chop.

When they'd finished smoking and cast the butts into the water, Sebastian gestured down at John's bag, to which he'd returned *Day's Horse Descend*.

"So, is it any good?"

John shrugged. "To be honest, I'm not entirely sure."

"How so?"

"I was reading it, but hardly remember any of it, if that makes sense. Went into a bit of a trance."

"It was a heavy night."

John took out the baggie of drugs he'd taken from under Sibyl's bed, held it up. "Yes. And I snorted some of this when I got back. Stole it from the stripper. Not sure it was a good idea. Made my nose bleed."

"Jesus." Sebastian grinned and shook his head.

"Well, like I say, not sure it was a good idea."

Sebastian stood up, stretched. "I think it's time to wake the others, have a bit of breakfast, and then get going. What do you say?"

They roused the other stags, prodding and kicking, and then all sat around for a bit chatting and moaning about their heads. Some went into town to find breakfasts and painkillers. Others rolled joints.

John joined those heading into Wroxham. It was one of the strangest places he'd ever been. The whole centre of town appeared to be one big general store, made up of lots of smaller shops, all in the same dreary creams and browns. He grabbed a bacon roll at a fast-food place, then returned to the barge.

Finally they got on their way. They were headed downriver. As the others had had a go steering the boat in the previous couple of days, John was given a turn at the tiller. He found it quite difficult, but supposed he'd get used to it.

But before they could get out onto the open broads, they needed to pass through the town. In the centre there was a low arched bridge over the river. Holidaymakers were not allowed to navigate this hazard on their own; they had to wait for a bridge pilot to take them through. So John joined a queue of other boats moored against the bank.

It was going to be a while, and the rest of the party all dozed, either in the bunks, or in the sun on top of the narrowboat, so while standing idle John thought he'd take out *Day's Horse Descend* again. He read the remainder of the book standing there. Again the poems themselves were lost to his memory, apart from a few of the titles: "The Mud of Men Spits Blood into the Sky", "Your Tears Will Water a Gibbet Seed", "The Spider and the Swan, Heads Wrenched Off, Dance". He recalled an overwhelming sense of delirium and ecstatic dread though, the equal of the feeling of communion evoked by the earlier section of the book.

His harrowed stupor was broken by the bridge pilot hopping on board. Their turn had come. The pilot was a jovial man, who seemed to have cultivated an almost comically nautical appearance—he had a florid face, thick white beard, and bushy eyebrows, wore a sailor's cap and blue-and-white striped jersey, and smoked a pipe. When he jumped on board he did a quick head count and, finding there were fourteen of them, told the stags that with him they exceeded the maximum number allowed on board, and that someone would have to get off and walk round while he took them under the bridge. One of the stags, whom John didn't know well, a guy called Dave, agreed and disembarked.

The pilot then took the narrowboat under the bridge. It didn't look easy, and John was glad he'd not had to do it. On the other side, the pilot steered the boat close in to a mooring, handed the tiller back to John, and stepped off. Dave was a little way away, trying to chat up a woman dressed in a drab shop uniform. The stags shouted for him and he ran back over. But by the time he reached the bank, the narrowboat had drifted a little, and the gap was too wide for him to leap. Another barge had also pulled in and moored just in front, leaving little room for manoeuvre.

John threw the throttle into reverse, trying to take the boat closer. But it was a struggle. The thing wasn't easy to steer. And he didn't want to strike the mooring. So he tried going ahead, but that was no better. He ended up going back and forth, occasionally getting closer in, but then accidentally veering away again. And Dave refused to jump even at times when he could clearly have made it. The whole thing was a farce. John was really starting to crash hard, felt sick and awful. And the horror evoked by the second half of *Day's Horse Descend* lingered. The hungover, high, and stoned stags were falling about or lying on the roof of the barge howling till tears came to their eyes. And a crowd of onlookers had formed, lining the wall of bridge and standing on the concrete mooring deck. Pointing and grinning. John reddened, but it was all good natured. Amid the gaggle on the bank, there was a woman with her two young sons. They were feeding bread to the birds. Some ducks, moorhens, coots, and two swans had gathered in the water between the boat and the mooring to jab at the soggy hunks with their bills.

The stags were laughing, those gathered on the bank and the bridge were laughing, even John was laughing, red-faced, frustrated, and shaky though he was. Someone on the bridge shouted out, "Get on with it, lads!" Then John caught sight of a hulking and writhen shadow a little way off on Wroxham's main street. At that moment, another boat passed by, having just gone under the bridge, apparently without waiting to be guided by the pilot, not a barge, but a gleaming white modern cruiser, and it was going too fast. Its wake rocked the narrowboat and washed it up against the mooring.

The barge wallowed in slow and heavy. John saw the mother reach out with her hands to cover her boys' eyes. There was a crunch as the hull struck the mooring. And blood spurted into the air, spattering John, the stags, some of those standing by the river.

There was a general gasp, then quiet.

The narrowboat rolled away from the bank and John saw what had happened. One of the swans had been trapped between the barge and the mooring. Its head had been lopped by the impact and lay on the concrete, jetty eye still glimmering with life. The body floated in the river amid a slick of blood.

The hush was broken by a drawn-out wail from an old man on the bridge. Dave did a running jump and got on board at the front of the barge. Not knowing what else to do, John tried to sail off. But he was blocked in by the boat in front and couldn't get the bow out. There was angry murmuring from those on the bank and bridge. Some of the stags suppressed hysterical giggles.

Then a thickset man pushed to the front of the crowd on the bank, bellowed at John. "Oi, son, you've just injured a swan."

John turned to him. "Yep. It's injured all right." Then, abandoning the tiller, he went and sought refuge in the barge's toilet.

The mutters outside swelled to a tumult of rage. Stones were thrown at the narrowboat. But one of the other stags must have taken the rudder and steered them out of there, for the boat lurched, then started moving away, and the howls and yells faded behind.

Once he felt enough time had passed, John unlocked the toilet door and went back out on deck. Sebastian was at the tiller. He was pale.

"Jesus, mate," he said. "What have you fucking done?"

John peered at him. "You saw. It was an accident." He caught movement out of the corner of his eye, and turning saw there were two stags looking down at him from where they sat on the edge of the barge's roof, Dave and another, who was called Greg.

He appealed to them. "You saw, didn't you?" They shrugged.

Sebastian tugged John's sleeve, and he turned back.

"Mate," Sebastian said. "You killed a swan."

"I fucking know that. Nothing that can be done now is there? And it wasn't my fault."

Sebastian grimaced.

"It wasn't! You saw that woman letting her kids feed the birds. Fucking stupid place. And nothing I could do about the wash from the boat went past, was there?"

"John," Dave called down. "You know swans mate for life, don't you? The other one'll pine away now."

"Shut the fuck up." John balled his fists.

"John," Sebastian said, putting his hands on John's shoulders. "We're all just kidding. You need to go up on the roof, enjoy the sun, drink a beer, have a smoke. It'll be fine. But just calm down."

John took a deep breath, nodded. "All right. Sorry."

"No worries. Now go on. Relax."

Round the table at Michael and Lorenzo's we all stared open-mouthed at John. Not just because of the nasty turn his story had taken, but also because of the hold he seemed to have over us—chatting afterwards we all recalled wanting to interrupt, to tell him to stop, but being unable to speak—and because of the way time was either clotting or stretching fit to break—it felt like he'd been talking for a good while, yet by our watches, by the clock on the wall, it seemed it had been no more than twenty minutes.

About a mile or so down the broad, just as John was beginning to relax a bit, a cruiser came motoring up behind them. In the prow was a man in a blue uniform and peaked cap who gestured for the stags to pull over. They put out the couple of joints they'd been passing around, made sure the barge was as clear as could be of signs of the previous night's debauch, then Sebastian, who was still at the helm, slowed down, manoeuvred into the bank.

"Uh oh," Dave said, turning to John. "You're for it. Clearly after a vicious swan killer."

John smiled and rolled his eyes, but sweat beaded on his forehead.

The cruiser drew up alongside the narrowboat, and the man in the cap hailed them.

"It's all right, lads. Just a warning. Speed limit on this stretch is four miles an hour."

Sebastian called back. "Sorry! Didn't know that. And I've nothing to tell me how fast this thing is going."

"Just don't push the throttle over three quarters, you'll be fine."

Sebastian was about to respond when there was a low eerie hiss from the river bank. Turning, the stags saw there were people thronged in the reeds, mouths agape. All ages, from children and teenagers, through to the elderly. The noise they were making swelled to a burst of static, then abruptly stopped. Amid them, John recognised faces: the young mother and her two sons, the bridge pilot, the secondhand bookseller, the crooked old man who'd wailed at the swan's death. Several carried shotguns, broken over their arms, but still menacing. At the front stood Sibyl, wearing a paisley summer dress, stained with blood, and cradling the body of the dead swan in her arms, and, by her side, her boyfriend, who held a willow-pattern dinner plate on which lay the waterfowl's head. They both sneered at John.

Folk came forward from the mob and dragged the stags off the barge. The river police shrugged and went on their way. When down in the reed bed, the stags were made to kneel, up to mid-thigh in the murky water, and their arms were tied behind their backs with hempen cord. Then headdresses, from which branching antlers jutted, were placed on their heads, tied under their chins. All save John. Instead the body of the swan was hung round his neck, and he was given the plate, on which its head rested, to carry. Then the stags were hauled to their feet and driven before the rabble, away from the river.

The tramp was agony for John. He staggered along, pulled down by the weight of the dead swan, his head pounding, struggling to put one foot in front of the other. The other stags, burdened by the cumbersome horns, stumbled. Early on, Greg tried to make a break for it. He didn't get far before a shotgun blast, pellets droning by his left ear, stopped him. He was dragged back to rejoin the rest.

They slogged across marshy reed beds, clambered over dykes and ditches, fought through thickets, and finally trudged across miles and miles of fenland, the stench of the mire in their nostrils, filth spattering up at each step. Most of the throng remained behind the stags, but the bridge pilot and the young mother went in front. It seemed they were the leaders. John kept glancing round trying to catch someone's eye, but no one would look at him. Save the bookseller, who peered haughty over his glasses, and Sibyl, who mouthed, "Fuck you." The mob were passing round cheap bottles of wine, guzzling the stuff down, even the children.

Then the throng reached a roughly circular patch of mud, clear of rushes and sedge. And there they stopped. John knelt down, panting, trying to get his breath back. Those carrying shotguns stood with them cocked and aimed at the stags. All had lips and teeth stained black by wine.

The bridge pilot gestured for hush, then the young mother bawled at the ragtag band.

"Smell that stink," she said, snuffing the air. "That's the good old fen stink. That's blood and fire, that is. That's life and death."

Cheers and whoops went up.

The bridge pilot took his pipe from between his teeth, pointed with the stem at the earth. "There's magic in this dung."

"Are you ready?" the young mother said. "You know the old gods of the fenland will love you for this. Remember that when you do well in your exams, or you get a raise or promotion or new job, or your house goes up in value, or you win some money."

More cheers and whoops.

"Those of you still with wine, pour out a libation!" Someone passed her a bottle and she glugged it out on the clag, then tossed it overhand out into the fen. Others followed her, emptying their bottles onto the ground and chucking them away.

"Come on then," the bridge pilot bellowed. "It's time! Blindfold the stags, then form them into a ring. Apart from you, you, you, and you"—he pointed to the four burliest looking among them, three men and one woman—"you can come forward and help with sundering."

The swan and its head were taken off John and laid on the mud next to him. He was pushed to the ground. The other stags were blindfolded, then stood in a circle facing outwards. The mob formed another ring about them.

Then the young mother called for silence. "Okay," she said. "Now's time to begin. And you four"—gesturing to the men and woman chosen for their strength—"you hold him down."

But John would have given in to his fate anyway; he felt again that sense that everything was connected, a kind of chain of being, welling within him. So he lay back.

A chant went up. "Blood and fire. Life and death." Over and over. Dave whimpered and the denim of his jeans' crotch darkened a shade. Looking up, John saw the bridge pilot standing over him holding a long-handled billhook. The blade was rusty, but its edge, keen. Above, the sky was clear blue with just a few shreds of wispy cloud. John sighed and closed his eyes.

The chanting droned on, growing louder. John sensed someone hunkering down beside him, felt fingers trace a line across his neck. The hands holding his ankles and wrists, holding him down, gripped more tightly.

He opened his eyes again and saw the bridge pilot standing over him, pipe back in his mouth, puffing away, tensed to swing the billhook. Then it whistled down, hacked into John's gullet, and askance he glimpsed the neck of the swan snaking towards its severed head. Behind, beyond the circle, he thought he saw a tall misshapen shadow looming. Then came terrible pain and John blacked out.

John stopped then. Looking round at those of us seated at Michael and Lorenzo's dinner table, he grinned. He'd undone the collar of his shirt and with his finger was tracing distractedly a red welt that ran across his throat. It felt like we'd been listening to him for hours and hours, but when I looked at the clock I saw it had only been about thirty minutes. I couldn't understand it. I felt odd, disorientated, and looking about me could see the others did too.

"Then what happened?" Beth asked.

I think we were all wan and staring. Julia trembled, and there were tears in her eyes, glistening in the fitful flicker of the candles.

"I don't really know," John said. "When I came to myself, I was back on the narrowboat. Sebastian was standing over me, asking if I was all right. Saying I'd fainted, saying it was the heat and what I'd drunk and taken the night before."

Julia stood up from the table. Her fists were clenched. "So your scar isn't from an operation?"

John got up from his seat, went round to her, went to take her hand. She made as if to snatch it away, but then relented, let him.

"I don't know," he said. "I don't understand any of it."

He reached out with his thumbs and tenderly brushed away the tears beading her eyelashes. They hugged.

"Was it delirium?" she asked, a catch in her voice. "What happened to your neck?"

John rubbed his eyes. "The others were acting oddly. Dave especially kept away from me, and I'm sure he smelt of piss. No sign of the book. *Day's Horse Descend*, I mean. Maybe chucked in the river? None of them will see me now." He shook his head. "I just . . . I don't know. Sorry, love."

"Love?" Julia said, a faint smile on her lips.
"Oh Jules. You make me really happy, you know that?"

It was touching. So touching it mostly dispelled the dread we'd all felt. And we weren't at all surprised to hear, not too long after, that John had proposed to Julia and that she'd accepted. Then, a short time after that, they had a sweet small ceremony, at which they announced they were moving to Toronto, where John had got a new job. That was about four years ago now. Beth has kept in intermittent touch with Julia since.

Till recently then, apart from the odd bit of news from Beth, I hadn't really thought much about John. And I'd pretty much forgotten the strange story he'd told at that dinner party. Though it affected me at the time, I suppose I came to think of it as some kind of bizarre joke, for all that he'd seemed sincere. But I've had reason to think of John and his tale again in the last weeks. About a month and a half ago or so, he contacted Beth to let her know he was organising a fortieth birthday party for Julia, and that he wanted to get her over to Canada as a surprise. He said he'd pay for everything, flights and so on. I was a bit resistant, especially since we now have a little girl, Daphne, and I was worried about looking after her on my own. But Beth was so keen to go, celebrate with her old friend, I realised in the end I was being selfish and said I'd get by.

Then two weeks back, I was reading a new book on Gothic fiction, its influence and legacy, which I'd been asked to review for a journal. In a section on Charles Robert Maturin's late-Gothic novel, *Melmoth the Wanderer*, I came across the following aside:

It is well known that Oscar Wilde, who was Maturin's great-nephew, took the name Sebastian Melmoth, after the eponymous anti-hero of Maturin's Romance, during his final years of self-imposed exile on the continent. What not many are aware of though, is that in one of the commonplace books he kept during the last year of his life, when he was living in penury at the shabby Hôtel d'Alsace in Paris, drinking heavily, broken in spirit, and ailing, Wilde tells of a visit by a creature who offers him some kind of diabolical trade. Wilde writes:

"On wakening this morning, from a horrid dream in which I again supped with the dead at a long table laden with maggoty offal, my fellow diners leering and wan in the fitful sputtering of tallow candles set in bone holders, I saw something in the wallpaper by my cot, a shadow nearing, with a general outline chimerical and nightmarish. There was a stench, rank and ruttish. A compact was proposed. But I have been saved by he who gave himself for our sins and am deaf now to that kind of horror."

Whether this was knowing fiction or fevered vision, surely Wilde must have been thinking of the infernal bargain the Wanderer offers poor desperate unfortunates in his great-uncle's book?

I didn't bring this up with Beth, my misgivings too nebulous, but I went online and checked out several used-book sites, seeking a copy of *Day's Horse Descend*. Needless to say I found no mention of the book, or of Hendrick Van der Decken, on those marketplaces, or anywhere else on the internet.

Early this morning, Beth headed off to the airport to catch her plane. She got ready quickly and quietly. When the taxi arrived, she shook me awake, went through to Daphne's bedroom, leant over her bed to kiss her goodbye, careful not to disturb her. Then she took her suitcase downstairs, went outside. I followed her down, waved her off from the front door. She should be landing soon. She said she'd give me a call once she was settled at Julia and John's, after John had surprised Julia with her, so I have my phone beside me.

Later, after I'd got Daphne up, given her some breakfast, sat her down in front of the television, and gone into my study to get on with work, the post arrived. There were a couple of bills, a few circulars, and a package addressed to me.

It sits unopened on my desk, next to my phone. Drab cardboard, innocuous. I take it up often, put my ear to it. Mostly it's silent and has the heft of a slim hardback book and the vanilla scent of aging paper and glue. But sometimes it's lighter, and I can hear cheeping and scritching, if very faint. At yet others there is a waft of carrion. When I hold it, my heart beats against my ribs like a caged bird frantic to be free.

Day's Horse Descend

Following the disappearance in 2002 of Emily Stirk, the poet who wrote hermetic verse as Hecate Shrike, there was a feverish, if brief, waxing of interest in her work. So when Ernest Todhunter, who'd been sent one of the cryptic letters Stirk had posted out just before going missing, along with a key to the suburban bungalow she'd inherited from her parents and lived in most of her adult life, let slip there was a room in there filled with damp and mouldering heaps of paper, drafts in Stirk's small and neat hand, a tantalising, if somewhat foetid, corpus, the gannets flocked to tussle for scraps. No one could work out why Todhunter, a joke on the London occult scene, a dilettante really, a sometimes director of "art" films that were little more than cheap porn, had been given this trust, and indeed, though he tried to fend off the scavengers, flapped his hands, he, whey faced and feeble, failed to put many to flight, and they made off with whatever they could stuff into the pockets of their long black woollen overcoats, worn even at the height of summer, or into the brown leather satchels poets are so fond of forever carrying about. The editor Hayden Morrison, who ran an obscure poetry journal, Flatlands, managed to get hold of a morsel in the frenzy, a previously unpublished essay, a piece Stirk had written about a troubling influence, the little-known French decadent Hendrick Van der Decken. He published it in the next issue of his magazine, where it was probably read by just twelve or thirteen people (and made sense of by fewer).

This essay is an account of my research into the creative practice of a minor French decadent, a poet. But it is also a ghost story of a kind, I suppose. Sometime in the late '80s, I was browsing the shelves of a secondhand bookshop in Bedford—that market town founded at a ford on the River Great Ouse, thought to have been the burial place of King Offa of Mercia—when the acid-yellow wrapper of a slim hardback caught my eye. I took the book from the shelf, examined it. It was a '60s translation of a volume of French decadent prose poems of 1870 entitled *Day's Horse Descend*. The name of the poet, Hendrick Van der Decken, meant nothing to me; the translator had chosen to remain anonymous. But I was intrigued by a claim on the back of the dust-jacket that in an early draft of *The Picture of Dorian Gray* the book that so corrupts Wilde's eponymous protagonist was recognisably this collection, before presumably it became a thinly disguised *À rebours*: *Le Secret de Raoul* by Catulle Sarrazin in the final typescript, a title and name censored by Stoddart before the *Lippincott's Magazine* printing, and subsequently the nameless "yellow book". So I took the volume to the counter, bought it.

After leaving the bookshop, I found a quiet pub nearby, an old fashioned place, lots of real ales on draft, wood-panelled walls covered with pump badges. I bought a pint, sat down—it was pretty much empty, I had my pick of the tables—and started to read. From the brief introduction by the translator, to the collection, I learned that Van der Decken was a pen name, taken from that of the captain of the legendary *Flying Dutchman*, and that the writer had been a Wallonian, Gilbert Moreau, who as a youth had moved to Paris, and in early 1871 had died there, during the siege, aged only twenty-nine. The English, *Day's Horse Descend*, had been Moreau's original title—a pun on either "*des os de cendre*", "of the bones of ash", or "*des os descender*", which means something like, "of the bones go down". The book had apparently an infamy as a work of ecstatic dread, a terrible book. There were more details about Moreau's life and the work, but I've forgotten these.

Before I could begin reading the poems themselves, I was accosted by a man who approached my table. Overweight, probably in his late fifties, he wore a white linen suit, crumpled and stained. Behind him, on a wheeled trolley, he pulled a gas cylinder, connected by a long tube to a clear plastic breathing mask he clutched in his hand. Standing there, in front of me, he held the mask over his nose and mouth and took a long pull. Whether it was oxygen or nitrous oxide, I've no idea, but he seemed antic, sinister.

"You here for the Kiddie Fiddlers?" he asked. At least I think that's what he said.

I frowned up at him.

"Band. They're playing later. Very good, you're in for a treat."

"It's only three," I said.

"They'll be on before you know it. I'm going to join them on the washboard. You know." And he mimed it, stroking a whisk broom over the ridged metal, then huffed on the gas again. I sat watching him.

"Ooh yes, it'll be a special turn, all right."

I shrugged, went back to my book, hoped he'd leave me alone.

But he didn't. "What's that you're reading?"

I grimaced. "Just something I bought at the bookshop round the corner."

"Lemme have a look-see?"

I hesitated, just for a moment. Before I could react, the man had, suddenly fleet, grabbed the book from my hands.

"Hey! What're you doing?"

He sneered at me. "Just having a look."

I got up to snatch the book back, but stumbled over the man's gas canister, which he'd put in my way, and he danced back, out of my reach.

But then the publican, an older man with round glasses and a grizzled beard, noticed what was going on and growled. "What have I told you, John? Stop harassing folk! I'll bar you again, this time for good."

John turned. "Sorry Colin. I get a bit carried away."

"Just give the lady her book back, will you?"

An ingratiating smile suddenly plastered on his face, John handed *Day's Horse Descend* back to me, then skipped out of the pub, dragging his gas cylinder after him. I put the book back in my bag, downed the rest of my beer at a draught, then left to head to the station, catch a train back to London. It wasn't till I got home I looked at the book again. I found that somehow there had been a switch, that within that lurid dust jacket was now a copy of some tawdry crime novel. The man, John, must have been a master of sleight of hand to have done it. I cursed him, but wasn't too put out, I was bound to be able to pick up another copy online, or so I thought.

But I was wrong. I searched everywhere for a copy, but was unable to track one down. Eventually, I gave up. But, haunted by its strange title, supposed dark reputation, and the poems themselves, which I'd not had a chance to read, I would from time to time look into Moreau and his *Day's Horse Descend.*

For years though, I turned up nothing. The Wilde angle led nowhere—I could locate no mention of that early draft of *Dorian Gray*. And the translation into English was also no help—the anonymous translator was of course a dead end, and I could find no record of the press that had put it out. I was beginning to think I'd either dreamed the whole thing or been the victim of an elaborate, and pointless, prank.

But then, some years later, while reading the Goncourt brothers' journals, I came across the following passage:

[W]e sat down [. . .] at a café opposite the Théâtre-Français. A waifish young man prowled round to us [. . .] and sat down to have a glass of beer. It was Gilbert Moreau, no relation to the more well-known Gustave, a typical literary Bohemian or unknown poet, known to us from the salons. His hair, though kept short and swept back, was unruly, and though he was handsome enough, we supposed, there was something about his features that was awry. His nose was like the beak of some great bird, and his lips were too plump, almost grotesquely sensuous. The hairs on his chin were soft and downy, like those of a pre-pubescent boy. His eyes were rheumy and poignant, like the eyes of a doe or an anchorite, his pocked, pallid skin, with its sheen of sweat, was that of an opium eater or chronic masturbator. Altogether something sickly and ghoulish . . .

After that, I began to research Moreau in earnest. But still I turned up nothing for an age. Then, by blind luck, I stumbled over, in an article about *Le Grand Jeu*, a reference to a hagiographic piece by René Daumal, apparently written in 1930 or '31, perhaps for the unpublished fourth issue of the magazine. After some digging, I managed to unearth it—it was among some private papers of Daumal's held in a Parisian archive. Frustratingly, I was only able to consult it once, as on a subsequent visit I was told it had been misplaced. Luckily, surreptitiously, as it was against the rules of the institution, I'd copied the whole thing out by hand that first time.

The piece opens with Daumal describing how he'd come across a copy of *Day's Horse Descend* in a secondhand bookshop in Montmartre in May 1929 and been, as he puts it, "beaten senseless". He goes on to give a fairly extensive biography of Moreau. It tallies with the spare details I recalled from the introduction to the translated *Day's Horse Descend*, though I still wonder whether it might not be a fiction on the pattern of Marcel Schwob's *Vies imaginaires*—it seems barely credible, and it's possible of course that the anonymous translator simply copied their facts from Daumal. Daumal had also been able, if he is to be believed, to track down a picture of Moreau, a *carte de visite* from around 1868, which was clipped to the papers and showed a young man with bad skin, lank hair, a nose like the gnomon of a sundial, wild eyes.

According to Daumal, Moreau was born in 1841 in Namur. Almost nothing is known of his early years, save that, his family being reasonably well off, his father a judge, they were comfortable, if not opulent. Moreau had always a slight, almost sylphlike build, and soft voice, and there were some who speculated he'd likely been christened Gilberta or Gilliane. At the age of eighteen, he left home and went to Brussels to attend the university there, but left aged twenty, without attaining his degree, to move to Paris, with the intention of becoming a writer, much to his father's chagrin. But the elder Moreau was not it seems irked enough to cut Gilbert off and continued to provide him with an allowance, enough funds to cover his board and lodging in a garret apartment in St.-Germain-des-Prés. So young Moreau was able to devote his time to literary activities. He wrote slowly, mostly at night, while apparently throwing a knife over and over at a picture he'd tacked up of Diderot, whom he is supposed to have irrationally hated. He attended the salons and in about 1863 started publishing his work, initially under his own name, in small editions printed at his own expense.

His early writings were apparently decadent poems, clearly modelled on Charles Baudelaire and the "charnel-house school" of Petrus Borel, Théophile Gautier, and others. Moreau was at this time interested in formal versifying, favouring the rhymed alexandrine. These works were fairly conventional then, even if in his use of tropes Moreau's work supposedly looked forward to the compression and imagistic potency of the later Symbolists. Moreau craved fame and was frustrated that his poems did not find favour with a reading public, though some contemporary *littérateurs* were impressed by them, including Auguste Villiers de l'Isle-Adam.

Then, late in 1867, Moreau seems to have had a sudden revelation. He abandoned his earlier approach and devoted himself to a new and bizarre poetics. Daumal writes:

> Tired of all that aping of *le romantisme frénétique*, Moreau committed himself to the hard path of renunciation, to the perpetual torment of a dread desire, and to the destruction of those carapaces he had put on to be a man and to live, committed himself to that void of lyricism which is more than death, that is the Black Sun which sears the Earth, calcines its clods. Committed himself as a monk or a tremulous lover to the "Great Black Anti-Sun".

This new method led, over the course of 1868, '69, and '70, to the composition of the prose poems that make up *Day's Horse Descend*. The volume was then published in early September 1870. One hundred and seventy-three copies were printed, but only thirty-seven sold. The Moreau of earlier years might have been enraged by this, but Moreau the convert cared nothing for the acclaim of the public. He had broken though, as Daumal states, into a "black peace, an Erebean quietus".

Here is Daumal's account of what happened to the remaining 136 copies of *Day's Horse Descend*:

> Moreau stalked the streets of Paris, with the damp stare of a syphilitic, a crazed prophet, or of Coleridge's Mariner, pressing copies of his book on passers-by. Most will have ended up being thrown into the Seine, used to light fires, as door stops, or to block up chinks around the window frames of draughty garrets, but maybe some were read, and some men wandered the city, wild, raving, ecstatic, eyes opened to the void by the Stygian glister of *Day's Horse Descend*, even if they doubtless went unnoticed amid the general madness.

"General madness", for, on the 19th September 1870, Prussian forces surrounded the city and began a four month blockade. Moreau was one of the casualties of that German adventure. The story goes that sometime in late January or early February 1871, he bolted from his flat, out into the biting February morning, wearing only a silken robe and a pair of felt *pantoufles* or slippers, and ran off down the road. Some acquaintances afterwards suggested he may have been suffering from *la folie obsidionale* or siege-madness, a commonly observed condition of that time, but Daumal hints at darker forces.

Moreau was scurrying past the Gothic church of Saint-Séverin, in the direction of the Ile de la Cité, when a stone gargoyle—perhaps juddered by the heavy bombardment of January, when the Germans fired some 12,000 shells into the city over twenty-three nights in an attempt to break Parisian morale—fell from a flying buttress, and struck him on the head.

Here is Daumal description of Moreau's death:

As he lay there on the pavement, with his brains leaking out and running into the gutter, shivering, holding closed, for modesty, his robe with his left hand (there were onlookers who swore to softer curves beneath the sheeny fabric than there ought to have been, but those who collected up and buried Moreau's carcass, kept his secret, if there was one to keep), trying to hold his smashed skull together with his right, he told the mob who'd gathered about how disgusted he'd been by the taste of a steak cut from the flank of either Castor or Pollux, the Jardin des Plantes's elephants, who were killed and eaten in late December 1870. Moreau had apparently been one of those who'd dined on the beasts, and it was his dying pronouncement that the meat was, *"dure et graisseux"*, and that its *"goût amer"* had not been ameliorated by the *"sauce poivrade"* it wallowed in.

Raving about the "rank and awful horror" of *Day's Horse Descend*, Daumal calls Moreau "a paragon of the bleak absurd", remarking that his work "reaches such extremes of dread ecstasy, that the reader's agitated brain may grow an egg tooth and butt it against the fragile shell of its cranium".

He also goes on to discuss another text by Moreau, a short outline of his method found among some correspondence he had with Isidore-Lucien Ducasse, the self-styled Comte de Lautréamont. Daumal claims to have discovered letters indicating an acquaintance between Moreau and Lautréamont, author of the famously bizarre, *Les chants de Maldoror*. Apparently the two men met at a salon and struck up a friendship. They admired each other's work. Ducasse's side of the correspondence is assumed forever lost; the papers and unpublished texts found in Moreau's rooms after his death were burnt by his father, who'd been horrified on discovering the morbid tenor of Moreau's work. But, according to Daumal, Moreau's letters to Ducasse were full of admiration for Ducasse's style, criticisms of contemporaries, gossip from the salons, and intriguing, oblique references to an atonal symphony they were composing together, "four movements of cacophony, infernal music!"

And they also contained a kind of explanation of the poetics that lay behind the creation of the prose poems of *Day's Horse Descend*.

In 1867, when insight flashed upon him, Moreau had, he told Ducasse, abandoned the frenetic oneirism of the decadent writers of his earlier influence for something far stranger. Daumal explains that:

In one of his letters to Lautréamont, Moreau wrote that he'd spent most of 1868 isolated in his garret, rarely venturing out, studying the alchemists, reading all the great works of Hermetic philosophy, from Hermes Trismegistus himself to Zosimos of Panopolis, from Agrippa to Paracelsus, Dee to Brahe, and even forbidden lore, such as that contained in Ludwig Prinn's *De Vermis Mysteriis*. At the end of that year of solitude and contemplation he emerged, like a moth from a cocoon, an adept of the Great Work.

Daumal writes that Moreau in one of his letters to Lautréamont told how, from his occult readings, he'd developed a new poetic practice. This practice involved coming up with a resonant phrase, then creating a sigil somehow from that sentence. Then after meditating on the sigil till his mind was a void, Moreau would begin writing in a kind of trance, watched over by an entity he called the "Great Black Anti-Sun". Daumal speculates, though he doesn't explain why, that this being was represented for Moreau by a *roi des rats* he had found in the street and, an amateur taxidermist, stuffed and preserved.

After this period of automatic writing, Moreau would then subject the text created to a series of transformations designed to mirror certain alchemical procedures. At first I thought it would be impossible to reconstruct much of this aspect of Moreau's method from the elusive hints Daumal gives from his letters. Obscurities such as this from a letter to Ducasse dated 11th November 1870:

I dreamed I was walking along a black strand beside a vast underground lake, a sunless sea, when I came upon a fane consecrated to dire rites where, on a stone altar, between two black candles set in bone holders, was a triptych depicting a garden of ecstatic transmutation, with above the scene in gilt blackletter a legend, "From the small bones of the middle ear—the hammer, anvil, and stirrup—can be fashioned a key." When I woke I realised the dream was telling me to transpose certain luminous words in my poems into others, blackly gleaming.

But the more I pored over the extracts from Moreau's correspondence, reproduced by Daumal in his essay, the more I realised they suggested specific textual operations—operations I could incorporate into my practice. So I determined to attempt to create work using parts of Moreau's poetic method. Having little to go on in Daumal's account, I based the creation of my sigil on the approach of the early-twentieth century British magician and artist, Austin Osman Spare. I attempted Moreau's process with a line that had come to me in a reverie, when I was sitting at my desk, afflicted by writer's block: "The antenna sets my pineal gland thrumming." I sat in contemplation of the sigil for a short while, a pen in my hand and cheap notebook in front of me, but nothing happened, my mind was a blank.

So, in a bitter, sardonic frame of mind, I decided to create my own version of Moreau's Great Black Anti-Sun, to try again under the watchful eye of a weird fetish I'd make, something which seemed at the time playfully grotesque, but now . . .

My idol sculpted, I tried once more. This time I soon fell into a trance. In that fugue I wrote automatically, short poem after short poem. I emerged blinking into the light after nearly an hour, my notebook filled with pages of scrawl. I then took the pieces I'd written and rearranged their text according to the formulas I'd conjectured from Moreau's letters. The awkward, clunky poems were transformed, became things ugly and morbid. Things disconcerting, laced with the vatic. Things nightmarish, beyond nightmare and into the realms of the dread ecstatic.

Would that I'd never done any of this, that I'd never heard of Van der Decken, never come across that copy of *Day's Horse Descend* in that bookshop in Bedford. But, since I have, I think I shall publish these poems, and flood this world, this miserable world, with revelation and darkling bliss.

The Song of the Goatsucker

After a long cold winter, the weather had turned and that night it was mild, though still damp and dreary. It was said that by the time the grisly offerings were found in a clearing in Bluebell Wood outside Luton, by a butcher from nearby Farley Hill out at daybreak walking his dog, they had already begun to stink and were crawling with flies, though they could only have been left there sometime during the night before. Carrion birds had been at the eyes and torn hunks from the jowls. It was a pair of red kites, a rare sight in those days, circling overhead, piping shrill, now and again stooping down, that had drawn the butcher to the glade, where he found the heads of six Friesian cows and one horse, a white mare, impaled on stakes.

"Never seen such an effing mess," the butcher said to people ever after, to the police, to family, to friends, and finally to strangers in the town pubs where he took to heavy day-drinking and sometimes soiled himself. "Ain't right." There had also been something about the sunlight that morning, he said; though it had been early, the sun still low in the sky to the east, in the clearing it had been glaring. The light had been, he would say, like it is in the Hollywood pictures, not at all like the wan light of an overcast spring dawn in England. Saying that, he'd shudder and pull nervously on a cigarette. The dazzling colours in the clearing that morning had filled him with a deep and awful joy he couldn't ever shake.

The papers were quick to connect the shambles in Bluebell Wood to the repeated desecration of a grave at Old St. Mary's, a derelict church, a roofless ruin, on a hill above Clophill, a picturesque village about thirteen miles to the north of Luton. Over the previous weeks, the bones of an eighteenth century apothecary's daughter had been dug up several times, on moonless nights. It was thought mostly to be aimless vandalism, the work of bored teenagers, but the original violation had borne clear signs of a knowledge of dark rites. That time, the skeleton had not just been scattered, but laid out inside the ruin in a pattern associated with the Black Mass. A Maltese Cross had been daubed on the floor in what was thought, from feathers found strewn about, to have been cockerel's blood. Graffiti scrawled on the wall read, "the mAw", "hell IS here", "Beelzebub 666", and "The Cloven Will Rise". There were also many crude sketches of eyes and a painting, done with some care, which depicted a naked human form, female above the waist, male below, but with cloven hooves instead of hands or feet, bat wings, tatters of leathery skin flung out behind, and a black ram's head with whorled horns.

The press reported the link between the incidents as fact. The police were less sure. The one person who knew for certain they were connected never revealed it to anyone. A watch, with a lurid yellow face and the initials G. F. scratched on the back, was found strapped to the stave on which the horse's head had been spiked. The police showed it to a Jane Fountain whose daughter Gill had gone missing. Jane had last seen Gill going up to bed the night the apothecary's daughter's bones had first been disinterred.

Jane told officers she didn't recognise the watch. She was never sure afterwards quite why she'd lied, save that she was strangely afraid.

Jane lived in a pokey little house on the old track in Clophill that ran up to the abandoned church of Old St. Mary's. On the morning after the night Gill disappeared, before she'd discovered her daughter was gone, Jane was standing in her cramped kitchen in pyjamas and dressing gown, her hair unkempt and sticking up in clumps, drinking a cup of weak tea, when she heard a ruckus outside. She peered out through the window. It was a grey, drizzly day. There were two children in the dirt road in front of Jane's house, a boy and a girl, both in blue denim dungarees. They were kicking something to one another and swearing. At first she was merely irked. "Bloody louts," she said to herself. But when she saw what it was they were passing back and forth, she was aghast, put her mug down and opened the window.

"Oi! What do you think you're doing?" she called out.

The children stopped booting the skull about and turned to her. The girl was perhaps twelve or thirteen, the boy a bit younger, maybe ten. They looked alike enough to be siblings. The girl grinned. "Nice barnet, missus. Very stylish."

Jane was taken aback. "Don't be cheeky! What are you doing? Won't your parents be ashamed of you, disrespecting the dead like that?"

The girl shrugged. "I shouldn't think they'd be much bothered." The boy giggled.

Jane leant out the window. "Where did you get it?"

"Wouldn't you like to know," the girl jeered. The boy stuck his tongue out.

Jane could now see the skull was yellow with age and mottled with dirt. "Have you dug that up?"

"Naw. We found it."

"How old are you anyway?"

"Old enough." This time it was the boy who spoke.

"Where are your parents?"

The boy shrugged. The girl smiled sweetly at Jane. "We ain't too young to be out on our own, if that's what you're thinking. We're older than the hills, me and him."

"Up from Luton are you?" Jane asked.

Both of them ignored her, sneered down at their boots, started scuffing them in the dirt.

"Well," Jane went on. "I wish you'd just go back."

The girl glared at her. "Perhaps we *ain't* from Luton," she snarled. "Perhaps we wish we *could* go back an' all. Perhaps we don't know *how* to get back." Then she bent down, picked up the skull, and flung it at Jane.

It fell short, struck the paving of Jane's front path with a dull crack. But she cringed back and when she looked up, the girl and boy were gone. "Good riddance," she muttered. But she was unsettled. And it wasn't just that there'd been something odd about those kids. She couldn't later explain to the police why she'd run inside, run straight to Gill's bedroom, even though it was a Saturday, and she would normally have let her have a bit of a lie-in. But she did, heart in mouth. And found the bed empty.

The police concluded that Gill had run away. She'd been a loner, with few friends, ostracised by the other girls at school because she was a bit of tomboy, kept her ginger hair cropped short, and preferred catapults and climbing trees to make-up and boys. Jane told the investigating officers she didn't think Gill had ever really got over her dad dying when she was ten, and that in the last years, she'd become more and more morose and withdrawn. She fitted the profile, one of the detectives had said. Just another lost soul. Except girls like Gill usually turned up, working the streets of London or Birmingham, hooked on drugs, or huddled in a doorway, dead of exposure. Gill didn't. Jane waited nearly a year before she lost hope and tried to make an end of things with an overdose of sleeping pills. She survived, but lived from then on as a shade.

And Gill never turned up. Neither did the bodies of the six Friesians and the white mare.

The crone's cheeks were sunken and pocked and her lank grey hair was loosely knotted on top of her head. She hunkered in the graveyard, the bodice of her tattered floral-print dress draped loose over her rawboned frame, its skirt stretched tight between her spread knees. There was a whickering brass oil lamp on the ground beside her, canted slightly by a tussock. Next to it was a light grey duffel bag.

Dark clouds clotted the sky, blotting out the moon and stars, but the girl could make the crone out by the fitful light of the lamp, which, falling slantwise across her face, glassed her eyes and sparked its glimmering flame there. From a nearby field could be heard the pained bray of a colicky donkey, and from the trees at the edge of the graveyard, the tinny burr of a nightjar. It was late spring, but still damp and chilly.

Digging in the dirt with broad, calloused hands, delving with long gnarled fingers, thick yellow nails, the crone heaved up clods like a mole. As she dug, she sang, her mouth slack, the loose skin of her throat flapping over taut tendons. Though her voice was weak and quavery, the girl could still make out bits of what she sang:

I've been a-rambling all the night,
And the best part of the day . . .

The wavering tune was strangely sweet and made the girl's heart ache.

The girl—who'd had a solid post-war name, a name stolid, though with a faint hope about it, a name lopped to one syllable as a feeble sop to childhood, a name she hated, a name which, though she didn't yet know it, she'd been robbed of by entering that liminal space—watched from the shadows inside the shambly church. She'd hid herself there because she'd heard some of the sixth-formers came out to the old church under cover of darkness to drink, and fight, and maybe get naked, and she'd wanted to see that. Her house was just down the hill and she'd often sneak out at night. It was easy, her mum took sleeping pills and no amount of noise would wake her. The girl had been up to the church several times before, but this was the first time she'd seen anyone else there.

The other children at school called her carrot top, because of her hair, and other crueller things, and she wished them all dead.

The donkey cried out hoarsely once more, then the breeze carried another snatch of the woman's song to the girl's ears:

Come give us a cup of your sweet cream,
Or a jug of your brown beer . . .

The crone was by then squatting in the hole she'd dug, throwing up dirt, arms flailing.

The girl remembered little of her father, just the stench of beer on his breath, the stink of cheap cloying perfumes, of the kind her mother would never wear, on his clothes, the swish of a belt buckle whipping through the air, welts on her back, buttocks, legs, her mum's battered face, tears leaking from her puffy, blackened eyes. The girl's mum had told her many times they needed to make allowances, that her dad had seen terrible things during the war, things they couldn't understand, but the girl had still hated the man and been glad when one night, on the way back from the pub, he'd fallen in a ditch and drowned. But her mum had changed since and now cried all of the time. The girl missed her smiles and laughter.

Hiding inside the old ruined church, watching the crone dig, the girl thought back to the first time she'd crept out in the middle of the night, about two years before. Of what she'd seen then by the light of a full moon. She'd hopped on her bike and ridden a short way to a field off the main Luton to Bedford road where she knew there was a pond where frogs thronged. She'd been there about half an hour, firing stones at the frogs and toads with her catapult, jeering at their frantic hopping and lumbering, when she heard a car pull into the lay-by where she'd left her bike hidden in a bush. She listened to the engine idle for a short while, then shut off. There were angry shouts. She shrugged. Probably a couple having an argument. She'd heard her parents fighting so many times. She went back to slinging stones at the frogs and toads. But then she heard two loud cracks. She ducked down and clapped her hands over her ears, just as she had done one afternoon in a picturehouse in Bedford when the hero and villain of the Western her dad and she were watching, facing off on a dusty street of clapboard buildings at high noon, both went for their guns, drew, and fired at almost the same time. Her dad had smacked her hard on the back of the head then, told her to stop being feeble—alone in the field she stayed crouched down, shivering. Then she heard a woman scream, "You bastard! You shot him. Why did you shoot him?" Taking her hands from her ears, the girl made out a low mumbling, and then, more distinctly, a man with a nasal voice say, " 'E frightened me, didn't 'e? Why did 'e 'ave to turn so swift like?" The woman babbled, begged to be shot too, or let go. This went on a short time, before the man hissed, "Be quiet will you. I'm finking." The woman stopped yammering, began to sob. "It's alright, love," the girl heard the man say. "Why don't you give us a kiss?" Keeping low and still, the girl jammed her fingers deep in her ears and stared out at the writhing mass of frogs and toads.

The later night, hunkered inside the derelict church, the girl was jolted by the donkey barking again. The old woman had, by that time, dug down quite far and, bent over, was out of sight. Then she stood and leant with her elbows on the side of the hole, puffing and panting. When she'd got her breath back, she warbled another verse of her song. This time the girl could make out her words clearly:

> When I am dead and in my grave
> And covered with cold clay,
> The nightjar will sit and sing
> And pass the time away.

Just then that bird's churr came again, louder this time, and peering, the girl made it out, swooping down from its perch in an old yew to alight on the edge of the pit. It puffed its chest, and the crone grinned and turned to it.

"Hello, my little goatsucker," she said, chucking it under the chin. "Come to sing for me, have you?"

It opened its stubby beak to let out one last trill, then began to preen its feathers.

"I've a use for you," the crone said to the bird. "You know what it is, don't you?"

The nightjar cocked its head and peered at the old woman. Then seemed to nod.

When, on that night a couple of years before, the girl had taken her fingers from her ears after some minutes had passed by, there was peace. Thinking she was safe to return to get her bike, she slunk back through the field. Getting to the lay-by, she hid behind the trunk of an old wych elm and peered out, saw a car still parked there, a grey Morris Minor. There were pulpy splashes thrown up against the windscreen and a body hanging half out of the open passenger-side door, a gore-soaked cloth wrapped about its head.

Then a man with wild, staring eyes in a doughy face, and short, unkempt hair, wearing a cheap grey rumpled suit, came out of the field to her left buttoning up his fly. The girl cringed back. There was a pistol in the pocket of the man's suit jacket, grip jutting up. After blowing his nose on a filthy handkerchief, he went back to the car and began dragging a woman out of the back seat by her ankles. Her clothes were torn and dishevelled and the make-up around her eyes was smeared, but she was quiet, her face set. She didn't even make a sound when she was dragged out of the car and her head hit the tarmac.

The man stood over her with his arms crossed. "Get up," he said. "Get 'im out of the car and lug 'im over there, will you?" He pointed behind him.

The woman groaned and staggered to her feet. Without a word, she took hold of the dead man under the shoulders and heaved him out of the car and hauled him to the verge at the edge of the lay-by. She then sat down next to the body, put her head in her hands.

"I'm not finished with you yet, love. I need you to show me how this bleedin' motor works."

The girl gawped out from behind the tree. In the moonlight all the blood looked black.

On the later night, a short while after the nightjar had come to perch on the edge of the pit, the crone crowed and threw up a few mouldering scraps of timber, stood and sang again:

> You can take the Good Book up
> And read a chapter through,
> But when the day of Judgement comes
> No god will think on you.

She bent down once again. After a few moments more scrabbling, there came a howl of delight and she brandished a long yellowed bone, perhaps a thigh bone, aloft, and began capering in the pit. The nightjar hopped about on the edge on its short legs, as if it too were beside itself. The girl's eyes almost started from her head and she gasped, then, fearing to be heard, clamped her hand over her mouth. The crone ceased cavorting, reached down again into the hole, picked up another, shorter bone, then clambered out.

She arranged the bones so the shorter crossed the longer at one end and held them tight in her left hand while she reached up with her right, drew a long strand of hair free of her topknot, and yanked it out at the root. She then wound it round and round the two bones to bind them.

She's making a crucifix, the girl thought.

Deadman's Cross. That was the local name of the place where the girl had seen those awful things in a lay-by two years before. After the woman had shown the man with the doughy face how to operate the gears and switches of the Morris Minor, she'd sat back down by the dead body, squeezing one of its hands in both of hers. The girl had prayed the man would drive off, leave the woman alone, but it seemed there was no one listening, for he got out of the car, walked to the woman, and stood over her, his head cocked. She pulled out a pound note, waved it at him. "Here, take this, take the car and go!"

He shook his head, walked several paces back toward the car, then turned, emptied the gun at the woman, reloaded, fired several times more. As the first bullet hit, she keeled to the ground, blood spurting. Several more struck her, and her body jerked like a rag doll. The girl put her hands over her ears, shut her eyes tight, and stayed as still as she could, holding her breath.

Then she heard the car drive off, with much grinding of gears. She opened her eyes and got to her feet. The woman lay still on the tarmac, blood running from her wounds. The girl panicked, grabbed up her bike, rode home.

She was horrified to later learn, from the new reports, that the woman hadn't been killed. That she'd just played dead, and after the shooting had spent some time trying to attract the attention of passing cars by waving a strip torn from the hem of her petticoat, before losing consciousness. She'd followed, with feelings of guilt at first, then increasingly listless, the investigation of the crime, the arrest, trial, the victim in court in a wheelchair, and the hanging of the doughy-faced man.

Deadman's Cross. But the girl soon realised she was wrong about that for, when the Crone had finished wrapping and knotting the hank of hair around the bones, she began to cut and thrust with them, holding the end of the femur under the crosspiece. It was a sword, a sword of bone.

The crone pointed the weapon at the church and turned to the nightjar, which still preened on the edge of the pit. "Now I need to array the rest of the bones within that place," she said. She put the sword down, jumped into the pit again, and began to root about.

The girl watched agape as the crone threw up more bones—a rib cage like a trap, vertebrae like esoteric sigils, a pelvis like an ossified imago, a skull with a gap-toothed grin—all yellowing, all brittle.

A short while longer, then the old woman stopped and clambered out of the hole. "That's it," she said. "Done." She unzipped her duffel bag and began picking up the bones and chucking them into it. The sword she placed in last, more carefully. Then she picked up the bag and the lantern, and came up the hill, headed for the church. The nightjar came with her, fluttering about her head.

The girl's guts lurched. She had to find a place to hide. She darted her eyes frantically about. They alighted on the spiral stairs in the tower, which, amid all the ruin, still stood, seemed sound. She crossed to them, began to climb, and was out of sight before the crone came in under the crumbling stone lintel.

She went on up, gyring higher, till she came out on the flat roof of the tower, surrounded by low crenellations. She crossed to the side from which she could look down into the nave, open, as it was, to the sky.

The moon had torn free of its shroud, and the girl stared a moment at the view before her—a patchwork of green wheat and fallow fields of witchgrass, ragwort, and cow parsley, stitched together by hedgerows of sere hawthorn, hornbean, and scrub alder. All was silvered, glistening with dew. Beyond were hills crowned with copses, which, swagged with mist, seemed fairy knolls. She could hear the wistful calls of night birds. Then she looked down.

In the nave of the ruined church, the crone was working a timber lintel into a chink in the rubble work of one wall.

The unearthed bones had been strewn on the flags of the floor, between which weeds sprouted, and by them had been set down the lantern, duffel bag, and sword of bone. After wedging the lintel into the wall, the crone laid the bones out beneath it. Then she took a small pot of paint and a brush from her bag, and began to daub a demonic beast on the wall. She took pains and it took some time. The girl watched, a cold quaking in her bowels. When it was done, the crone took a small cockerel, a saucepan, and a serrated breadknife from the bag. The fowl fluttered weakly in her hands. She drew the knife across its throat. Blood spurted and spattered, further staining her mud-smirched dress, but she managed to catch most of it in the pan. After throwing aside the body of the dead cock, she began to smear a pattern on the floor with the blood, around the bones.

Finally, she took up the skull, rested it on the lintel, and stepped back to look at what she had wrought. Just then the nightjar, which had been flitting about, alighted on the brainpan. The girl watched from up on the tower, frightened, yet curious. The crone nodded at the nightjar who perched, head cocked on one side, peering at her with a jetty eye.

"It is time now for our ritual. Bow your head little lich fowl."

Then she took up the sword of bone, held it out before her, and began to intone slow, sing-song:

It's well budded out.
I'll call on you next year, nightjar,
Should you live to tarry the town.
All, both great and small, my song is almost done.
I cold clay.
I cold clay.

The nightjar joined her on the refrain, a wordless churr:

> The nightjar will sit sweet
> When I am dead and say,
> "Before your door I stand."
> The best part of you,
> A branch of May.
> A branch of May.
>
> And now I am my right arm,
> My right arm raised up.
> And the Lord will think on my grave.
> God bless away,
> God bless away.

The crone drew a deep breath. The girl thought for a moment she scented the cloying perfume of bindweed flowers and the salt tang of blood or brine, and heard a faint yowling, but then it was just manure and the wonted sounds of night time once more.

The crone went on with her litany:

> And when, on the day of Judgement,
> I have been rambling
> All the hedges and the fields.
> I will have a bag on.
> A bag on.

She reached solemnly down, took up the duffel bag, now empty, put it over her head.

"Now," she said, "we go through."

At the far end of the church there was an arched opening, once a stained-glass window which would have spilled a tranquil light on the altar, but, panes and lead long since gone, was then a raw hole that gave onto tussocky grass mottled with garish ragwort and whited fleabane, the flowers bright in the moonlight. The crone, bag over her head, brandishing the sword before her, strode off, out through this opening.

The girl waited awhile, peering into the graveyard to see where the crone had got to, but there was no sign of her. So she climbed down from the tower and, reaching the bottom of the stairs, shrugged, crossed over to the lamp, which the crone had left behind, picked it up, then followed the witch out. Moments later the nightjar took flight and came after the girl.

Things seemed a little different out there. The moonlight had something of an oily sheen and the calls of the night birds were no longer mating cries or shrieks of the hunt, but low mocking whickers. The crone was a little way ahead, lying on her side on the ground, the bag still over her head, the sword waggling in her hand, her legs kicking out as if she were still walking, like a dog dreaming of chasing rabbits.

Going up to her and crouching down, the girl took the bag off her head. The crone's legs slowly stopped churning and she rolled to turn to the girl, grinning broad.

"Now, don't be afraid," she said. "Don't forget I've studied the lore of this place and know its perils well. The box of prophecies we seek is a mere half a day's walk to the north. All will be well."

"Lore?" the girl asked.

"That church. This hill. In pagan times a place of blood rites. Later a leper colony. When the church was new, the Black Death came here, and the villagers locked the afflicted inside, left them to die."

"What?" said the girl.

"This place—"

But the girl grimaced, wrenched the sword of bone from the crone's grasp, and struck her with it several times, though gently, not meaning to hurt. But still the crone curled into a ball, wrapping her arms about her head, and the girl walked off, brandishing the sword, leaving her behind. The nightjar came after, then alighted on the girl's right shoulder, began to churr, eerie and thin. She turned to look at it. Its stubby beak was wide, its pink throat pulsing within.

A short while later, the girl clambered over a low stone wall and found a man in a cheap rumpled suit, slumped forward, on the other side. Putting the sword under his chin, the girl tilted his head back. It was the man with the wild eyes and doughy face.

"I thought they hung you," the girl said, peering at him, holding the lantern in his face.

The man squinted in the light. " 'Anged," he corrected.

She flicked the man's head back with the blade, and it lolled to one side. She could see the mark of the rope about his neck.

The girl jabbed the sword hard at his flabby mouth a few times.

"Leave it out," he said, spitting teeth and blood.

"All right," the girl replied. "I'll be on my way then."

She put her foot on his shoulder and pushed, and he flopped bonelessly onto his side. Then she walked off whistling a jaunty air, the nightjar, still perched on her shoulder, whispering strange and awful things.

She went on towards those fairy knolls she'd seen from the top of the church tower. After a while she came to a brake of bracken, gorse, and bramble and started to hack through with the bone sword. From overhead came the whistling of a kite, a noise like a boiling kettle. The nightjar looked up warily and gave a throaty burr. The girl petted it. "Don't worry," she said. "I'll keep you safe. You stick with me." The nightjar winked and told her about the monsters she'd soon face, how it was her destiny to vanquish them, or die in the attempt, about the treasures of the country that would be hers if only she was brave enough. About how, if she kept her wits about her, she could be the greatest hero the land had ever known, celebrated on feast days, remembered in song.

The girl came out of the thicket, went on, stumbling across a new-ploughed field. After a while she saw a faint reddish glow low in the east. It waxed, then the sun rose above the horizon, climbed into the sky. She looked down at her watch with its bright yellow face. The big hand was on the seven and the little hand between the five and the six. She couldn't make head nor tail of this. Knackered, when she reached the hedge at the end of the field, she lay down in a ditch with some ferns for a pillow and drifted off.

She dreamt that on the following morning she'd come across a crock of honey jammed in the entrance to a badger sett and that the nightjar would tell her to take off her shoes and socks and smear the sticky mess over her feet and drowse till late afternoon, all through the hottest part of the day. That, on waking, she would find her feet clotted with insects who'd swarmed to the sweetness and got stuck and were slowly dying. Crane flies struggling weakly, fluttering their papery wings, their legs like black dancing filaments. Cockchafers, elytra opening and closing feebly. Bluebottles with sheeny carapaces, droning slow and fading. Wasps buckling to plunge in stingers, but unable to sink them through the gloop. Stag beetles, clacking their mandibles, frantic.

"Girl," the nightjar would say to her, "now you can go on. Booted in chitin, you're ready to tread this new earth."

The girl slept on soundly. The lowing of cattle in a nearby field did not wake her. Neither did a milk van driving by on the other side of the hedge, its headlights sweeping the verges, bottles clinking in crates. A bit later alarm clocks started to burr and folk to stir in their beds, sit up, rub their eyes, and steel themselves to face the working day.

The Pale Moon Shines at Night

After university, my friend Jess moved back to the drab town we'd grown up in, worked in a pub there, the Man in the Moon. On the sign swinging from a bracket over its shabby frontage a wan flabby face hung in a night sky strewn with stylised stars. The landlord liked having Jess behind the bar; she was very pretty in a sickly English rose kind of way—dark unkempt hair framing a round face, pallid complexion with a hectic flush to her cheeks—which brought in the punters. Not that they needed much encouragement—the beer was always acrid with the taint of line cleaner, but was so cheap it made boozing in the local Spoons seem wanton. If more pleasant—the garish patterned carpet in the Man in the Moon was always sticky in inverse proportion to the prices.

Among the pub's regular day-drinkers was a short man with a coxcomb of grey hair. His skin was not so much sallow as grey, like plumber's putty. He mostly sat sullenly sipping from glasses of cheap Scotch with chasers of strong Czech lager, but when drunk would now and again sing a snatch of an old song in a soft quavery voice:

And when I wander here and there,
I then do most go right.

He would also become animated when at quiet times Jess played '80s music videos on the pub's TV. He'd point at the screen and say, "That light. Those colours. That's what the light *there* is like." Jess would humour him and nod. His English was good, but he had a strong accent she couldn't place. "And the *pale* moon shines by night." He placed an emphasis on the adjective. "That's why I first came in here," he went on. "The sign outside."

Jess shrugged. "But that moon's got a face?"

"Yes . . . " He trailed off and swigged at his whisky.

One day he hid in the toilets when a group of lads in some kind of archaic fancy dress came in. It was a stag party maybe. After that, he never came back.

Jess sometimes wondered what had happened to him. Then she started having dreams in which she wandered under the sickly light of a strange moon. Tramped across moorland of sere witchgrass and sprawling gorse. Slogged over hills rocky and bleak, where kites soared and piped, circling for carrion. Fought through rank woods where reddish swine rooted and rutted in tangled undergrowth. They unsettled her, she said, these dreams, but felt little different from any ordinary nightmare. But then the border between sleep and waking seemed to grow porous. One time she dreamt of cowering in a hedge, hiding from a rabbit the size of an elephant with blood red eyes, then woke with burrs in her hair. On another, she spent the night shackled in a basement with the smell of loam and camphor in her nostrils, being force-fed a bland mush of boiled tubers by folk with faces painted blue and feathers in their hair. That time, when she'd been roused by her alarm, she'd felt sick, and her ankles and wrists had been bruised and chafed.

Eventually the dreams got so bad that to dull them Jess began drinking heavily herself. I lost touch with her after that. An old acquaintance told me she'd gone up north to move in with a someone she'd met online, but I thought it odd she hadn't let me know.

A few years later, I was back in town, visiting my parents, and went out for a drink with some friends. On the walk back home at the end of the evening I came across an unhealthy looking man in motley rags, who was ranting about how he'd been beaten and robbed. I talked to him a bit, then gave him some money to get into the local shelter for the night. When I got back to the house, I found a corner torn from a newspaper tucked into my coat pocket. Scrawled on it were the words, "It was the sweet o' the year."

I don't know what to make of all this. Jess I've never seen or heard tell of again. But I sometimes hear that man singing in my dreams, that man whose skin was the flat grey of spoilt fish:

Why, *he warbles*, then comes in the sweet o' the year.
For the red blood reigns in the winter's pale.

To Have a Horse

You work on it during the hours of darkness, on some waste ground abandoned to witchgrass, cow parsley, yarrow, nettle, and scrub alder and willow, at the edge of town, past a railway siding and brakes of briar. Once, long ago, there was a workshop on the site that made soft-whip ice cream machines, and you sometimes stumble over half a decaying brick or turn up, with the toe of your boot, a nozzle that glints in the starlight.

The moon goes from full, through new, and back to waxing gibbous before you're finished. Some nights it's above you, looking down on your work, on others it never rises, or is hidden behind a high thick wrack of cloud scudding away to the west. Each dusk you walk out of town, cross the tracks of the siding, threading the abandoned commuter trains, canted carriages splashed with tags, once garish, now dull, faded, and pick your way through the tangle of mallow and bramble. And each dawn you return. Sometimes under a sky the colour of salmon left too long on the fishmonger's slab, sometimes under a sulphuric haze.

And then one night, clear, with a spatter of stars and that mangled moon overhead, you realise it's ready. An armature as if of bone cobbled from twisted spars of dull metal scavenged from the wreckage of the old car plant. Joints moulded from a putty made from boiling up squirrel and rat carcasses, then scraping the residue out of the pot. Sinews of rusting barbed wire. All draped with a mould-furred tarpaulin. The skull is two pieces of hard grey plastic from the casing of an old photocopier carved in clumsy apery of the wicked bone callipers of a real horse's skull, jaw articulated with baling twine. It stands tottering on swollen hocks, as if afflicted with bog spavin. Had it been real, a horse like this would have been sent to the shambles or the glue factory. But there are no real horses, which is why you have made this sham.

You clear a patch of earth and start a small fire with the smashed pieces of an old table you've been saving. For kindling, you light a hank of steel wool cupped in your hands, before tucking it into the nest of broken-up timber. It burns quickly and like a tracery of burst blood vessels, then flinders away to nothing. But you blow softly and steadily, and sparks puff up, and before long the wood catches. Then you stop and intone the invocation you found in the old book (and which you spent some days translating from medieval Latin with the aid of a primer taken from a classroom of the public school in town):

> I conjure you demons from the south,
> And by the seven frogs and these winds;
> I conjure and adjure you:
> That you should speedily and without delay,
> And without deception,
> Terror and trembling and injury to my body,
> Bring me a horse prepared and ready to do my will.

Then you sit down by the fire and wait. Staring into the flames, you think about how you used to now and again feel, as a jolt, the interconnectedness of things. Of the squabbling starlings, chittering blackbirds, and tits that perched in the bushes of your back garden; of the mangy one-eyed fox that often skulked at the foot of it and survived on kebab leftovers and fried chicken bones; of the scurrying rats in the alleyway that ran down one side of your house; of the tangle of dogrose, hawthorn, and poppy of your frail elderly neighbour's overgrown garden, and of the midges, mosquitoes, blowflies, wasps, and bees that whined, droned, and buzzed through this thicket, alighting on red and pinkish blossoms, russet berries; of the dead hare in a nest of thorns and the pallid grubs that made the carcass to shimmer; of the kite that soared, circling, overhead, its shrill piping like the whistle of an old-fashioned kettle; of the newts and frogs in the storm sewer off down towards the river; of the bream, roach, perch, and tench swimming in its waters; of the flukes burrowing into their flesh; of the knot of elver squirming in the shadow of the bank a little way upstream; of all the people going about their days or nights, sleeping, eating, working, drinking, arguing, fucking, and lying benumbed or rapt before the coruscations of the TV; and of the inanimate too, the housing estates, all the derelict industrial buildings, the air, the sun and moon, the blue sky and the clouds, and the scattering of stars that could faintly be seen, points of light in a net of contrails, in the west of the lightening sky.

But now everything is a smash-up, a wreck, and there are just strewn shards and splinters.

After some time you start, thinking you see a glimmer in the socket of the skull you roughly hewed, but it is only firelight glistering from the threads of a web a spider has swiftly spun there. In the end, bone-weary and lulled by the wavering flames, their faint warmth in the night's chill, you can't keep awake, your chin falls to your chest, and you slump forward.

You wake up screaming. Somehow the fire has spread to your hair and jacket. Running stumbling about the waste ground, you bat at your head and chest with your hands, before throwing yourself down in a sump at its edge to hiss and steam. When you get to your feet again, your hair is mostly gone, your hands and scalp are blistered, and the manmade fibres of your jacket have melted into a thick carapace. Then you remember the dream you were woken from.

In it you were somewhere else, at another time, at some kind of festival in a country village. The Carousing of the Grey Mare. A rabble went through the streets from house to house, following a man leading, by reins of woven bramble, a figure draped in a sheet, blue with gold stars, who held aloft on a pole the yellowed skull of a horse, adorned with ribbons and tatters that streamed behind in the wind. In the sockets of the skull had been placed two white flowers like trumpets, which gave off a cloying scent of nectar and dung.

At each house the leader would knock on the door while the Mare pranced up and down, its lower jaw clacking, and the mob would chant, with one voice and the solemnity of a liturgy, an old folk song of some sort:

> Bonefaced, with eyes of stars,
> Deathless and dark-matter shod,
> Gravid have I been
> Since spores first drifted cross the void
> And seeded this spinning ball of clay.
> But now I feel the birthing pangs,
> And seek a place to foal.
> Won't you let me in?

You sit on the cold ground, in your shell of char, the stink of burnt hair, skin, and plastic in your nostrils, looking out into the girding dark and musing on the meaning of this dream.

Some time will pass, then you'll see a brief slash of light overhead. And at the same moment, hear a faint whickering from behind you. Your breath will catch in your throat and your eyes will fill with tears. Without looking round, you'll incant the second part of the formula from the old book:

O good horse I conjure you
By Dedya, Stelpha, Draco, Drogancio, Barabas,
And Medya, who is the mistress,
And he who rides upon a black mount,
And she, upon a red,
That you may have neither in your body,
Nor in your mind,
Nor in the most unclean part of your body
The will to make me fall at all,
But that you should bear me to my place
Healthy and uninjured,
According to my will.

Then you'll wait a moment before turning, all the while thinking about the journey ahead, the hard time you'll have of it, that which awaits you at its end, and about the last time you cried, so long ago, on that night when you choked on the salt tang of blood or brine and the cloying perfume of bindweed flowers.

Sources

"What the Old Bones Told Hecate Shrike" was first published in *Tales from the Shadow Booth Vol. 1*, edited by Dan Coxon (Privately printed, 2017).

"Three Relics" is comprised of three stories, originally published separately. "Cast a Cold Eye" first appeared in *The Far Tower: Stories for W. B. Yeats*, edited by Mark Valentine (Swan River Press, 2019); "Sad Presentiments of a Proud Monster" first appeared in *Chiaroscuro Void: Goyesquean Fictions and Visions*, edited by Alcebíades Diniz (Raphus Press, 2020); and "A Chance Encounter in Barnsbury" first appeared in *Faunus 21*, edited by James Machin (Friends of Arthur Machen, Spring 2020).

"With Scourges, with Flowering Sprigs" was first published in *The Book of Flowering: An Anthology*, edited by Mark Beech (Egaeus Press, 2019).

"Under the Sign of the Black Raven" was first published online by *3AM Magazine*, selected and edited by Susan Tomaselli (May 2012).

"The Purblind Bards" is reprinted in this volume only in part. It was first published as a chapbook by Zagava (2020).

"And Yet Speaketh" was first published in *Murder Ballads*, edited by Mark Beech (Egaeus Press, 2017).

"The Yellow Book" was first published in *The Scarlet Soul: Stories for Dorian Gray*, edited by Mark Valentine (Swan River Press, 2017).

"The Song of the Goatsucker" was first published in *Harvard Review 56*, edited by Christina Thompson (Houghton Library at Harvard University, 2020).

"Under a Certain Old Street Lamp", "We Recognise Our Own", "Let It Be a Blood Ape on the Prowl . . . ", "Day's Horse Descend", "The Pale Moon Shines at Night", and "To Have a Horse" appear in this volume for the first time.

Acknowledgements

First among those I must thank here are the editors of the anthologies and magazines where some of these tales first appeared, without whose encouragement and support I might have abandoned this path long ago: Mark Beech, Dan Coxon, Alcebíades Diniz, James Machin, Jonas Plöger, Christina Thompson, Susan Tomaselli, and Mark Valentine. Further gratitude goes to those friends (you know who you are) with whom I have, long and late into the night, talked of things bookish—my understanding of how the supernatural tale works has been shaped by those many discussions. And thanks to my family for all their support.

Many thanks also to the Swan River team of Meggan Kehrli, Jim Rockhill, and Steve J. Shaw—they are absolutely the best at what they do. The cover art is by øjeRum, an artist whose work I have found a constant inspiration—it is a thrill to see these collages paired with my tales. Without Brian J. Showers, this book would not exist, not only because he has taken a chance on these stories, but also because of the way his friendship and our conversations over the years have informed my writing of strange fiction. And lastly, to Liliana Cârstea for her patience and encouragement, all my gratitude.

About the Author

Timothy J. Jarvis is a writer and scholar with an interest in the antic, the weird, the strange. His first novel, *The Wanderer*, was published by Perfect Edge Books in 2014. His short fiction has appeared in *The Flower Book*, *The Shadow Booth Volume 1*, *The Scarlet Soul*, *Murder Ballads*, and *Uncertainties I*, among other places. He also writes criticism and reviews, and is co-editor of *Faunus*, the journal of the Friends of Arthur Machen.

SWAN RIVER PRESS

Founded in 2003, Swan River Press is an independent publishing company, based in Dublin, Ireland, dedicated to gothic, supernatural, and fantastic literature. We specialise in limited edition hardbacks, publishing fiction from around the world with an emphasis on Ireland's contributions to the genre.

www.swanriverpress.ie

"While small publishers often produce beautiful books, few can match those from Swan River Press."

– Washington Post

"It [is] often down to small, independent, specialist presses to keep the candle of horror fiction flickering . . . "

– The Irish Times

"Swan River Press—cutting edge of New Gothic."

– Joyce Carol Oates

"The redoubtable Brian J. Showers [keeps] the myriad voices of Irish fantasy alive there in Dublin."

– Alan Moore

AGENTS OF OBLIVION

Iain Sinclair

"Generally speaking the dead do not return," pronounced Antonin Artaud. But the dead are permitted to visit those who welcome them. Their spectral, machine-made voices echo in deep tunnels under London. Voices without hosts. Without agency. They make their oracular pronouncements even when nobody is listening on the vast empty platforms of the Elizabeth Line. They have their codes and their secret meanings.

Four stories starting everywhere and finishing in madness. Four acknowledged guides. Four tricksters. Four inspirations. Algernon Blackwood. Arthur Machen. J. G. Ballard. H. P. Lovecraft. They are known as "Agents of Oblivion". And sometimes, in brighter light, as oblivious angels . . .

As host, as oracle, Iain Sinclair moves through this quartet of tales, through a spectral London that once was, or might never have been.

" . . . a hugely entertaining addition to his canon."

– Fortean Times

"Sinclair illuminates and sometimes terrifies the soul!"

– Michael Moorcock

*"Nobody can do more with a sentence's cadence,
diction and imagery than Sinclair."*

– Washington Post

THE DUMMY
& Other Uncanny Stories

Nicholas Royle

Nicholas Royle's stories are "immaculately sinister", according to Olivia Laing in the *Times Literary Supplement*, while Phil Baker, in the *Sunday Times*, described Royle as "a real craftsman of disquiet".

In his third collection, *The Dummy & Other Uncanny Stories*, Royle focuses on archetypes and phenomena that, through their particular melding of the familiar and the unfamiliar, produce uneasy, or uncanny, effects. In these stories he writes about doppelgängers, ghosts, dummies, disconnected body parts, impaired vision, the dead and the prospect of death, not without a macabre sense of humour.

These stories reflect Royle's continuing development as an exponent of the form, in which he is always seeking to learn and to grow, and to push against boundaries.

"Royle's dark fiction is always worth reading . . .
His storytelling is impeccable, his plots always interesting
and his characters credible."

– Mario Guslandi, *SFRevu*

THE SATYR

Stephen J. Clark

In the final throes of the Blitz, Austin Osman Spare is the only salvation for Marlene, an artist escaping a traumatic past. Wandering Southwark's ruins she encounters Paddy Hughes, a fugitive of another kind. Falling under Marlene's spell Hughes agrees to seek out her lost mentor, the man she calls The Satyr. Yet Marlene's past will not rest as the mysterious Doctor Charnock pursues them, trying to capture the patient she'd once caged. *The Satyr* is a tale inspired by the life and ethos of sorcerer and artist Austin Osman Spare.

Another three novellas of occult enchantment follow: a bookseller discovers that his late wife knew the Devil, in the Carpathian Mountains refugees shelter in a museum devoted to a forgotten author, and in Prague a portraitist must paint a countess whose appearance is never the same twice.

"This book will adorn your shelves, where it will be at ease in shadowy converse with your copies of À Rebours, The Picture of Dorian Gray, The Great God Pan.*"*

– Mark Valentine

"Clark's subtle prose, vivid and disturbing imagery, and the concepts he weaves into his stories make them irresistible to those whose senses have been jaded by more common fare."

– Black Static